"I'm leaving."

Scott gripped Carrie's arm, his eyes blazing. "I don't know what you expected by coming here and telling me this, but if you thought I wouldn't give a damn, you're mistaken. I don't walk away from the problems that drop into my lap uninvited. I never have before and I'm not about to start now."

She glared. "Belle isn't a *problem*. She's a little girl who's lost the only father she's ever known." She yanked her arm from his grip. "And you've got plans, so why don't you do us both a favor and continue with them? It's Christmas. Go be happy with your family."

"It seems one half of my new family is standing right in front of me."

Dear Reader,

It's time for *Christmas at the Cove!* I am so excited to introduce my first ever Christmas story and the fourth book in my ongoing series set in the fictional U.K. town of Templeton Cove.

Thank you so much for the emails and Tweets asking me to write the stories of so many of the secondary characters who have appeared so far. I am overwhelmed with the love for Templeton Cove and its residents! I have just finished book five, which features a hero and heroine from book three, *What Belongs to Her* (Harlequin Superromance, March 2014), so I hope you'll look forward to that.

Christmas at the Cove stars Carrie Jameson and Scott Walker, who met a few years before when Carrie was visiting the cove. The sexual heat between them was too much to resist, and soon after Carrie returned home she discovered she was pregnant.

Deciding a baby was the last responsibility a gorgeous bad boy would want, Carrie chose to raise little Belle alone, then later in a marriage with a good and devoted man. Carrie has always been tormented by the guilt of not telling Scott he is a father, and after her husband's death, she returns to the cove to lay her guilt to rest so she can live an authentic life.

After thinking about Carrie for years, Scott is thrown for a loop when she returns...and even more so when she tells him he's a daddy. Scott is devoted to his mother and sisters and won't turn his back on his daughter, but he needs to know that he can trust the woman who kept Belle a secret.

I so enjoyed writing this book, and the glittering Christmas lights and warm homely scenes only added to my creative joy. Merry Christmas, everyone!

I'd love to hear from you, so feel free to follow me on Twitter or email me anytime.

Rachel Brimble

Twitter: @RachelBrimble
Email: rachelbrimble@googlemail.com

RACHEL BRIMBLE

Christmas at the Cove

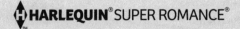

Recycling programs
for this product may
not exist in your area.

ISBN-13: 978-0-373-60881-2

Christmas at the Cove

Copyright © 2014 by Rachel Brimble

HARLEQUIN®

Printed in U.S.A.

™ www.Harlequin.com

ABOUT THE AUTHOR

Rachel lives in a small market town only a short distance from the famous Georgian city of Bath, England. Becoming an author is a dream come true, and Rachel now writes contemporary romance and romantic suspense for Harlequin, and Victorian romance for Kensington. When she isn't writing, Rachel likes to read, knit, watch far too much TV and walk the gorgeous English countryside with her husband, two daughters and beloved black Labrador, Max. *Christmas at the Cove* is Rachel's fourth book with Harlequin, and with book five finished, she has many more books in mind for Harlequin Superromance and her beloved Templeton Cove. Watch this space! She loves chatting and connecting with readers and romance authors alike and would love to hear from you!

Website: www.RachelBrimble.com
Blog: www.RachelBrimble.blogspot.com
Twitter: @RachelBrimble
Facebook: www.Facebook.com/RachelBrimbleAuthor

Books by Rachel Brimble

HARLEQUIN SUPERROMANCE

1835—FINDING JUSTICE
1869—A MAN LIKE HIM
1912—WHAT BELONGS TO HER

Other titles by this author available in ebook format.

This one is for all my fabulous,
wonderfully kind and devoted readers—
I couldn't continue to live my dream without you.

Merry Christmas!

PROLOGUE

Summer, Three Years Earlier

THE DOOR OF The Coast Inn swung open and Carrie looked up from her shot at the pool table. The stranger in the doorway was tall and broad, his face in shadow as the freak summer downpour flowed in torrents behind him. She straightened, inexplicable tension lifting the hairs at the back of her neck. The reggae track that blasted from the jukebox faded, and the chattering laughter all around her subsided.

He stepped inside the bar and shook the rain from his dark hair, pushing his fingers through the wet strands. She tried to drag her gaze away but instead openly stared at his wide, powerfully built chest. He didn't wear a jacket and muscles rippled beneath translucent white cotton. Her gaze wandered lower over his flat stomach to linger shamelessly at his groin encased in blue jeans.

"Carrie? What's wrong?"

Carrie blinked and plastered on a wide smile. She turned and met Michaela's slightly wine-glazed stare. "Nothing's wrong. I'm working out my strategy for this next shot." She focused on the task at hand, her grasp trembling around the cue. "Hold on to your hat. You're going down."

She shot the ball and missed by inches.

Michaela gave an inelegant snort. "Oh, yeah, you've got this game in the bag."

Carrie shrugged and tossed her hair over her shoulder. "Fine, let's see if you can do any better."

She stepped back when Michaela elbowed her out of the way. The music and chatter had re-emerged and Carrie breathed a little easier. With her friend's back turned, she looked at the stranger again. He faced away from her, laughing with the bartender as he snapped the top off a beer bottle and slid it across the bar. When her object of fascination lifted the bottle to his lips, the skin at his throat shifted and moved as he drank, hitching every nerve in Carrie's body to high alert.

Never in her life had she looked at a guy and wanted to keep looking like she did now. *I have to talk to him.* Her head swam with too much wine and too little food. What else could be the cause of this momentary lapse in the sensible and steady personality she'd worn with ease her entire adult life?

She was here for a fun weekend with her girl-friends. A hardworking, ambitious woman work-ing as a TV producer for a national network. A woman who went through life with methodical precision. A woman who dated and carefully considered…who never leaped into bed with a guy she'd only just seen.

So why did she want to do exactly that?

She couldn't think past walking over to him, sliding her hand into his and leading him out of the bar to the hotel where she and her friends were staying.

She swallowed and hungrily ran her gaze over the back of his head, continuing her perusal. Muscles flexed and relaxed beneath his shirt; his butt was firm…the side of his thigh muscular and thick. Her body yearned with a desire she couldn't explain.

He turned and her breath lodged in her throat.

Their eyes locked and his laughter came to an abrupt stop. His smile dissolved as the beer bottle hovered at his mouth and everything quieted once more. She tried to move, to turn and rejoin her friends, but her feet remained welded to the wood flooring.

With his eyes still on hers, he put the bottle on the bar and stepped toward her. Panic rushed through Carrie and she shot a glance over her shoulder. Her three friends watched him approach, their cheeks flushed and their eyes agog. Carrie's heart pounded and her mouth drained dry. She turned to face him.

He stopped directly in front of her and she tipped her head back to look into his eyes. In the muted light, they shone a bright blue, striking against his deep olive skin. His gaze roamed over her face, down to her breasts and back again.

She wet her lips and forced a smile. "Hi."

"Hi." The seconds beat like minutes before he took another step closer. "I'm Scott."

"Carrie."

"I haven't seen you before."

"I'm visiting for a few days." She glanced behind her. "These are my friends."

He turned to Michaela and the others and dipped his head before facing Carrie once more. "You look as though you're having a good time."

She lifted her chin, forced nonchalance into her stance. "I am. Templeton seems a nice place."

"How long are you staying?"

"Until tomorrow."

His gaze bored into hers. "Then we don't have much time."

She stiffened. *No. He can't mean...* She huffed out a laugh. "For what?"

His eyes gleamed. "You know what."

She crossed her arms to hide the trembling, to stop from reaching up and grabbing his jaw to bring his lips to hers. "Do I?"

"We need to get out of here."

Oh, my God. "I don't think so."

"Why not?"

Carrie glanced toward Michaela and the others and bit back a bubble of nervous laughter. Her friends wore identical, jaw-dropped expressions of fascination. "I can't just leave—"

"You don't strike me as the type of woman who lives to other people's schedules." His gaze glided over her face in a steady, soft caress that made her feel like the most beautiful woman in the world. A way she'd never felt her entire life. He lifted his shoulders. "Or maybe I'm wrong."

Carrie drew in a long breath as her habitual need to maintain control rose. *He's a player. Walk away. Go back to your friends.* "You're right, but I don't know you."

His gaze darkened and settled at her mouth. "Ditto."

"Then I should stay here."

He lifted his gaze to hers and said nothing.

Time stood still as her heart beat fast and her mind whirled. How could she not go? Every nerve in her body screamed for this man; every second that passed felt wasted. She waited for the rush of her returning sanity, but instead, relief swam through her. Relief he'd suggested they leave together first, that this madness was his idea, not hers. Could she do this? Just go with him and to hell with the consequences?

"Do you do this often?" She lifted an eyebrow,

going for the breezy rather than the terrified. "Approach women in bars and ask them to leave with you?"

"Never. You're the first."

She looked into his eyes and nothing but sincerity shone back. God, she wanted to go with him. Desperately. "You could be an axe-murderer for all I know."

She said the words, but no part of her was afraid of this man. Instead, she wanted to comfort him, to soothe the deep frustration emanating from him. The look in his eyes wasn't full of male ego but intense inquiry, mixed with a hint of disbelief that she understood only too well in that moment.

He exhaled. "I could be, but I'm not. I'll look after you, Carrie. I promise." He raised his hand. "Scott's honor."

Her stomach knotted and laughter bubbled in her throat once more. "Well, in that case..." She smiled, still apprehensive. "I'll grab my purse."

For the first time since he'd left his barstool, he smiled. A smile so soft, she sensed his mutual relief. Sensed he was as unsure about what he was doing as she was. On shaking legs, Carrie approached her friends and glanced at each of them in turn, desperate for the words to explain she had to make love to this stranger or regret it for the rest of her life. She wanted him to take her and feel the weight of his body pressed down on hers. She wanted to smell him, touch him and hear him groan.

She focused on Michaela, her best friend and only hope of being understood.

Michaela frowned. "Carrie?"

Carrie smiled, even though nerves and doubt danced in her stomach. "I have to go with him."

She moved to walk away, but Michaela gripped her wrist. "You don't know this guy."

Aware of Scott watching, Carrie pulled back her shoulders. "But I will."

"Carrie—"

"I have to do this." She eased her arm from her friend's grip. "I'll call you. If you don't hear from me in a couple of hours, call the police." She winked and pushed away the seriousness of the implication.

"That's not funny." Michaela glanced toward Scott before facing Carrie again. "If you want to go, I can't stop you, but for God's sake, call me later so I know you're okay."

Carrie smiled even as unease rippled through her. Michaela's concern was justified. Wouldn't she have been saying the same things to her friend if the roles were reversed? She squeezed Michaela's hand. "I will. I promise."

After a final worried look in Scott's direction, Michaela smiled and raised her hands in surrender. "Fine. Then get out of here."

Grinning, Carrie faced Scott. "Ready?"

He nodded. Her heart stuttered, but still Carrie slipped her hand into his and led him from the bar.

HER SKIN WAS like smoldering silk beneath his hands. Scott relished his exploration over her back and along the bumps of her spine and ribs as she lay facedown on the hotel bed. Her body delicately quivered and a soft mew whispered from her lips. He burned it all into his memory because there was every chance this would be their single time together. An event never to be repeated.

The tension in her shoulders when he smoothed his fingers across them and the way her toes remained curled against the mattress spoke of a woman doing something alien to her. The thought he'd never see her again sent panic ricocheting through him, but he had no right to expect more. He'd approached her. He was the one who'd been pulled from his barstool as though hypnotized.

He was no angel. He enjoyed the chase and the conquer. This was neither. He was hers for the taking. The feeling was unwanted…and scary as hell. For the first time in his life, it was important he found a way for a woman to entirely trust him…to understand he'd take care of her. That he wouldn't walk away from her as he had others.

A crack of summer lightning lit the peach-and-cream hotel room and she stiffened beneath his fingers. He smiled. "Shh."

Her body relaxed into the mattress. The drapes lifted as the wind gathered ferocity and washed into the room through the open window. When the sun had burned hot that afternoon, he wouldn't have believed they'd need to seek shelter from this seemingly impenetrable storm. He swallowed. How could he have imagined any of this?

He didn't pick women up in bars and sleep with them. He dated them, romanced them and ensured they had a good time whenever they were with him. He didn't understand nor need the unspoken seriousness of his reaction to Carrie. She mattered. Something in her eyes spoke to his heart. It was as though he already knew her…and she possessed the power to change his life in the blink of an eye. He laughed, joked, played pool and hung with the boys. He didn't fall in love.

He'd been struck; caught in her invisible snare.

Yet despite the emotional risks to his heart, he didn't leave her bed. He didn't gather his discarded clothes and escape the room in a bid to salvage what was left of his sanity. He continued to touch her. Adore every damn inch of her.

She'd shaken her long, blond hair from its clip the moment they stepped inside, her brown eyes boring into his, dark with desire. *Carrie.* The urge to say her name over and over rose to his tongue and he swallowed it down. He wanted to know where she came from…and, more important, would she stay with him.

But he wouldn't push her. Her need to be in control permeated the room. If he didn't let her lead this moment, it could be over before it began and he couldn't allow that to happen.

He sensed her tension, her confusion and it was equally as potent as his. His heart hammered and his cock hardened as he smoothed his hand lower over the dimples at the base of her spine to the soft curve of her ass. She stretched beneath his touch, languishing like a panther against the stroke of his fingers. Scott clenched his jaw. He sensed one wrong move on his part and the spell would be broken.

But for now she was his.

Something had gripped them both, and its claws dug deep. Her hair was thick and long, almost reaching to her waist, her figure the hourglass perfection akin to Marilyn Monroe. Unbelievable curves in all the right places. She had the sexiest body he'd ever had the honor to touch. He didn't need to question if doing something like this, with him, was in any way the norm for her. Her insecurity showed over and over in the flashes of doubt that whipped across her gaze, before she blinked and they were replaced with determination.

He didn't dare question her reasoning for fear

he wouldn't like the answer. The moment he laid eyes on her, fate had reached in and gripped his damn heart.

She turned over and his gaze dropped to her full, creamy white breasts. He smoothed his thumb across one pink nipple and then the other. They instantly hardened. He smiled softly and met her huge eyes in the semidarkness. They were wide with wonderment, yet confident and sexy as hell.

"I want to make love with you." She reached up and smoothed the fallen hair from his brow. "Then you leave. Can you do that?"

No. I can't leave. I can't not look at you or touch you again. He looked deep into her eyes, desperate to understand her. "Why?"

"It has to be this way. I have things I want, things I need to do. I can't give or promise you anything." She closed her eyes. "I need to hear you're okay with that. Otherwise this stops now."

What the hell was going on here? It was usually he who laid the ground rules so a woman didn't get hurt, he that made them understand he wasn't the type of guy they wanted to hang around with too long. Yet now, with Carrie…he swallowed. He had no idea how he'd leave. Scott's heart beat fast, but he held her steady gaze. "I won't ask you for anything."

She smiled softly and opened her eyes. "Good."

His gut knotted with regret as a woman turned

the tables on him for the first time. He wanted her. All of her. He slid his gaze from her face to glide languidly over her body. His heart twisted. She'd been honest, which was a quality he held above all others. This was about tonight and tonight only for her. He'd deal with the aftermath because not doing this, not taking her while he could, wasn't an option. He met her eyes. "Will I see you again?"

A faint blush colored her cheeks, but her gaze never wavered. "I don't know."

Pain hit his chest but still he nodded. "Okay." Scott let the silken strands of her hair drift through his fingers, and inhaled a long breath. "I haven't the time for a relationship right now, either." *Liar. You'd make time for her.* "My life…is stressful, to say the least." He looked deep into her eyes, hating the way he wanted to keep her with him. He smiled. "I'll make love to you and then leave."

He lowered his lips to hers and she surprised him when she met his kiss with ardent intensity. Their tongues explored and dominated, surrendered and resisted. They touched each other's skin. Caressed, rubbed and teased. Scott's blood pumped fast and hot; his penis ached and his balls tightened. She consumed him.

His entire being had come alive with an electricity only she could ground.

"Now. I want you now." Her breath rasped against the side of his face.

He slid his fingers through her delicate patch of pubic hair and found her hot, wet and ready. He massaged her and she shook her head, her cheeks flushed, her teeth clenched. "Now, Scott. Please."

The desperation in her voice stroked his ego and confidence bloomed, where moments before it had wavered. He leaned over the bed and snatched a condom from the side table. He sheathed himself, moved over her and hovered. When her gaze locked on his, he slid deep inside her silky warmth. She closed her eyes and he thrust deep, drew back and thrust again, intent on taking them to a place neither would forget. He clenched his jaw, his heart hammering. *God, don't let her forget me...*

CHAPTER ONE

CARRIE STARED THROUGH the murky window of the train station café as she waited for her mother to return from the bathroom. Her heart beat fast and her hands trembled around an oversize latte. When her stomach heaved with trepidation, she pushed the drink away.

Never in a million years did she imagine she'd be in her current position.

Successful, hardworking and entirely independent…but also mum to a two-year-old little girl. A little girl with jet-black hair and bright blue eyes so like her father's. Carrie swallowed. Maybe Belle didn't need to know her biological father. *Maybe I don't need to find a man I slept with over and over again in the sexiest and most fantastical week of my life.*

She snapped her eyes open and inhaled a strengthening breath. No. She had to do this. It was Christmas, and Lord only knew when she'd have a decent amount of time away from the studio again. She had to put things right. She'd promised herself she'd do everything she could do to find Scott. No more deceit. No more secrets. New year, new start.

Tears burned and Carrie closed her eyes against the images of her deceased husband's cut and bruised face. Gerard's green eyes had pleaded with her as he lay in a hospital bed, holding on to the last minutes of his life.

"Find him, Carrie. Find Belle's father. She'll want to know him one day." Gerard tightened his grip on her hand. "Find him. Be happy."

In that moment, everything became clear. Carrie had looked into Gerard's eyes and known how badly she'd failed to convince him Scott was nothing to her, that the night, that had so quickly become a week, was only a distant memory. Tears burned. She'd never forgotten a moment of it. She'd never forgotten Scott....

"Your train's here, sweetheart. Time to go."

Her mother's voice filtered through Carrie's memories and she abruptly stood, hitching her tote bag onto her shoulder. "I am doing the right thing, aren't I?"

Her mother's concerned gaze ran over Carrie's face. "You're having second thoughts?"

Carrie swallowed and closed her eyes as, once again, guilt pressed down on her that her reasons for finding Scott weren't entirely motivated by their daughter. What kind of person grieved her husband for a year and then began to have thoughts about a man she hadn't seen for three years? She opened her eyes. "I'm just scared of what will happen once Scott sees me after all this time." She exhaled and stared through the open café door at the bustling platform. "I have no idea if he still lives in Templeton. Worse, we both made it perfectly clear we would draw a line under that time from the moment I left. Now, when I turn up out of the blue and tell him he has a daughter…"

Her mother frowned. "If you're not ready, wait. Belle is little more than a toddler. You have time."

Carrie sighed. "Do I? If Gerard's accident didn't teach me how quickly life can change, nothing will. What I want doesn't come into it. I have to do this." Carrie forced a smile in a bid to allay the worry in her mother's eyes. "I'm being silly. Everything will be okay. Belle has a right to know her birth father. Scott was a really nice guy. I'm sure he still is."

"Well, if he's in Templeton, you'll find him." Her mother gripped her hands and smiled softly. "I can still come with you, you know."

Carrie shook her head. "I have to do this alone." She winked. "Besides, if Dad has to look after Belle on his own for more than a few hours, God knows what we'd come back to."

Her mother laughed. "Well, there is that, I suppose."

Carrie lifted her chin, her stomach knotting.

"I should've done this years ago and then maybe the guilt I'm feeling wouldn't be quite so heavy."

"You were adamant you didn't want a stranger in Belle's life." Her mother cupped Carrie's jaw. "You didn't know this man. You still don't. You did what you thought was right at the time. No good will come of looking back."

Carrie frowned. "But what if I'm wrong now? What if...what if this is more about what I need to do to clear my conscience than what's right for Belle?"

Her mother's gaze filled with sympathy. "If you want to turn around and walk out of this station right now, we can. Lord knows, I'd be lying if I said the fact you're getting on a train to find a man you don't know doesn't frighten me half to death."

Trepidation and fear of the unknown battled as Carrie's heart hammered. "I want a fresh start in the New Year. I want to pick myself up and start living again. The chances are Scott won't want anything to do with Belle, or me, which is fine. I can come back home knowing I did my best by Belle and we're free to live our lives, just the two of us." *Liar. Scott's her daddy. Her family...and you've not had a single day in the last three years when he hasn't snuck into your head.*

Despite the lines wrinkling her mother's brow, she smiled and her gaze softened. "You're a brave woman taking control of your life." She glanced toward the window and the idling train beyond. "No matter how much your father and I are going to worry about you the entire time you're in Templeton."

Carrie looped her hand through her mother's arm. "No matter what happens next, Gerard was my husband, and I'll never forget how much he loved us, but I have to do this."

"Then don't let the lessons he taught you about love be wasted. You're human and you need to let this guilt go. Belle is the best thing in your life. She's your daughter and you love her. Tracking down her biological father will never change the fact that little girl is yours."

Carrie exhaled, uneasy, before picking up her suitcase. "Come on. I need to hurry before the train leaves without me."

They walked from the café onto the platform. The smell of bacon, burgers, grease and oil gripped Carrie's stomach as she glanced toward the train waiting to take her on the most terrifying journey of her life.

The conductor's whistle blew, making her start. Her mother pressed a firm kiss to Carrie's cheek. "Your father and I will keep Belle so busy she won't give you a second thought. You'll be home for Christmas and we'll have a wonderful time. I promise."

Carrie grasped the handle of her suitcase and

pulled back her shoulders. "I'll call as soon as I'm settled in the hotel. Give Belle a big good-night kiss from me, okay?"

Her mother wavered as tears glazed her eyes. "Of course. Now go. Quickly."

The whistle blew a second time and, with a final glance at her mother, Carrie rushed for the train. "Hold that door."

The burly conductor scowled as she leaped past him into the carriage. Carrie walked along the aisle as the train rumbled into motion. She drew on every ounce of inner strength that had gotten her through losing her loving husband and Belle's real father…no matter what DNA might argue.

She hefted her suitcase onto the overhead rack and slid into a vacant seat, resolutely turning her face from the platform for fear she might see her mother and bolt for the exit.

The train picked up speed and left the station. Barely a mile or two had passed before the slowly darkening sky surrendered its cargo and spat sleet violently against the window. Carrie flinched. It was as though God showed His disapproval of her plans. Only He knew what the next few days held, but either way, she had to go through with tracking down Scott. The past few weeks had been filled with her constant contemplation of whether or not she and Scott could've had a chance of making it work. And she couldn't go on another day wondering, worrying…maybe even hoping.

Gerard's death had caused a huge shift inside her and Carrie refused to continue to live with the punishing belief she'd walked away from Scott out of pure, unadulterated fear.

Fear of the passion he brought out in her.

It had been spellbinding and stripped her of her usual sensibility; made her feel she could conquer the world…albeit without responsibility or thought of anything or anyone.

Heat rose in her face and she forced the traitorous smile from her lips. No one lived like that.

Yet still she wondered if he would look the same or if he'd recognize her. All Carrie remembered of him was his wild, intense, vivid blue eyes and unruly jet-black hair…and his body. Always his damn body.

She dropped her gaze to her clenched hands and stared at her wedding band. Gerard was gone. Killed having suffered severe internal injuries in a motorbike accident. Never to return. Never to hold her in his big capable arms and tell her everything would be okay. Time and again, Gerard had suggested they find Scott and tell him about Belle… and time and again, Carrie suspected his motives were based in his need to ease her anguish, than wanting to invite another man into the life of the little girl he considered his own.

Carrie inhaled. She'd always told him there was no need; that she was happy. His dying request and the look in his eyes proved all too clearly he knew she wasn't as happy as she should've been.

She swallowed. She'd been selfish in her reasons, weak in her motivation. The fear that the sudden and powerful pull she'd felt for Scott the week Belle was conceived would reignite the moment she saw him again had held her back. How would she fight it when it consumed her so completely before? She hadn't looked for Scott all this time for the pure terror of hurting Gerard. She loved Gerard, adored him, but not once had he evoked the same passion.

Carrie swiped at her face. She was a coward and now Gerard had been taken from her. It was a lesson. A lesson she learned fast and felt deeply.

Guilt clenched around her aching heart. She'd clung to Gerard like he was a buoy in the turbulent ocean during the emotional upheaval of an unexpected pregnancy. A quiet, intelligent and funny writer she'd dated on and off and whose company she loved—yet the special frisson she sought in her heart and in her life hadn't materialized between them.

Pregnant, afraid and unsure of the future, Carrie had been prepared to raise Belle alone, but Gerard had softly and patiently shown her she didn't have to. After months of his pursuing her, she'd welcomed his love with open arms and given hers freely. When they married, just a few months after Belle was born, Carrie stood tall and proud before the registrar on that hot August day and pledged her love and life to the man who had shown her his heart.

Now it was time to start again. To face all the fears she'd had when she made the decision not to tell Scott about Belle.

With her parents' love and support, Carrie had gotten through the past twelve months, knowing her precious baby was surrounded by people who loved her. Scott was a stranger. A man who could insist on seeing Belle when Carrie knew nothing about him. If she'd told Scott about Belle when she was born, he might have asked Carrie to move to Templeton, away from everything she loved and worked for at home. She hadn't been prepared to do that then…and wasn't sure if she would be now. Either way, she had to reconnect with Scott so she could live her life authentically. No more secrets.

She stared through the window at the passing countryside. She might finally be doing the moral thing, yet the feeling that returning to Templeton would be her undoing lingered. She couldn't allow anything to dissuade her from her plans to build a life of her own making…for her and her child. Relying on Scott hadn't been an option in the past, and it wouldn't be now.

Everything in her life would be open, honest and real.

She stared at her wedding band. She wanted to start again, but this only remaining token of her marriage was the hardest to remove.

Scott had made love to her as she'd never been made love to before or since. She'd never forgotten the stranger filled with passion and a brooding intensity that was thrilling and exciting—entirely impossible to resist, but lust didn't last. Scott's skillful hands and rock-solid body had taken her to places she would've never known…but lifelong trust wasn't built on good sex.

The aura of complexity surrounding Scott sparked an instinct in her that he wasn't ready to love and cherish her. It was very probable she'd feel the same if and when she tracked him down in Templeton.

Carrie closed her eyes.

Hindsight had shown her that her marriage with Gerard was rife with the unresolved, lingering issue of Scott and his paternity to Belle. She refused to allow a hurtful boulder like that to remain in her life any longer.

Her nights with Scott were meant to be a single moment in time…then they'd conceived a child. The first time they made love they'd been careful…the other times need had overtaken caution and neither of them had thought of protection.

She'd never done anything so impulsive as to call work and say she'd been struck down with a stomach infection so she could spend a few more nights with a man she'd only just met. She never lied. Period. Scott had brought out all sorts of unpredictable behavior in her...and instead of her fearing the liberty, Carrie found herself craving it.

Desperate for distraction from the cruel thoughts racing in her head, Carrie snapped open her eyes and yanked her tote bag from the seat beside her. She extracted a paperback and smiled wryly at the cover. *Living Your Life Your Way.* She opened the book and made a resigned effort to immerse herself in spirited decision-making.

THE TRAIN RUMBLED beneath Carrie as it slowed and she shifted forward to get a better view through the window. The track ran high through the hills above the Cove before proceeding on a downward spiral toward the heart of Templeton town center. When she'd last seen this view, it had been a balmy July evening and the sun had lit the small seaside town in all its picture-perfect glory. The multi-colored houses, the rows of quaint thatched cottages on the outskirts and the beach with its tumbling rock formations had been idyllic.

Now the town shone beneath a twinkling blanket of lights and huge, illuminated Christmas decorations. Carrie smiled as the reds, golds and greens flickered and danced. Dusk would soon fall and she didn't doubt the seaside town would look more beautiful than ever. Her smile faltered and she slumped back into her seat. She couldn't be seduced by its beauty…and she couldn't be seduced by the thought of anything substantial existing between her and Scott, either.

The train shrieked to a stop and the gray evening light turned dark under the shadow of the platform's metal lattice overhang. Passengers stood to retrieve cases and bags, but Carrie remained stock-still in her seat.

It was six days before Christmas. She'd find Scott, tell him about Belle and if he reacted in any way she couldn't handle, she'd get the first possible train out of there. Everything would be fine. It was nothing more than a case of ripping off the Band-Aid and exposing her open wound to the air so it could start to heal over. Yes, she'd been selfish in her decision-making as far as Scott was concerned, and even though Gerard's sudden death had rocked her soul and broken her heart, she was stronger than ever before. She knew her heart and mind, made her own decisions and molded her own destiny. The first step was making this the last Christmas she kept her secret hidden.

The New Year would be a different year for her, and possibly Scott.

Carrie shook off her melancholy and pushed

to her feet, forcing her chin high. She heaved her case from the rack and purposefully headed toward the nearest exit.

She was in Templeton, but this time she was all grown up, her naivety well and truly quashed. The woman Scott had known was gone and now the mother of his child stood in her place. There would be no racing heart and pumping blood upon sight of him. No instantaneous need to have him touch her, kiss her and take her under again and again until she couldn't breathe.

This time, she'd be entirely in control.

SCOTT WALKER SNATCHED a rag from the engine of the car and wiped his grease-smothered hands. He stared toward the open double doors of his garage and wandered closer. The sleet came down harder than when he'd disappeared under the car's hood half an hour before. He grimaced.

Less than a week to Christmas and he had yet to buy a single present for his mum and three younger sisters. If he didn't sort something out soon, they'd undoubtedly team together and strip him naked before working him into the ass of the Christmas Day turkey.

Then there were the women he'd taken out over the last few weeks…

Damn. He was stuffing whichever way he looked at it. To men, a few dates meant a nice time and a little kissing and flirting. To women, a few dates often meant a hell of a lot more. Guilt slithered over his shoulders and he steadfastly shook it off. He had nothing to feel guilty about. Honesty was his steadfast priority and he'd been careful his entire life not to promise a woman something he couldn't deliver.

He'd never cheated nor left a woman's bed without a kiss and his number, should she ever need to call. He enjoyed a busy social life and worked on plenty of cars that belonged to the women he'd dated after they amicably went their separate ways. He might be considered a bit of a rogue around town…but he wasn't a liar, and the women he dated knew that. Scott clenched his jaw. Or at least, most of them did.

Wandering back to the car, he shook off the niggling irritation over the split with one particular ex and stuffed the oily rag in his back pocket. He planted his hands on his hips, surveying his completed handiwork. The car was now running like a dream and he'd cleaned it all down as well as topped off the oil and water.

Slamming the hood closed, he strolled around the other two cars waiting to be serviced before ascending a set of iron steps to his office. He closed the door and headed for the small fridge. He pulled out a beer and snapped off the top. Taking a long slug, he strode to his desk, collapsed into the chair and lifted his booted feet onto the desktop, crossing them at the ankles.

The cold beer slid welcome down his throat as thoughts of what he had planned for the next year filtered into his mind. He'd worked long and hard, bought the garage and made it enough of a success he would be bidding on an auction for garage number two in the New Year. He smiled. He was on his way.

Financially stable and continuing to provide for his family, he found life was good and settled, just as he planned. He took another drink. Even though he was nothing like his AWOL father, he couldn't deny the thought of relationships, marriage and babies sent him running for cover.

That didn't mean he would up and leave his family anytime soon. He was just fine and dandy living his life single and on his terms. Ignoring the ache in his chest, Scott took another pull on his beer.

The fact remained he still avoided serious relationships like his life depended on it. He couldn't go there even if he found a woman he wanted. Not until he was ready to be a father and a provider and, by God, he wasn't ready for either yet. There had been one woman that made him think he'd risk everything he held dear to be with her forever.

Forever lasted less than a few days before she disappeared out of his life again.

Scott took another drink. So he'd done his duty and continued to focus on looking after his mother and sisters as he had for the seven years before that fantastic week. He couldn't deny his blood pumped with adrenaline, pulsed with a need for excitement and adventure...even some good old-fashioned romance from time to time, but he wouldn't do that to himself, or a woman, until he was sure they'd both be around for the long haul.

The tension that knotted in his gut when he considered a committed relationship told him all too clearly he was nowhere near ready.

Scott hefted his feet from the desk and approached the office window. His Benelli motorbike was parked near the entrance of the garage, ready and waiting, primed to within an inch of her metallic life. Every time he revved her up, it was as though the bike urged him to just get the hell out of Templeton and onto the open road.

"No can do, sweetheart. No can do." The weight of his familial obligations pressed down on his chest and Scott drained his beer.

He tossed the empty bottle into the recycling bin and whipped his leather jacket from the back of his chair. He shrugged it on, snatched his keys from inside the top drawer of his desk and strode toward the door. He locked it behind him and hurried down the steps, eagerly approaching his bike.

His heart pumped with anticipation for the freedom he felt whenever he rode her. He kicked the machine off its stand and wheeled it into the yard. He narrowed his eyes to look at the jet-black sky. Rain spattered his face. The gathering clouds would soon cover any stars that dared to appear when the mid-December temperatures slowly edged toward freezing.

He took his helmet from the box at the rear of his bike, pulled it on and straddled his favorite female. He gunned the engine and satisfaction roared through him as the powerful bike ignited his adrenaline and need for speed. Snapping down his helmet's black visor, he accelerated onto the road toward Templeton's town center.

He eased off the gas as he merged with the chaotic holiday traffic crawling along High Street. Colored fairy lights danced across his vision and he glanced toward the decorated shops on either side of him. The bustling summer season felt like an imagined memory. The Templeton shop owners were nothing if not resourceful, and each year the shops that kept the tourists happy with little pails and shovels in summer kept the residents happy at Christmastime with an array of gifts, original artwork and knickknacks only a woman needed.

Knowing he had to do something in the way of appeasing his coven of female relations, Scott reluctantly pulled into a parking space outside one of the shops. Cutting the engine, he slid off his helmet and ran his hand through his hair. He glanced toward a latticed window donning a particularly festive display and grimaced. Christmas was about time with family, laughing and joking, while consuming far too much food and beer. It wasn't about sparkly red baubles, dancing reindeer or plastic Santas clutching their juddering bellies.

Get your ass in there and get this done, Walker. He swung off the bike and stowed his helmet.

Pocketing his keys, he took a deep breath and purposefully marched toward the shop. He raised his hand to push the door when it swung abruptly open. Upon sight of the woman's long blond hair and hourglass figure trussed up in a fur-collared winter coat, he stepped back and waved his hand to the side in a theatrical gesture of gallantry. She barely glanced at him as she continued to coo and chatter into the cell phone glued to her ear, but he saw enough of her pretty features to cause his entire body to freeze and his grin to vanish.

Her soft floral scent whispered beneath his nostrils and her mumbled "thank you" seeped into his ears, burrowing deep into his mind. She hurried away along the street. Scott stared after her, his heart a granite rock in the center of his chest. That hair. That figure.

He swallowed. The short length of her coat showcased stocking-covered, shapely calves that he'd never forgotten. He couldn't be mistaken. It was her.

He released his held breath and rubbed a hand over the back of his neck. Not now. Not after all this time...

CHAPTER TWO

THE CHRISTIE HOTEL was wonderfully, quintessentially English. As a lifelong lover of all things Agatha Christie, Carrie had fallen in love the moment she walked into the Art Deco lobby earlier that evening. Unable to resist her producer's habit of people-watching, she'd happily taken the key from the receptionist, dumped her case—after a little squeal of nostalgic satisfaction at the bedroom's decor—and hurried back downstairs.

Now, as she stood in the hotel's lobby, she released her held breath on an appreciative sigh. A gorgeous ruby-red carpet stretched out in front of her, leading to the closed beveled-glass, creamy-white doors of the bar at the far end. On either side of her, dual chairs were placed around low tables where people sat and chatted over a glass of wine or brandy. Plinths holding huge floral cascades of every imaginable color boosted the décor, the gilded mirrors reflecting the light in prisms around the vast space.

When her gaze travelled the height and breadth of the gloriously lit Christmas tree in the very center of the lobby, all thoughts of the dreaded task of tracking down Scott momentarily vanished. As she wandered closer, Carrie delighted in the exquisite 1930s ornaments and trinkets overflowing from its branches. She smiled, wishing for a sleek satin evening gown, and strolled toward the bar.

Despite being a habitual single-bottle-of-beer kind of girl, tonight she'd order a dry martini, just for the hell of it.

She slid onto a vacant barstool. The bartender, dressed in a black tuxedo, white dress shirt and bow tie, was young, good-looking and currently serving an elderly couple at the end of the bar. Carrie couldn't wipe her smile as she stared around the room. The subtle light emanating from old-fashioned lanterns cast the intimate space in a soft amber glow; the dark wood paneling, bar and stools added warmth and security. The open-topped, pristine-white piano in the far corner was the cherry to her visual cake. Heavenly.

"Can I help you, ma'am?"

The bartender's gaze darted in quick time from her face to the V of her sweater, but Carrie shook off the threat of annoyance, determined to wallow in the beauty surrounding her awhile longer. She forced a friendly smile. "Hi. Could I have a dry martini, please?"

His green eyes glinted with flirtation. "Coming right up."

While he mixed her drink, Carrie swiveled around on her seat, her imagination on perpetual overdrive. Each and every person relaxing in the bar served as a potential character in a future TV project.

"One martini, as requested."

She dragged her gaze from a man nearing eighty, and the woman on his arm who looked barely out of college, to face the bartender. "Thank you."

"You're welcome." He grinned and the glint in his eyes grew brighter.

Carrie lifted the elegant cocktail glass and took a delicate sip. "Mmm…that's lovely. Thank you."

"You're welcome. So…" He planted his hands on the bar and leaned closer. "Are you in the Cove visiting family for the holidays?"

She slowly replaced her glass on its coaster as wariness skittered over her skin. The less people knew about her, the easier her escape from Templeton would be. She cleared her throat and concentrated on the olive in her drink. "I'm hoping to catch up with an acquaintance. I don't plan on being here for Christmas."

"I see."

She met his eyes and he lifted an eyebrow, his intense gaze roaming over her face. "Does this acquaintance know you're here?"

She shook her head. "It's a surprise."

"A man, by any chance?"

Is that really any of your business? Carrie nodded. "Uh-huh."

Disappointment flickered across his face. "Damn, that's my hopes dashed, then."

Carrie laughed and wiggled her left hand, showing him her wedding band, hoping the bartender would change the subject. No such luck.

"Ah, okay. Is the person you're visiting anyone I might know?"

The lighter tone of his voice indicated his cooling flirtation as he wandered a few feet away and took some discarded glasses from the bar to stack in the washer. Feeling suddenly indecisive, Carrie studied his profile as he concentrated on his task. Her intention had been to spend an hour soaking up the nostalgic atmosphere and then head to bed so she was as refreshed as possible in the morning to start her task of finding Scott. However, putting out feelers on who he was today could prove useful.

Deciding this was too good an opportunity to waste, she sipped her drink and contemplated her next move. She guessed the bartender to be in his early twenties, probably five or six years younger than Scott. The likelihood they hung out in the same bar or place was highly probable. She hesitated. Of course, there could be trouble if the bartender saw Scott before Carrie did. Scott's knowing she was in town and asking questions about him could easily start things off on completely the wrong foot.

She inhaled a long breath and took a leap of faith. "His name's Scott."

"Scott who?"

"Walker."

Interest piqued in his gaze and he gave a slow, knowing smile. "Right."

A flash of irritation rippled through her and Carrie quickly quashed it. How could she get mad at the implication she was a woman chasing after a past lover if in reality that's exactly what she was? She lowered her glass. "Do you know him?"

He slammed the washer door and flicked a switch. The muted rush of running water flowed between them. He smiled and stood directly in front of her. "You know, there isn't a woman this side of Templeton who doesn't keep tabs on Scott. You'll have to fight to get to the front of the queue. Not that I've known the guy to ever get involved with a married woman."

Carrie glared. "And neither would I have an affair."

The barman at least had the decency to blush. "Right. Sorry."

"I assume you're telling me our mutual friend likes the ladies…as long as they're single, right?"

He grinned. "I think it's more of a case of the

ladies liking Scott, but the guy's only human and he doesn't turn down a good time."

Carrie fought a scowl as her stomach knotted with unmistakable disappointment. So Scott was the man she really hoped he wouldn't be...a man who loved them and left them. A man who most likely hadn't lingered over their week together as she had. How could she have thought anything other than sex was on his mind during the passionate, frenzied, entirely erotic time they spent together? How could she have been so stupid to even contemplate the possibility there could have been more between them?

She swallowed. "How well do you know him?"

He shrugged. "Well enough."

"So his reputation precedes him?"

"Something like that."

Irritation hummed through Carrie as she took another fortifying sip of her martini. So the man who fathered her child was a player. Perfect. Despite giving herself to him on a plate three years ago, a small part of her still wanted to believe she had Scott all wrong and their time together was as much a life-changing moment for him as it was her.

Had she imagined the soft fascination she'd seen in his eyes when he looked at her? Had she really been wrong in assuming there was nowhere else he'd rather be than with her…just as she had felt about him?

Shame infused her and Carrie inhaled a deep breath, dragging up her unending tenacity. Everything would work out for the best. Belle's beautiful face filled her mind's eye. It had to.

She studied the bartender as he moved back and forth behind the bar, and narrowed her eyes. She cleared her throat. "So, Scott is still in Templeton?"

He came toward her and planted his hands on the bar. "If we're talking about Scott Walker with dark hair, works out, has a smile that makes women weak at the damn knees because he's got that whole miserable, broody thing going on…"

Carrie smiled. "Yep, that sounds like him."

The bartender grinned. "So, you go in for misery rather than mirth, huh?"

"I'm not in for either right now. I'm in town for a few days, so I thought I'd look him up." Carrie struggled to retain an aloof facade as her knee bounced out of control against the bar. "It's been a while since I last saw him."

He whipped a cloth from the waistband of his trousers and slapped it onto the bar. "Well, I might be reading things wrong here, but from where I'm standing, Scott Walker's the only guy around here confident enough to let a woman as beautiful as you slip through his fingers, that's for sure."

She lowered her eyes. "Maybe."

"Hey."

She looked up. "What?"

The bartender's teasing expression softened. "He's a good guy. Scott's just not interested in settling down, and he makes sure he doesn't ever lead a woman on to think otherwise. He's one of the good guys."

Carrie nodded, fighting the urge to spit feathers. This guy actually sounded in awe of a bona fide womanizer.

"Nope. Despite his reluctance to get involved, I've never seen Scott treat women with anything but kindness and respect." He winked. "If it makes you feel better, I'm sure he'll be more than pleased to see you. I haven't seen him with a woman for a while. He must be getting kind of lonely."

The ill-disguised innuendo in his tone set Carrie's teeth on edge. "Didn't I just show you my wedding band?"

"Sure, but who wouldn't want you turning up the week before Christmas, looking pretty enough to decorate their tree?"

Carrie glared. "I'm not here for some grandiose idea of an illicit affair. He's...a work associate, that's all."

He lifted an eyebrow. "Really?"

She held his gaze. "Really."

He studied her for a moment longer before he shrugged. "If you say so."

Frustration and the need to stick the guy in the eye with a needle hummed through her, so Carrie took a deep breath and glanced around the bar. "So…do you know where I can find the town's Casanova, by any chance?"

"Where he always is. He'll be working at the shop tomorrow. I suspect he'll be there right up to Christmas Eve. He's a hardworking guy." His eyes glinted with amusement. "But if he's a work associate, shouldn't you already know that?"

Carrie glowered. "Fine, I lied. So, what's the shop?"

"The garage on Stiller Street. It's his. He owns it." He moved along the bar to serve a businessman scowling at a bottle of Scotch behind the bar like it was a mirage in the middle of the desert. "Yes, sir. What can I get you?"

Carrie studied the bartender through narrowed lids. Decorate his tree? Pleased to see me? Well, no doubt she'd soon obliterate Scott Walker's love-'em-and-leave-'em lifestyle the minute she told him about Belle. It seemed her daughter's biological father was about as ready to be a daddy as Santa Claus was to go on a diet.

Picking up her glass, Carrie finished the martini in a single gulp and winced against the rush of liquor. The need to flee home pulsed through her but she tamped it down. She had to find Scott or else the perpetual cloak of guilt she wore for keeping Belle a secret from him would never be discarded. How could she face Belle's inevitable questions about her father in the future without knowing she'd done her utmost to involve him in her life?

At least the bartender's words had lessened her fear of being as attracted to Scott today as she was when they met. Time and experience had changed Carrie in the last three years and there was little chance of her to succumbing again to a pair of deep blue eyes and a body like brick.

She stood. She'd go to bed and pray for Scott's disinterest in both her and Belle. That would be the best Christmas present she could ask for. Tomorrow, she'd track down his garage on Stiller Street and face Scott head on. Tell him about Belle and if his attitude was as vile as she suspected it would be, she wouldn't even have to suggest they find a mutually satisfying way of taking their parenting forward. Belle was her priority and Carrie had no interest in exposing her to some Lothario who had zero interest in being a daddy.

If he didn't want anything to do with Belle, so be it. She hadn't returned to Templeton on a witch-hunt.

She placed some cash from her purse onto the

bar and left, renewed determination echoing in every click of her high-heeled boots against marble.

THE FOLLOWING MORNING, Scott winced as the wrench he held slipped from his grasp and scraped roughly across the knuckles of his other hand, splitting his skin wide open. "Goddamn it."

The metal tool clattered to the darkened pit floor and he kicked it against the wall in frustration. It was barely lunchtime and his concentration was shot. Snatching a rag from the car's engine, he wrapped it around the wound and glared at the underside of the car suspended above him. How the hell was he supposed to get any work done when nothing but a blond-haired woman with the sexiest figure known to man circled his damn mind?

Just like the first time he'd seen Carrie years before, the same lightning struck him immobile. He had no idea what it was about her, or why, but Carrie's allure was too strong to ignore. All he cared about was his family, yet this woman had the ability to make him think about the life he led before and after her. It was as though she was a pivotal part of his very existence…and he hated it.

If it was her he saw last night, then what? He had plans. Plans that didn't involve a woman who took his damn heart and then tossed it aside.

Scowling, he braced his good hand on the top of the pit and heaved himself out onto the garage floor. She'd taken his heart, yet he couldn't ignore the fact his reluctance to get involved meant he hadn't made any attempt to find Carrie, either. He was equally as guilty of tossing her heart aside…if there was any chance she felt the same way he did.

Yanking open the buttons on his overalls, he shrugged them down to his waist and stalked over to the sink. He removed the rag and washed his injured hand, memories rising in his conscience. He was all too aware of his reputation as a womanizer around town and he'd done little to correct the gossip, not caring what people thought…but now, with the potential that Carrie could be back, the rumors worried him.

He turned off the faucet and replaced the rag with paper towels from the box on the wall. One by one the women he'd dated crept into his mind. None of them had hit the spot in his heart Carrie had, or even come close. So he walked away. Time and again. Did that make him a bad guy? Maybe, maybe not, but as far as Scott was concerned, he never intentionally hurt any of them.

His gut tightened. No? So why date them? Why romance them and sleep with some of them only to bail out in the end? *Just like your dad when it comes down to it, aren't you?* Scott squeezed his eyes shut as one particular ex's face rose up behind his closed lids. He'd run quicker from Amanda Arnold than he had the others. He told himself it was entirely because of Amanda's trying and demanding personality, but the fact she had a kid too ate at his conscience.

God damn it. Who says I have to want to buy into that crap? He marched across the garage floor, his mind a mess. Was it such a damn crime if he didn't want to add more family obligation to the mountain he already carried?

Making a snap decision, he grabbed his cell phone. He needed reinforcements. Friends and allies out in the field looking for Carrie. One way or another, he had to know if the girl he'd seen in town last night was really her. If she was, he wanted to know why the hell she was back in Templeton.

He punched in his best friend's number.

"Hey, man." Nick Carson yawned loudly. "What's up?"

Scott pushed his fingers through his too-long hair and wandered around a three-foot circumference. "I need a favor."

"Uh-oh. You sound pissed."

"I am."

"Because…"

"I think she might be back."

"Who?"

"Her."

"Her? You're going to have to be more specific than that."

"The blonde."

"The blonde? Nope, still need more."

Scott halted his pacing and glared. "Her. The blonde. The only woman to ever totally mess with my head. Her."

A long moment passed before Nick sucked in a breath. "Ooohhh, her."

Scott scowled. "Didn't I say that clear enough the first time?"

"Hey, just take a minute, okay?"

"Take a minute?" Scott squeezed his eyes shut. "I haven't had a single minute of head space since I almost knocked her off her feet in town last night. Jesus, Nick, you've got to do something."

"*I've* got to do something? What does that mean? I never saw the woman."

Scott stopped pacing. "You're my friend, aren't you? You've got to help me find her."

Nick huffed out a laugh. "What's the matter with you? Even if it was her, you've got enough sense to stay the hell away, right?"

Scott opened his eyes and glared toward the open garage door. Dark storm clouds gathered in the distance like an omen. Nick was right, finding her would surely lead to trouble. Trouble he didn't need...but there was no way in hell he could let this go. He had to know if she was really Carrie. What he'd do about it if she was, he hadn't figured out yet, but right then, not knowing ate at him from the inside out.

"Scott? Did you hear what I said?"

"I heard you."

"And?"

"And what?"

"I'm guessing you haven't spoken to her, so forget her."

"How could I have spoken to her when I barely saw her?"

"Then what's the problem here, man? If you haven't spoken to her—"

"She smelled the same." Scott closed one eye against the pain of his pitiful feelings.

"What?"

"She smelled the same. Exactly as I remember. Her hair is shorter but just as thick, just as pissing sexy as it was then."

"You hear yourself, right? This is ridiculous. What is it you want me to do exactly? Come down there and put you in a damn straitjacket?"

"I've got plans, Nick. You know I've got plans."

"Damn right I do. Plans that will make you rich after all the blood, sweat and tears you've put into that garage. So, what's the problem?"

"She is. Having her turn up here."

"I don't understand. You're saying if this mystery woman is the one you spent a few nights with, it changes everything? Don't talk crap, man. This is one woman. A woman who disappeared. Who never called. I'll be honest with you. I hope to God it isn't her. She's a hassle you don't need."

"How can either of us know that?" Protectiveness for Carrie burned like a fireball inside Scott's chest. He clenched the phone. Memories of the way her body felt in his hands, the texture of skin as smooth as silk beneath his lips...

"Because of you. That's how." Nick sighed. "You love women, but you've never loved a woman like you did her. You fell like a shot, man. Bam! Face down on the floor with no idea how to get the hell back up. You don't need that again. I'm telling you right now, if it's her, get on your damn bike and leave the Cove today."

"Sure. I'll just run away. Don't bother telling Mum or my sisters what I'm doing..." The click-clack of high heels yanked Scott's head up like it was attached by a rubber band to the ceiling. He stared toward the door, his heart picking up speed.

Click, clack. Click, clack.

"Scott? You still there?" Nick's voice filtered down the line.

Tension rippled through Scott's body and his heart beat fast. Carrie came through the open door and halted. Their eyes locked.

Scott's mouth drained dry. "I've gotta go." He snapped the phone closed.

She stepped farther into the garage and closed

her umbrella. He might have been mistaken, but he could have sworn her eyes widened as she cast her gaze over his chest. Before his ego could inflate an inch, their eyes met. God, she was beautiful. Her cheeks were flushed but her gaze steady as she clutched her purse at her stomach.

She tilted her chin. "Hello, Scott."

That voice. He swallowed and crossed his arms, fighting a wince when his elbow knocked his injured hand. "So it was you I saw in town last night."

She stiffened. "You saw me?"

"Yes."

"Where?"

"Does it matter?"

Time stood still and he cast his gaze over her face and body before he could stop himself. Desire burned and mixed with the shock pulsating through him. The atmosphere crackled, showing him all too clearly nothing had changed about his hot and crazy sexual attraction to this woman. He still wanted her, would willingly take her against the garage wall right then if she asked him.

She came closer and halted less than five feet away. He curled his hands into fists to stop from reaching for her as her gaze wandered over his face and chest, lingering at his bandaged hand before she met his eyes once more. "I have to talk to you."

Her soft, husky voice whispered over his senses, raising every hair on his body, making his dick twitch awake as though it'd been dormant for three long years. He purposefully slammed his defenses into place. "Is that so?"

Her eyes flashed with a fire he remembered only too well when they'd been face-to-face at The Coast Inn. "Yes." She glanced around the garage. "I'm sorry to turn up unannounced like this, but I'm here and we need to talk."

He stared at her in disbelief as questions, demands and weaknesses hurtled around inside him, battling with the intense sexual frustration storming through his body. "Just like that, you turn up and say, 'We need to talk'?" He shook his head and turned away from her, lest he get caught in the snare of her wide, impossibly gorgeous eyes. "Go away."

"No."

Keeping his back to her, he uncrossed his arms and planted his hands on his hips. He tipped his head back and smiled as insanity rushed his bloodstream. He wanted to grab her, shake her, kiss her and make love to her. God, he wanted to drop to his damn knees in front of her and beg her to tell him where she'd been and now she was back, was she back for good?

"Scott?"

He closed his eyes, barely resisting the urge

to cover his ears and block out her voice, achingly laced with the unmistakable sound of a plea. "Whether you want to see me or not, I have to talk to you, and I won't leave the Cove until you listen to me."

Her heels clicked closer and his body tensed, waiting for what came next. The dangerous, musky scent of her perfume wafted under his nostrils and he inhaled. She approached the bench beside him and put down a business card. "My number's on there. I'm staying at the Christie. Call me when you're ready to talk. It's important or I wouldn't have come."

He glanced at the card. Carrie Jameson. Producer.

She turned and walked away. He let her go, feeling like a smashed-up car after a hurricane, tossed and turned through the air before being spewed crudely across the highway, left to rust and burn.

He picked up the card. What the hell was he supposed to do now? Carrie was back and his libido told him only too clearly there was no way in hell he wouldn't go to her. How was he supposed to let her leave again when he'd lived the last three years regretting he didn't stop her the first time?

CHAPTER THREE

CARRIE LEFT THE garage and strode into the street, her legs trembling. She clasped her hand over her mouth and ducked into an alleyway. Dropping her head back against the damp brick of the building, she welcomed the heavy rain as it battered her skin.

My God, he looked…amazing.

Scott Walker was still gorgeous, sexy and alive with a fire she stupidly thought she remembered so clearly—but hadn't remembered accurately at all. The irresistible intensity surrounding him hadn't lessened with time. It still seeped from every pore. His inexplicable manliness appealed to her senses and scored over her skin, like nothing she'd ever known with another man. It was crazy—yet so very, very real. She closed her eyes.

God, why did I come here expecting to control the situation?

When he stood in front of her, broad chested, with grease-smeared overalls hanging loose at his hips…Carrie drew in a long breath through flared nostrils as her center shamelessly pulled. The man burned with passion. When she looked into his eyes, his shock over seeing her scorched right through her skin and deep into her heart, making her want to kiss him...comfort him. Apologize. Ask him to forgive her. But how was she supposed to talk to him about Belle and get the hell home as quickly as possible when he affected her like this?

From the dark fall of his thick hair to the shadow of stubble at his jaw and upper lip, he was so entirely masculine she couldn't stand how weak with desire he made her. This wasn't who she was. She was a mum. A producer. A daughter. A widow...

Confusion and shock rocketed through her and she pushed away from the wall. She needed to get a grip. This was about Belle. Not her. Not Scott. There was no way she'd leave Templeton and go back home without doing what she came to do, so she'd better find a way to deal with his pull on her and find it quickly. She couldn't let her fear of Scott's potential to take her as easily as he did the first time change the reality he was Belle's father. And she'd promised herself she'd tell Scott the truth.

Smoothing the front of her coat, she hitched her belt tighter and inhaled the moist winter air. Belle was growing and growing fast. Carrie could scarcely believe this was her daughter's third Christmas. God, she should have done this months ago—why had it taken Gerard's death to make her take responsibility for her actions?

Because I'm a coward. Because I was scared of this. Scared that I'd still be as attracted to Scott today as I was then. Scared that the suspicion in Gerard's eyes whenever I spoke of Scott would be proven justified. Scared I would have to accept what Gerard knew all along...Scott matters to me.

Carrie's tears slipped from beneath her closed lids and trickled a warm path down her icy cheeks. Gerard was a brave man. A selfless, wise and mature man. Her antithesis and, as far as she could tell, Scott's too. Hence why she'd taken over a year to grieve and gather the strength to get through what she now had to do alone. Carrie shook her head. She'd convinced herself the time was right because with the time that had passed since she'd seen Scott, surely her attraction would be gone, obliterated by a loving marriage and a beautiful child teaching her so much about motherhood.

But no. It was still there, maybe burning more dangerously than before because this time she and Scott had a child together. The potential was there to know each other for the rest of their lives; to be side by side at Belle's parent-teacher interviews, birthday parties, Christmas holidays...

Oh, God. Carrie paced left and right as though looking for an escape as the alley's walls closed in on her. *I have to take control. Arranging for*

Scott to see Belle at some point in the future is all that matters here. He doesn't want me. He's never wanted me. I have to remember that. If he felt half of what I felt, we would have found a way to be together. She gave a curt nod and swiped at her face as sanity returned.

She glared toward the opening of the alleyway and belatedly opened her umbrella. Her carefully styled hair now hung in limp rats' tails down her back. The next move was Scott's, and she'd learn to be patient. There was nothing else to be done today. It was only fair she gave him a little time.

She exited the alley and, at the entrance, cast a glance toward the garage. She half expected him to be standing in the doorway, watching her with those midnight-blue eyes. The area in front of the garage was achingly empty.

Ignoring the jab in her chest that felt far too much like disappointment, Carrie dragged up the courage she needed if she had any hope of getting her mission done. Gripping her umbrella in front of her face against the wind and rain, she hurried along the road that would take her back to High Street. The rain hammered on her umbrella, matching the chaos screaming inside her.

The welcome sight of a bakery with lights burning through the cottage-style windows came into view. Tinsel and baubles glinted and twinkled behind the glass, beckoning Carrie inside. She

yanked her umbrella closed and stepped gratefully through the door.

The bakery was deserted. Not a single customer
sat at the pine tables or booths to keep her company…or better still, keep her hidden from ob-
servation. Yet, the smells were as close to heaven
as a girl could get, and Carrie firmly closed the
door. She'd enjoy a cup of coffee and then head
back to the hotel.

Scott had twenty-four hours to contact her before she'd return to the garage and confront him
a second time. He might have shaken her today,
but she was determined that wouldn't happen tomorrow.

She fluffed her hair that was already beginning
to frizz and met the gaze of the woman standing
behind the counter. She had a welcoming smile,
but Carrie was shrewd enough to recognize the
baker's intense appraisal.

Carrie planted on a smile and approached the
counter. "Hi."

The woman's gaze softened. "Good afternoon,
lovely. What can I get you?"

Inexplicable warmth replaced the chill in Carrie's bones that had bothered her every second
since seeing Scott. She dropped her tense shoulders. "A cappuccino would be great. Thank you."

"Anything else? I have freshly baked Christmas
cookies and sweet mince pies, too."

Carrie dragged her gaze from the woman's sparkling brown eyes and looked through the pane of the glass-covered display counter. Her stomach grumbled with insistent demand. Every Christmas cookie imaginable was laid out on red, gold and green trays. Iced cakes and chocolate éclairs, grinning marshmallow snowmen and sparkling angel biscuits cruelly arranged and made purposely impossible to resist.

She sighed as her diet vanished...again. "Why not?" She smiled. "I'll have one of the Santa cookies."

The baker beamed with satisfaction. "Good choice. Why don't you take a seat and get out of your wet coat? I'll bring your coffee and cookie over in two ticks."

"Thank you." Carrie looked around before heading for the booth farthest away from the counter. She took off her coat, tossed it over the seat and slid close to the window. Rain slid in continuous zigzags down the glass, blurring the view of the street. She pulled her cell phone from her bag and hovered her finger over her mother's number. She longed to hear Belle's voice but knew it would be pathetic to call again so soon. She'd only left her at her parents' house the day before. If she was going to do what she came to do, she had to be strong.

Yet, as strong and succinct as she was in her working life, Carrie couldn't remember a time she'd felt so alone since burying Gerard. Seeing Scott again had not only evoked dormant sexual yearning, it had brought on an explosion of further guilt and betrayal toward Gerard. How was she going to handle these conflicting emotions? Heat rose in her face. She was a horrible, horrible person.

The soft brush of approaching footsteps broke through her melancholy and Carrie looked up. The woman from behind the counter placed Carrie's cappuccino on the table, followed by a brightly decorated Christmas plate donning her grinning Santa cookie.

The baker slid onto the opposite seat and set down her teacup before meeting Carrie's gaze. "I'm Marian. Welcome to Templeton." She offered her hand and glanced toward the window. "I promise the Cove isn't always this gray and damp."

Carrie shook Marian's hand and smiled. "Carrie Jameson, and I know just how sunny Templeton can be. You have a beautiful town."

"We do…and a lot of visitors."

Carrie tensed and braced herself for whatever was coming next. Marian might appear friendly but her gaze was dark with curiosity. Small towns, more often than not, equaled little anonymity.

Marian lifted a brow. "So you know Templeton? I don't remember seeing you around here before."

Carrie took a sip of her coffee and its delicious

rich and chocolaty taste slid warm and comforting down her throat. "That's because the last time I was here, coffee was way down on the agenda."

"Want to tell me what was on the agenda…and when?"

"You're not very backward in coming forward, are you?" Carrie struggled to fight her smile.

Marian grinned. "Nope. If you're here to stay for the holidays and like your coffee, you'll soon get to know me and realize how keen I am to know who's who in town. I love Templeton as much as I love my George. I like to know who everyone is."

"Well, as delicious as your coffee is, I won't be here for the holidays. I was here a while ago on a weekend trip with friends." Carrie smiled wryly. "Although, that seems a lifetime ago now."

Marian frowned. "But you had a good time?"

Far too good. Carrie forced a smile. "Yes. Templeton's lovely."

"So you like the Cove, but you're not here for the holidays." Marian frowned. "Are you here on some unfinished business?"

Despite Marian's unabashed interrogation, Carrie warmed to this gray-haired baker with soft, motherly curves and keen inquisitiveness. She glanced toward the window. "I'm here to deliver a message. Then I'll be heading straight home."

"I see." Marian raised her teacup to her lips, her gaze steady above the rim. "And I guess by the sudden hint of sadness in your eyes, the recipient of this message is a man."

Carrie's wavering defenses slotted back into place. "Maybe."

Marian grinned. "There's no maybe about it. What's his name?"

"You don't give up easily, do you?" Carrie raised an eyebrow.

"Nope."

"I don't like to be rude, but I'd rather not say."

Marian's smile dissolved, but she shrugged good-naturedly. "Fair enough."

They lapsed into silence and Carrie watched Marian as she drank. For some reason, she could imagine her in a big, dusty bookshop, browsing the shelves and gossiping. Although, she suspected the baker's laughter was a loud boom rather than a snigger and might not be too welcome in a book-shop. Yet, Carrie would bet money it was a laugh that people loved.

She shook off her burgeoning fondness for this woman and looked toward the window. She had to be on her guard and not get drawn into any sem-blance of friendship while she was there. One look into Scott's eyes told Carrie the man was private. Guarded. She wasn't entirely different. The last thing she wanted was to inadvertently add more fuel to an already burning fire by spreading their business all over town.

The bell over the door announced a new arrival and Carrie darted her gaze to the entrance. The man who came in was tall with blond hair and a fit, athletic physique. He ran his hand over his short-cropped hair and looked to Marian. His face broke into a wide smile. "There she is. One of the usual when you're ready, my darling."

"Can't you see I'm having a sit-down? Come here and meet Carrie. She's in town visiting awhile."

Carrie inwardly grimaced. She didn't want any more people knowing her name. She'd been in Templeton less than twenty-four hours and it seemed everyone was far too keen to introduce themselves to her...thus forcing her to be civil in return.

The man strode forward, his head bent as he shrugged out of his jacket. He looked up, and the moment he met Carrie's eyes, he drew to a sharp stop. "Oh, no. You're blonde."

Carrie glanced from his wide-eyed stare to Marian and back again. "So are you."

He glared. "Not funny. You're new in town and you're blonde."

Marian shifted in her seat. "What's the matter with you, Nick? That's no way to say hello to a lady the first time you meet. Now show some manners. This is Carrie Jameson." She smiled at Carrie. "Carrie, this is Nick Carson, Templeton's resident superstar DJ."

Carrie held out her hand despite her unease. "Nice to meet you."

Nick stared at her with open dislike. He took her hand in his but instead of shaking and releasing, he held it firmly. "Are you in town to see Scott Walker, by any chance?"

Shock caught Carrie's breath in her throat and she snatched her hand from his. She shot her gaze to Marian. "I'd better go. It was nice—"

"Have you seen him yet?"

Nick's demand turned her head and Carrie narrowed her eyes, her spine rigid. "I don't know who you're talking about. I really need to go." She shimmied along the seat and stood.

He crossed his arms. "Scott doesn't need any trouble. Why don't you go back to wherever it is you've come from and leave the man in peace? He's got plans. Plans that don't need altering."

Irritation flared like a lit flint behind her ribcage and Carrie glared, grateful to vent some frustration on this arrogant idiot…all semblance of friendliness vanishing. "Is that so? Well, unfortunately for Scott, plans change…but, believe me, I'll do my utmost to make sure his life, and mine, stay just the way they are."

"So you are her. The blonde who's going to mess up his head again."

"Will you stop calling me 'the blonde'? I have a name, you know." She snatched up her coat and turned her back to him as she buttoned it, yanking the belt tight.

"He's made a good life for his family. Why are you here? What do you want from him?"

His family. *Scott's married? Has kids?* Carrie opened her mouth, but no words formed as her heart thundered. *Oh, God. Why didn't I consider he could have a family?*

Marian cleared her throat. "I'm not sure what's crawled into Nick's backside and turned him into a Neanderthal, Carrie, but please don't hurry off on account of his lack of manners. If anyone should be leaving my bakery right now, it's him."

Carrie turned as Nick's words reverberated in her mind. Trepidation gnawed at her stomach. Scott could have a wife. He could be a father to other children. Why had she not thought about that? Why hadn't she thought about his life, period?

She looked at Nick and his anger permeated the air between them. She clutched the strap of her bag to hide her trembling. "I don't want anything from Scott. You can think what you want, but I came to Templeton to tell him something important and then I'm leaving. Why don't you do me a favor and tell him that, okay?" Carrie looked to Marian who glared at Nick's profile. "It was nice meeting you, Marian."

"You too, sweetheart."

"Where are you going now?" he demanded.

"None of your business." Carrie faced Marian once more and smiled. "Thanks for the coffee. Maybe I'll see you again before I leave."

She nodded, still glaring at Nick. "Make sure you do."

Carrie snatched her umbrella from the stand and threw open the door. She walked out into the rain, her heart racing and her chin high. Nick Carson's animosity had done her more good than he could imagine. It had made her more prepared and given her prior warning of Scott's life now.

The biggest worry was, if he had other children, would he want Belle more than she could have anticipated...or would he completely reject her? He might not want another child. Carrie's stomach dropped. What if he was married when they spent those crazy, lust-fuelled days together? Was his wife away on business? Is that why they never left her hotel room?

"Oh, God." Heat burned her face and in her chest. Had she slept with another woman's husband? Partner?

Sickness rolled through her. She might have kept Belle a secret from Scott for longer than she should have, but infidelity? Being the other woman? No, no, no.

She exhaled a shaky breath as further shame engulfed her. Before the possibility of Scott already being a father came to the table, a father who was present in his children's lives, things had been laced with a romantic ideal in her mind. She had to face the truth that she had come back to the Cove as much to find out about her feelings for him as she had for Belle's sake.

She would tell him about Belle then leave. If he loved and provided for his existing children, the chances were he'd want to love Belle, too. Carrie worried her bottom lip. Would she have to deal with a wife who'd lived in marital bliss, only to now find out her husband had created a baby with a past lover?

Carrie vehemently shook her head. She had to believe Scott was single when he slept with her. She had to or everything had just gotten a whole lot messier. She strode along the street, her head spinning. What confused her was Scott's intensity seemed no different today than when she'd met him years before, and wouldn't children soothe him? Belle had certainly softened Carrie's need to work twenty-four-seven. Carrie now preferred instead to spend time at home doing close to nothing as long as she was with her daughter.

What was going on with Scott that his children hadn't healed the hurt she had sensed when they lay side-by-side, skin-to-skin in a hotel room?

Carrie narrowed her eyes. She wouldn't go there. The reasons behind his state of mind weren't her problem. Since losing Gerard, her resolve had strengthened more than any stranger would detect on the surface. Any man worth their salt should learn and learn quickly, never mess with a mother protecting her child. Ever.

STANDING TOE-TO-TOE with Nick in the garage office, Scott's anger poured into his blood, making his chest constrict with the overwhelming need to punch Nick clean in the face for the first time in their twenty-year friendship. "What the hell do you mean you faced her off? What did you think you were doing?"

Nick planted his hands on hips. "I was looking out for you, that's what. She's trouble. I saw it in her eyes. Whatever it is she wants from you, she won't be going anywhere until she's got it. Why would you even want to find out what that is? Just use some common sense and stay the hell away from her. If she finds you, shut the door in her face."

"You had no damn right."

"I had every right. I'm your friend and it was you who called me, remember? You asked for my help, and I'm not going to sit back and let her walk all over you a second time."

"I asked you to help me find her, not find her and get in her face."

"She was there. I did what I had to do."

"God damn it, Nick." Scott shoved his hand into his hair as he scrambled for the right words. "The woman meant something to me."

"Yeah? You never went after her though, did you?"

Scott glared, words failing him. He hadn't gone after Carrie for fear of the unknown. He didn't want commitment…and after their amazing time together, he couldn't risk hurting her. He'd let her go because he couldn't promise her anything. A woman like Carrie deserved to be promised the world.

Nick's shoulders slumped. "Look, she might be back…but this time she's wearing a wedding band. I'm sorry, man. I'm trying to do the right thing here."

Shock struck Scott's chest. *She's married and come back looking for me? What the hell does she think she's doing?* He shrugged as he struggled to maintain some semblance of nonchalance. "Well, if she's married, this isn't about us hooking up again then, is it? At the end of the day, this is between me and her, not you." Scott moved to walk past him but Nick gripped his arm. Scott scowled. "What?"

"If she isn't here to hook up with you, what the hell is she here for?"

"How the hell should I know?"

"Then I did the right thing by sending her on her

way. Whichever way you look at this, her turning up can only mean grief."

Scott pulled his arm from Nick's grasp. "Whatever… You still shouldn't have gone off at her."

Nick glared. "So we don't watch each other's backs anymore? Will you listen to yourself? She clearly gave you a better time than any other woman has in months. What's going on with you?"

Scott screwed his eyes shut. "I have to see her."

"Didn't you hear what I just said? She's married."

Scott opened his eyes and clenched his jaw as he searched for the reason why he battled the overwhelming urge to sprint from the garage and track Carrie down. It was an answer he didn't have. All he knew was as soon as she stood in front of him, he wanted to kiss her, touch her, make love to her and have her smile at him in the same soft, sexy way she had when she was in bed with him before.

He shook his head, snatched his keys off his desk and pointed them toward the door. "You need to go."

"What?"

Their gazes locked as Scott's blood roared in his ears. "If you think she walked all over me last time, we've nothing else to say to each other. How could she have walked all over me when we were barely together more than a few days, huh? What happened after she left has nothing to do with her. Don't you get that? It was me who hit bottom. It wasn't her fault."

Nick's eyes widened. "So you're going back for more of the same?"

"I have to know why she's back."

"No, you don't. You want to. What is it about this girl? Sure, she's pretty but God, man, it's like she's got hold of your damn dick."

Frustration coursed through Scott on a vibrating wave. He had no clue what it was that burned like an inferno between him and Carrie Jameson. The only thing he was sure of was the same shock mixed with desire had gleamed in her gaze at the garage as it had when she took his hand and led him from The Coast Inn straight to her hotel room.

Scott brushed past Nick. "I don't know what it is, but it's up to me to deal with, not you." He pulled open the office door and waved. "After you."

"You're going to see her right now, aren't you?"

"Yes."

"Fine." Nick raised his hands in surrender. "Do what you have to do. I'll be at the bar when you need a drink. Something tells me that will be sooner rather than later."

Nick marched out the door, his feet banging down the iron steps and through the garage. Scott refused to allow his friend's judgment to seep into his blood and make him resent Carrie when she'd done nothing wrong. She'd promised him nothing. He had to see her.

Locking the door behind him, Scott hurried down the steps and through the garage. He drew together the two iron doors and padlocked them before pocketing the keys in his jeans. Taking a deep breath, he lifted the collar of his leather jacket and, with his head bent against the wind and rain, jogged toward town.

The townspeople were out in their numbers as Christmas Day approached with a rapidity Scott couldn't think about right then. Some faces etched with happiness, others with stress—there was no avoiding the holidays would soon be here and Scott was far from prepared. He passed the temporary ice rink that was set up in the town square every year.

The sound of the kids' laughter and their joyful expressions as they whizzed around the rink did nothing to appease Scott's trepidation. It seemed a lifetime ago when he was carefree enough at Christmastime to spend it at the rink.

Forcing his gaze ahead, he pounded the distance and, with each hundred yards, his adrenaline slowed and his mind leveled. The gold-and-bronze canopy of the Christie Hotel came into view. Slowing to a walk, he nodded to the doorman and passed through the revolving door into the hotel's lobby. It was a fancy, old-fashioned place. Not necessarily to his taste, but that didn't prevent the image of Carrie, dressed in a column of sapphire silk and killer heels, from filtering through his mind.

Once again, his dick twitched awake and his blood heated. Even the knowledge she was married didn't cool his physical need to make love to her again. Her hair, her eyes…those damn, sexy legs covered with sheer black stockings. Never before had a woman held him so quickly and so strongly in her snare. Thoughts of her with another man, and married, caused a lash of inexplicable pain in his chest—a pain so much worse than the surges of jealousy that had torn through him for months after she left whenever he imagined her with another man.

He lifted his chin and shoved his thoughts into submission. He glanced around the hotel lobby and smiled wryly. Yep, the place suited her perfectly. Carrie had that whole Hollywood golden age thing going on. A woman with good curves in all the right places. Rita Hayworth, Jane Russell…He breathed deep and smiled. Real women.

He approached the front desk. The stout, English butler–type manager wore the air of a king overseeing his subjects. He met Scott's eyes with casual indifference. "Good afternoon, sir. May I help you?"

Scott cleared his throat. "Good afternoon. I believe a Carrie Jameson is staying here. Could you please phone her room and ask her to meet me in the lobby?"

"Your name, sir?"

"Walker. Scott Walker."

"One moment, please."

The desk manager picked up the phone and Scott turned, his nerves jumping and his shoulders tense. He looked to his left at a group of suited businessman and grimaced. His idea of hell would be having to wake up each morning and get trussed up in a suit and tie to work behind a damn desk all day. He looked to his right...

Carrie stood watching him. Her shoulders and chest rose as she took a deep breath and strode toward him. He pushed away from the desk. "Don't worry. I found her."

"Sorry, sir?" The desk manager coughed behind him.

"She's here. No need to try her room." Scott moved away from the desk, and he and Carrie came to a stop in the middle of the lobby. He stared, his gaze roaming over her hair to her face, lower to exquisite collarbones and smooth skin above breasts concealed beneath a red shirt—and, God help him, the revealed edge of a red satin bra.

"You came." Her words whispered from between scarlet-painted lips. "Thank you."

He met her eyes. "I'm sorry about Nick."

She smiled softly. "You know about that?"

"He came to me straight afterward." Unable to resist, he glanced at her hands clenched together in front of her. Her wedding band glinted. He met her eyes, his heart beating fast. "The man can be an ass, but he's only trying to look out for me."

"I got that." She broke eye contact and waved toward some seats to the side of them. "Shall we—"

"Why are you here, Carrie?"

A faint stain colored her cheeks. "Why don't we sit down?" She glanced around. "I don't want to do this standing up with everyone watching."

"Why does it matter?" He clenched his jaw. "Does your husband know you've come to Templeton? That you're here now? With me?"

Her color darkened and her gaze blazed with anger. "My husband has nothing to do with this. I'm sitting down. You can either join me or go. I'm not talking about this for everyone else's entertainment."

Scott glared after her as she stormed away. He hesitated as his gut churned with indecision. Whatever she had to tell him couldn't be good, but how the hell could he walk away without knowing what brought her back to Templeton? Not knowing would haunt him for the rest of his damn life.

Cursing, he pulled back his shoulders and strode across the lobby to where she sat at a low table, smoothing her hands up and down the length of her denim-clad thighs. He slid into the seat opposite her, his gaze once again flitting to the shiny gold wedding band on her ring finger. God, he was grateful for the table between them. A table that acted as a boulder. A boulder he deemed necessary if his urge to touch another man's wife was anything to go by.

He met her eyes. "Okay, I'm listening."

Her gaze bored into his before she dropped her attention to her lap. Her hands were clamped so tightly together, her knuckles showed white. Scott shifted in his seat. No part of him was used to making women uncomfortable or fearful. He wasn't a monster and he refused to let Carrie make him feel that way.

He reached across the table and took her hand. She flinched and her head snapped up. Her dark brown eyes were wide with caution. "What?"

"Whatever you have to tell me, just say it."

Time stood still.

Dread seeped into his veins, making him want to lunge forward and wrap his arms around her—

whether in a bid to comfort or silence her, he couldn't be sure.

Tears leaped into her eyes and her hand trembled in his grasp. "I had a baby, Scott. Your baby."

CHAPTER FOUR

CARRIE STARED AT Scott as his hand slipped from hers. He dropped his head forward, his gaze glued to the floor between his feet. Her heart pounded, drowning out the Christmas carols that played quietly on an endless loop throughout the hotel lobby. Bells jingled and faceless characters sang their rejoices, even as her life changed forever. Whatever happened next—whatever Scott said or did—their lives had altered.

She pursed her lips and fought the need to tell him how amazing his daughter was, that she was sorry and should have come clean before but had chosen not to rather than upset Belle's family life for a guy she barely knew. That she knew deep down he wouldn't be ready for a baby, but now he was older…they were older, and their baby was growing up quicker with each passing day and beautiful Belle had a right for the chance to know her daddy.

Carrie's heart beat fast as she waited for Scott to speak. His reaction would illustrate the way forward and what she said next. For now, she would relinquish her habitual need to be in control. Empathy rose for the man sitting opposite her. She remembered all too clearly the shock of the blue line appearing on the pregnancy test. Hadn't she pretty much shown Scott the exact same thing?

His sharp intake of breath broke the tension and he looked up. His dark, blue eyes blazed under the light and Carrie shifted in her seat. The intensity she'd found so appealing felt different now, making her stiffen with unease, rather than heightening her attraction. Uncertainty and shock showed in his expression, overshadowing the steadfast authority she'd gotten from him before.

"You're sure it's mine?" The color in his face faded.

Her first instinct was to be insulted, but she pushed it down. He didn't have any more reason to trust her than she did him. She nodded. "Yes."

"Girl or boy?"

Irritation bloomed and she raised her eyebrows. "Does it matter?"

He closed his eyes. "No. That was a stupid thing to ask. Sorry."

Carrie released a shaky breath. An apology was unexpected—and appreciated. She swallowed against the dryness in her throat. "Her name's Belle. She'll be three in April. She has dark hair and blue eyes. Like you."

His gaze stormed with a myriad of questions

and a depth of pain she'd neither anticipated nor prepared for. Her stomach clenched. She'd expected dismissal, denial, even accusation, but not this barely disguised anguish.

"You've raised her with your husband all this time?" His voice was low, laced with a hint of annoyance.

Further guilt slipped into her veins and sent her pride soaring to high-alert. "Yes. Gerard loved her like she was his own."

A flash of color darkened his cheeks and his gaze shot to her left hand. "Loved? Past tense? You're not married now?"

She glanced at her ring finger and her cheeks warmed. "No. Gerard's dead."

"Dead?"

"He was killed in a road accident over a year ago."

He stared at her for a long moment before glancing toward the people walking through the lobby. "I'm sorry."

"Thank you." She cleared her throat and fought the painful beat of her heart. She had to take control and veer the conversation away from her personal life. Belle, and Belle only. Everything else was out of bounds. "I'm not here because I want anything from you. You have the right to know you have a daughter. I shouldn't have kept it from you all this time. Before Gerard died we discussed bringing Belle—"

"Stop."

She froze.

His gaze ran over her face and lingered at her lips. "You don't get to do that. You don't get to tell me about your marriage or what happened before your husband died. Not yet."

Heat pinched her cheeks. "That's the last thing I want to do. I was trying to explain…apologize, for not coming here before now. I don't want to discuss Gerard with you any more than you want to hear about him, but he is a part of this. He was the only father Belle has ever known."

He glared. "And that's my fault?"

Carrie's heart picked up speed to see such anger in his eyes. "No, but—"

"Fine, then I'm not prepared to listen to you talk about the man who's effectively raised my daughter for the last two years. Not yet." He pushed to his feet and fisted his hand in his hair. "I need time to process the news I have a child I know nothing about. You disappeared, Carrie. Even knowing you carried my baby, you didn't come back."

Irritation simmered deep inside and Carrie glared. "I didn't disappear. I went back to my life after an insane few days with you."

His eyes locked on hers. "An insane few days?"

She lifted her chin, steadfastly refusing to acknowledge the hurt that flashed across his gaze before he blinked and it was replaced with defiance. "Yes."

His jaw tightened. "Right. That's all it was to you."

Carrie looked past him to the bustling lobby. "I didn't know how else to do this but to just come right out and tell you." She forced her eyes to his. "You've got my number. If you want to contact me—"

"That's it?"

She frowned. "You just said—"

"What did I say?" He glared. "That it's okay for you to tell me I have a daughter and then you're free to leave the Cove again? I don't think so. I need some time to think. You're going nowhere until I come find you and we decide what happens next."

Panic skittered up her spine and squeezed like a fist inside her chest. "What happens next?"

"Yes, Carrie."

She swallowed hard as protectiveness for Belle rose up inside her. "Nothing has to happen straight away. I wanted you to know because I can't live with this hanging over me anymore. I don't expect you to step up…or see her…or—"

"Be in her life any way at all unless it's by your rules?" He huffed out a laugh and snatched his hand from his hair. "Who do think I am, Carrie?

You've told me I've got a child. Now you wait for me."

"I wait for you?" Carrie barely stopped herself from teetering from the chair. "What do you mean *wait for you?*"

"You wait for me to get my head around this."

The anger emanating from him spilled like poison across the table between them. Carrie stood, her body shaking. "I'm leaving."

He gripped her arm, his eyes blazing. "I don't know what you expected, but if you thought I wouldn't give a damn, you're mistaken. I don't walk away from the problems that drop into my lap uninvited. I never have before, and I'm not about to start now."

She glared. "Belle isn't a problem. She's a little girl who's lost the only father she's ever known." She yanked her arm from his grip. "From what your friend Nick told me, you've got plans, so why don't you do us both a favor and continue with them? It's Christmas. Go be happy with your family."

"It seems one half of my new family is standing right in front of me."

Her heart shot into her throat. How was this getting so out of her control? Scott was a player, a womanizer, yet the man standing in front of her was reacting so differently than a man who didn't give a damn would or should. Panic flowed through her on a heated wave. She had to do or say something to stop the look of possession in his eyes. "Belle and I are nothing but strangers to you."

He glared. "You really think that?"

She lifted her chin. "I know that. From what your friend ranted at me this afternoon, you already have a family." Shame that she might have slept with a married man curdled like soured milk in her stomach. "So go and do what you need to do and call me whenever you want to talk, but I will not stand here and listen to you say Belle is your family."

He lifted an eyebrow. "Nick told you I had a family?"

"Yes." She crossed her arms to hide the trembling. "I didn't come here to cause you trouble. You can chastise me about my lack of thinking, but don't for one minute start blaming me for wanting to protect my child. You can't lay any claims or demands on me without knowing her or me. More importantly, without us knowing you."

His cheeks darkened. "You think you need to protect her from me?"

Tears burned and she nodded. "I don't know you, Scott."

He stared at her for so long Carrie took a step back, nerves jumping in her stomach. "What?"

"The family Nick spoke of is my mother and

three sisters." His jaw tightened. "I'm the furthest thing from a married family man you're likely to meet in this town."

Relief he wasn't married coursed through her, only to be snatched away again by the boldness of his honesty. "Right. So what are we arguing about? Clearly, you're happy with your life just the way it is. I can leave on the first train tomorrow and you won't need to see me ever again."

"You're going nowhere. Not yet."

Their eyes locked and Carrie opened her mouth to protest, to tell him he didn't get to lay down the rules, but nothing came out. No words of wisdom or wit burst forth to put the man in his place. She snapped her mouth closed.

He smiled softly. "Did you think I was married? Had kids?"

She crossed her arms. "And if I did, you find that funny?" She narrowed her eyes. "I don't sleep around, and I certainly don't sleep with other women's husbands or partners." Her body trembled with frustration as his gaze softened to careful curiosity rather than hostility. She blinked and glanced across the lobby. "I should go."

"If Belle's mine, she's my family. I care about my family more than you'll ever know."

Carrie snapped her gaze to his. "*If* she's yours?"

He shrugged.

"Get out of my way." She pushed him. It was like trying to move a rock with a feather.

"You're not leaving the Cove until we've talked some more."

She fisted her hands on her hips. "Are you trying to scare me? Bully me? Great way to convince me I should consider you being a part of my daughter's life."

He tipped his head back and closed his eyes as if trying to hold on to his self-control. She knew the feeling.

He sighed. "I said I need time. You owe me that. Tell me you'll stay and let me have time to process this. We'll meet tomorrow when, hopefully, I can think straight."

Her heart thumped and her body trembled. How could she refuse him twenty-four hours? He dipped his chin and his crystal-blue, black-lashed eyes bored into hers. As much as she wanted to sprint upstairs, pack and get the hell out of there, she wouldn't. She couldn't have done that to anyone…but especially not him. Not to the father of her child. God damn it, not when he was a man she wanted to touch so badly it made her want to scream.

More than that, how could she refuse his request when he looked at her in the exact same way Belle did when she was hurt, confused and desperate to understand what her mother had just told her?

Her shoulders slumped and she closed her eyes. "Fine. I'll wait for you to call."

"Promise?"

She huffed out a wry laugh. Belle would've said that, too. She opened her eyes. "Yes."

"Then I'll see you tomorrow."

His gaze lingered over her face, slowly evolving and changing. She stood rooted to the spot as his frustration abated and turned to something equally as fiery, but now its implication ran over her body in a way that made her yearn. Her breath turned harried as her body tingled with awareness.

Just as she recognized his intention, he gripped her hand and tugged her forward. Carrie opened her mouth to protest but it was too late. His lips touched hers as he held her firmly against his broad, hard chest.

Stop this! Stop this now! But she leaned into him, her toes curling in her boots and her core humming mercilessly. She could do this. She could match him blow for blow, kiss for kiss. A groan escaped and she raised her hand to grip his neck. She was in control… *Liar!*

She had never felt so out of control since the night she slept with him. Her body trembled with a desire that hadn't been ignited in any shape or form since Scott last touched her. This wasn't the desire she felt for Gerard during their lovemaking. This was fraught with danger and potential heartbreak of a different kind. She had to stop the kiss and stop it now.

Gathering her strength, she pushed her hands flat against his chest and shoved. "Happy now?" She raised her eyebrows, her body a mess. "Exerted enough authority to stroke your ego? Don't touch me again. Do you hear me?"

His gaze was feral. "I needed to know if it's still there. I've never forgotten you. I've never had a relationship or even sex with another woman that compared to what I had when I was with you. Don't you dare leave."

He stormed past her, toward the exit, before she had time to tell him to go to hell or even draw a breath. She raised her shaking hand to her tender mouth. What had she done? How could she have not seen Scott Walker was a man who took what he wanted whenever he wanted it and to hell with the consequences?

Despite her bravado, the need to slump to the floor reverberated through her weakened muscles. She cast her manic gaze left and right. People lingered, watching her curiously. Embarrassment replaced her shameful lust. Her first kiss in months and it was with the man Gerard always suspected she loved. Tears burned. Was this love? Did it make you lose your mind? Do things you normally wouldn't? Carrie trembled. Did it really hurt this much? Did it make you want to run and hide…yet still reach out for the person in question?

Inhaling a shaky breath, Carrie stormed toward the elevator. The seconds passed like hours as she waited for the doors to open.

"Good afternoon, madam. Which floor?"

She forced a smile at the elevator attendant's greeting, cursing the world that she wasn't alone to collapse to the floor. "Six, please."

He pressed the button and Carrie concentrated her gaze on the rising neon numbers above the door. When the doors pinged open, it took every ounce of her self-control not to sprint through the opening like a woman possessed. Instead, she tossed the attendant a wide smile and walked out with as much dignity as she could muster.

Just as the doors closed behind her, her cell phone beeped with an incoming text. Dread knotted her stomach as she slowly extracted her phone from her bag and looked at the display.

You owe me some time. I'll pick you up tomorrow morning at nine. Scott.

Carrie closed her eyes as the corridor walls drew in on her until she thought she would scream out loud.

Scott sat at his kitchen table, frustration curling his hands tighter on his coffee mug. Any man who ran his own business, paid mortgage payments on a three-bedroom detached house and owned a car, as well as his beloved bike, should be able to have a quiet cup of coffee with some good eggs while he contemplated his day ahead. Well, that was no more the case the morning after he learned he was father to a two-year-old little girl than it was any other day.

He glowered over the rim of his coffee cup. Once again, his three sisters had turned up uninvited, kissed their mother at her seemingly permanent position at the stove and then taken seats at his table waiting to be fed. The loud, and too often brash, tirade of conversation bounced from the walls and Scott squirmed as the hardened veneer that sealed in his frustration threatened to splinter.

Once again, the pressure of his familial obligation rose hot and heavy in his chest, burning and clawing at his need to escape. He worked hard and as he earned more money, he planned to be free of the responsibility his absent father had dumped in his lap years before. He planned to help his mother and youngest sister get their own places so he'd have his solitude back. He planned to employ someone else to manage the garage so he'd be free to travel the world, if and when he chose to do so.

Now it was possible that he was a father. The responsibilities had just gotten a whole lot worse.

He curled his fingers tighter around the handle of his coffee cup. A father. The simple fact was, if what Carrie said was true, it was his own fault. They'd made love once with a condom; the second time protection had been the last thing on his mind in his eagerness to have her. He couldn't remember her injecting any sanity or responsibility into the moment, either…

He closed his eyes as the noise and his sisters' presence clawed at his nerves. He took a gulp of his coffee and glared at each of them in turn.

As much as he hated it, the perpetual feeling of suffocation gathered strength. He didn't want his mother or sisters to change. He loved them and adored the unbreakable bond they held with each other—and him. Yet today, more than ever, he felt like a fraud.

The resentment he harbored toward his father fought its way to the surface. He had to find a way to separate himself once and for all from the man who sired him.

All the effort he'd put into not getting involved, not hurting a woman when she might want more than he could give…and now this.

A father to a baby conceived in the week he'd never forgotten…with the woman he'd never forgotten. How could he deny the suffocation didn't ease every time Carrie looked at him since she came back? She must be telling him the truth about the baby. She had no reason to lie. There was a little girl out there who'd never known him as he'd never known her.

His mind turned to his last break-up...or rather, to the woman's son. He liked the boy; had probably grown too attached seeing he had zero intention of settling down. No matter how much Scott told himself he finished the relationship because of the kid's mother, he couldn't ignore her accusations and criticisms. Amanda had made it perfectly clear she thought him no better a man to look after her son than she did the boy's absent father.

A sense of failure dried his throat. Maybe she had a point...but where the hell did that leave him if Carrie's daughter was his?

He glanced at the clock. Eight-thirty. Another ten minutes and he'd leave to go to the hotel and pick up Carrie.

"So it's true, then?"

Scott snapped his head up at his eldest sister's voice. He met Bianca's intelligent gaze. "What is?"

As if joined by an invisible wavelength when one spoke, his other sisters, Ella and Lucy, stopped babbling, their faces swinging between Bianca and him like they watched a damn tennis match.

Smiling smugly, Bianca stole a rasher of bacon

from the plate on the counter, ignoring her mother when she jabbed the back of her daughter's hand with a fork. "I saw Nick at The Oceanside last night. He asked me if you're okay."

Goddamn it, Nick. You know my sisters better than to ask them that. He shrugged. "So?"

Bianca's smile widened. "So, why would he ask that?"

"Didn't you ask him?"

Her smile faltered.

Scott grinned. "He wouldn't tell you, right?"

She scowled. "Fine. Don't tell us, then. See if your sisters care if your face looks like it's been steamrolled and you've got black trash bags stuck under your eyes. If you don't want to tell us—"

"I don't." He stood sharply and the chair legs screeched against the terracotta tiles.

Silence descended.

Scott steadfastly met four pairs of narrowed, almost identical blue eyes and lifted his chin. "I'm going to work."

His mother's wise and far too inquisitive gaze held his and his detachment wavered. His mother's heart was his weakness; her happiness the major pull at his conscience. Was he looking at a woman who was now a grandmother?

She stared a moment longer before nodding curtly and clapping succinctly three times. "Girls, go." She held her arms wide, the fork she'd prodded into Bianca's hand now swapped for a spatula. Grease steadily dripped from it onto the floor. "Breakfast's over."

Cursing inwardly, Scott lowered onto his chair. If he walked out now, his mother was likely to slap him up the side of the head with that spatula. One by one his sisters rose from the table, glancing at their brother, curiosity etched on their pretty faces. None of them argued; none of them risked her mother's wrath.

He smiled softly, his temper cooling as laughter tickled his throat. There was nothing any of them could stand more than being out of the loop on the prospect of some juicy gossip. To add fuel to their already raging snoopiness, he lifted his hand and wiggled his fingers. "See you later, gorgeous sisters. Don't work too hard."

The tension hummed as bags were whipped from chairs and files picked up from kitchen counters. Slowly, his sisters left the kitchen and filed down his narrow hallway to the front door. When it slammed, Scott let his shoulders slump and faced his mother. "Thank you."

She smiled. "You're welcome." She walked across the kitchen and grabbed the coffee pot and a mug. "We need to talk."

He stared at the woman he loved more than any other, his heart turning over. Every fiber in his body screamed for him to tell her about Carrie right then and there. Get it over and done with so he didn't have to bear the burden alone, but to do that, without knowing for sure what Carrie said was true and the little girl she told him existed was even his, would be selfish.

He had to be sure Belle was real and he was her daddy before he made his mother the happiest woman on earth. A grandchild. He couldn't think of anything that would fill her soul more perfectly.

"I'm ready whenever you are." She sat in the chair beside him and filled her cup before topping off his. The glass pot clattered against the earthenware stand in the center of the table. She held her cup between her fingers in front of her, her gaze concerned.

He exhaled. "I met a blast from the past yesterday."

"Oh?"

"A woman."

His mother slowly put her cup down and leaned forward on her elbows. "And?"

"And it's shot me through a loop."

Suspicion darkened her gaze as she frowned. "What's going on, sweetheart?"

"She's not your average woman. She's…she's someone I cared for too much, too fast."

His mother narrowed her eyes, studying him. "Go on."

He shifted in his seat, indecision about how

much to tell her about Carrie rippling through him. How could he explain what she meant to him when he didn't understand it himself? How could he describe the gnawing anxiety deep in his gut that kept him awake half the night? Or how the need to kiss and touch Carrie still burned just as strong yesterday as it had before?

Closing his eyes, he fought the impending headache pulsing at his temples. "We hooked up and she left. I never expected to see her again. Now she's here and—"

"There's every possibility you're going to care too much, too fast again?" His mother smiled and took his hand in hers. "Is that such a bad thing? You've built a good life, sweetheart. You deserve to find someone special to share it with. Don't you want to get married? Have babies?"

Scott opened his eyes, his gut tightening. "Mum—"

She laughed. "What? Is that so bad?"

"You don't understand."

"Then talk to me."

Guilt wrenched like a hook in his chest. "I'm not ready for that. Not yet. You, Bianca, Ella and Lucy are what's important right now."

His mother arched an eyebrow. "And there's not room for anything more in your life? That's silly, Scott. Worse, as a mother, it makes me feel entirely responsible. Have we made you feel you can't have your own life? That you have to be on call to us twenty-four-seven?"

He closed his eyes. Making his mother feel bad was the very last thing he wanted. *God damn it. This is coming out all wrong.* He opened his eyes and squeezed her hand. "No, of course not. That's not what I meant. What I mean is—"

"You deserve someone, Scottie. The girls and I appreciate everything you've done for us…especially since your father left. But—"

"This isn't about him."

"Of course it is. You've looked after us for too long. You were so young when you took responsibility for this family." She smiled and lifted her hand to his chin. "It should be your time now. Why won't you let yourself be happy?"

The truth of her words gnawed like dog's teeth in his heart and he slowly drew her hand from his face. "I'm fine." He planted his hands on the table, preparing to lever up from the chair when his mother gripped his wrist.

"Who is she?"

"It doesn't matter." Their gazes locked, but he stood firm under her scrutiny. Their brief conversation had heightened his impatience to see Carrie. When the time came to tell his mother everything, he needed to know what he told her was accurate and true. It was imperative he had all the answers she'd need if she was grandma to a child she never knew existed.

"Scottie?"

"Mmm?"

"How come I didn't know about this mystery woman when she was here the first time? There's not much you can hide from me..." Comprehension lit his mother's gaze. "Ah, unless..."

Scott frowned. "Unless what?"

"It was her, wasn't it? She was the reason you changed overnight a few years ago. One minute you were going about your business and working hard, the next you were brooding over something none of us knew anything about and was tetchy as can be."

"I was not tetchy—"

"You were...just like you are now." She shook her head. "Didn't I ask you straight if a woman was messing with your heart?"

Scott stood. "Whether she is or isn't, I'm not going to let that happen."

"Good, because I don't want you carrying on, growling and grumping your way through one woman after another like you did back then." She shoved back her seat and snatched their cups from the table.

"I did not—"

"You did." The crockery clattered as she placed them in the steel sink. "Do you know how many women came around here fussing and fawning over your sisters and me as though we were the way to get you to notice them?" She planted her hands on her hips. "If you like this woman, I hope to God you get on with it and she has the backbone to deal with you the right way this time."

The irritation simmering in his gut veered to outright annoyance. "And which way is that?"

"With gumption. You're a hard man to keep satisfied. You might be a man who's looked after his family and hasn't run off like your good-for-nothing father, but that doesn't mean you don't need a strong woman beside you to keep your feet under the table." She waved her hand in the air. "These soppy, fawning, batting-eyelashes, good-for-nothing girls I've seen you with so far aren't worth the polish on your boots."

"Well, that's good to know because she's different. I can guarantee you that."

"She is, huh?" His mother's eyes piqued with interest, her tone softening. "I like her already."

Scott scowled. "Believe me, the thought of you and her in the same room is as appealing as stepping in front of a moving train right now. She's strong, beautiful and undoubtedly a match for you and my damn sisters." He snatched his keys from the kitchen counter. "I'll see you later."

He planted a firm kiss to her cheek and left the kitchen, ignoring her knowing smile. He stormed through the hallway, whipped his jacket from the banister at the bottom of the stairs and his helmet from the beneath the coat rack. He opened the front door and slammed it behind him, gratefully inhaling lungfuls of cold, biting air. The day's weather was the antithesis of the day before. Bright sunshine filled a clear blue sky. Not a single cloud marred its perfection, causing the temperature to plummet another few degrees.

An interrogation from his mother was the last thing he needed, but it should've been expected. Worse, she now knew far more than he was comfortable with…which undoubtedly meant his sisters soon would, too. Cursing, Scott drew Carrie's business card from his back pocket and stared at the italic scrawl for the hundredth time since last night. *Producer.* He clenched his jaw.

Did she think his life was a movie she could direct as she saw fit? Did she come back to Templeton expecting a happily-ever-after regardless of whose lives she changed beyond recognition? He slid the card back into his pocket and straddled his bike. If she did, she was going to get the surprise of her life, because he hadn't played the role of provider for so long only to get trapped again without knowing the truth. All of it. He buckled his helmet, gunned the powerful engine and accelerated toward town.

CHAPTER FIVE

CARRIE GLANCED AT her watch as she paced the length of her hotel room. A fitful night had left her a mess of nerves and trepidation. How could she have let Scott get close enough to kiss her yesterday? To say she was disappointed in herself was the understatement of the year. She'd gotten off the train determined not to be the same woman she was when she'd been in Templeton the last time.

Yet she hadn't stopped the kiss…. God, she'd wanted more of it.

This couldn't happen; she couldn't let him get to her physically as he had before. But hadn't it been her, and not him, who'd deepened the kiss and pressed her body closer? Carrie covered her face with her hands and groaned aloud into the room.

Her nerve endings had sizzled awake; the memory of the contact making her stomach flip-flop and libido soar.

She snatched her hands from her face and glared out of the window. She'd come back to Templeton because she needed to own what happened between her and Scott. For better or worse, she wanted to move on. The guilt of keeping him from Belle had dug a slow and gaping hole in her marriage that she'd tried to ignore. Yet, Gerard never once held it against her that he wasn't Belle's father. All that time, she'd wanted the courage to face her truth and stand tall and proud, regardless of her child being conceived through a brief love affair. Why couldn't she have done that when Gerard was alive? She closed her eyes.

Because the prospect of seeing Scott, of telling him about Belle had frightened her beyond reason. How could she have guaranteed she'd keep her marriage vows and want to return to Gerard's safe stability, if Scott rocked that recklessness inside her again?

The powerful emotion and attraction she felt the moment he walked into the bar had been profound. She hadn't wanted something so intense and complicated in her life, so she'd convinced herself Scott wouldn't want the pressure of a baby.

Even if Gerard had wanted Scott to know about Belle in the hope that it would allay some of Carrie's guilt about keeping Belle a secret from him, would Scott have just walked away? She doubted it. One look in the man's eyes and his sense of possession was clear. She'd been right to keep him out of their lives so Gerard could enjoy Belle being his and his alone.

Tears blurred the busy high street below as she

gripped the windowsill. Now Gerard was dead and it was her responsibility to set the record straight.

She whirled away from the window and swiped at her face. Scott had the power to make her lose her mind and throw caution to the wind. How could that possibly be the right thing for Belle? Yet, she had to find a way of making this work if she was ever to be free to live authentically. Belle had the right to know her father.

Carrie pushed her fingers into her temples. More than anything she sought stability and security for Belle…and she would never find that in a guy who carried off black leather, denim and a permanent five o'clock shadow like he belonged on the cover of GQ. She toyed with her wedding band, hating the undeniable awareness and thoughts rushing through her mind. She was calm, professional and focused in every aspect of her life. Just once she'd acted on instinct rather than intelligence, and it had resulted in the mess she was in now.

She was thankful for Belle, but that's where the joy of her impulse three years ago ended. The fear, anxiety, uncertainty and foolishness Scott drew out in Carrie had made her life harder than it ever would've been if she hadn't met him.

She walked to the bed and snatched up Belle's toy dog. Pressing it to her face, Carrie inhaled deeply. It was one of her daughter's well-loved toys, and Carrie had carefully packed it in case of emergencies like the one she was enduring right now. She closed her eyes and filled her heart with Belle. Second by second, her tenacity and spirit gathered strength. *This is about my child, god damn it.*

Her cell phone rang on the bedside table, making Carrie jump. She rushed to pick it up. "Hello?"

"Hi, sweetheart."

Carrie's shoulders slumped with relief. "Mum. Hi."

"How are you feeling? You didn't sound yourself last night."

"Tired, but okay. I'm due to meet Scott downstairs in—" she glanced at her watch, her stomach knotting "—ten minutes."

"Okay, well, I just wanted to wish you luck… and advise you to keep an open mind to whatever he says. It's important you hear him out or you'll come home without feeling any better about the future."

Carrie swallowed. "I know, and I will."

"Good, because from the way you sounded when you called last night, the man clearly rattled you yesterday. Don't let him badger or intimidate you. You were both there back then."

"I know." She looked toward the window. "It's no surprise he doesn't immediately believe Belle is his under the circumstances."

"He said that?"

The disdain in her mother's voice was expected…and as far as Carrie was concerned, unwarranted. "Mum, I don't dislike him for asking the question."

"I do."

"He doesn't know me. How is he supposed to know I wouldn't lie for my own gain?" She exhaled. "I haven't exactly got a great track record as far as he's concerned, do I? I left and didn't look back, found out I was pregnant and didn't tell him."

"Fine, he might not trust you, but you have reason to be wary of him, too. He's a stranger you're considering bringing into Belle's life. As far as I'm concerned, he has to earn that right regardless of what happened before.

"I could easily be there with you, you know. I could leave Belle with your father and be there in the morning."

Carrie smiled. "I'm a big girl, Mum. It's Christmas, and I want you to be with Belle."

"Are you sure?"

"Yes." Carrie blinked back the tears as desperation to be with Belle brought an ache to her heart. She sighed. "I really thought he'd want nothing to do with me or Belle, but he was—" the confusion that burned blue-hot in Scott's gaze filled her mind's eye "—adamant I stay and meet with him today. I naively thought I'd be on the first train out of here by now. Instead, I'm scared to death he'll say more I don't want to hear." The nerves that had ebbed and flowed through her since dawn grew worse. "He's…complicated."

"And so are you. You can do this, sweetheart. You're in charge here, okay?"

Am I? I certainly didn't act like it when we kissed. She swallowed. "I'd better go."

"Okay. Call me later?"

"I will. Love you."

"Love you, too."

Her mother hung up and Carrie snapped her cell phone shut. She slowly inhaled in a bid to calm her racing heart as trepidation about seeing Scott resurfaced. If she lowered her defenses in even the smallest of ways, she couldn't say for sure it wouldn't be easy for him to take her, possess her and drive her to oblivion and back as quickly as he had the first time.

Guilt slithered over her shoulders. Gerard had taught her about real, enduring love and not a burning passion that surely would be impossible to sustain. She placed Belle's dog on the bed and snatched her purse from the dresser, dropping her phone inside. Belle was hers, and when they lost Gerard, Carrie had closed an airtight cocoon around her daughter, wanting nothing or nobody to ever cause her pain or fear. Until she knew more about Scott, she wouldn't risk him being near her baby. Part of her was angry at letting him close enough that they kissed…another part horribly ashamed by the hurt in his eyes.

With a final glance around the room, Carrie made for the door. She marched along the corridor and pressed the button for the elevator. If Scott wanted to be a part of Belle's life, she would learn to live with that, but that couldn't happen until her attraction cooled enough for her to see him clearly. More important, trust him entirely.

The elevator door whispered open and Carrie smiled at the attendant. "Lobby, please."

"Yes, ma'am."

The elevator descended and Carrie turned to the mirrored wall beside her. She fussed with her hair and clothes, her hands trembling. She and Scott had to set some ground rules. She could kick herself for not being mentally and emotionally prepared for his paternity question, but that was in the past. Now more than ever before she was determined to cement the way forward and would willingly do a DNA test if that's what he wanted.

When the elevator doors opened in the lobby, Carrie nodded her thanks to the attendant and pulled on her confidence like an extra coat. Scott might have slipped under her armor, but that didn't mean she was any less willing to do battle.

If Scott became a part of Belle's life, she would smile when he came to visit and block her nose to his musky, masculine scent that drifted so easily into her nostrils and struck at her femininity. Her bruised and battered heart still grieved for a man who treated her like a queen and Belle like a princess. She couldn't bear another loss of someone she loved…whether that be by death or betrayal.

Leaving the hotel, she looked left and right down the street before glancing at her watch. Nine-fifteen. He was late. She swallowed…or maybe he wasn't coming. Carrie narrowed her eyes. This would be his one and only chance. If he didn't show, she would leave Templeton and go back to her life without him.

A gruff, thundering and powerful motorbike approached far too close to where she stood and Carrie stepped back. She hated bikes with a passion. Gerard was killed on a death trap much like the one rumbling to a halt barely a foot away from her. The rider straddled the machine like it was an extension of his damn anatomy.

She crossed her arms.

He cut the engine and Carrie scowled. He lifted his helmet. The too-long, jet-black hair that should've been deemed messy rather than sexy caused her stomach to drop. *No. Please God, no.*

"Good morning." Scott's eyes shone bright, his smile wide. "Your helmet's in the box so there's no need to look so worried. You'll love riding once you've tried it."

"You think this is funny?"

His smile wavered. "What's wrong?"

Gathering her wits as shock turned to anger, Carrie strode toward him and fought the temptation to kick the damn bike with the point of her stiletto. "My husband was killed on one of those things. You're unbelievable."

His smile vanished and he swung from the bike in one fluid motion, his arms outstretched as he came toward her in two easy strides, his gaze apologetic. "How was I supposed to know that?"

Carrie waited as the seconds beat out between them and the cold winter air that blew along the street whipped into a sudden frenzy. She gripped the hair that swept across her face, opened her mouth, closed it and opened it again. "I don't know, but God damn it, I don't want that thing anywhere near me."

He dropped his chin to his chest, and when he exhaled, a puff of breath danced in front of his mouth. He bounced his helmet against his denim-clad thigh a few times before he looked up. She stared in fascination as his eyes cooled from ice-blue to midnight blue, soft with regret. He raised his hands in surrender. "The bike's out of here, okay? I'll go park it across the road and we can walk wherever it is you want to go. Deal?"

Her stomach knotted with something hard and fast and deep that she didn't want to contemplate.

His consideration was genuine, which unfortunately struck another hole in her weakening defenses. "Yes. Thank you."

He smiled softly, his gaze running like a caress over her face. "Good."

Turning, he approached his bike and Carrie released her held breath. He stowed his helmet in its carrier, tossed her another apologetic smile and kicked the bike off its stand. Frozen, she stared after him as he waited for the road to clear before he wheeled his bike toward the parking lot on the other side as though it weighed little more than a tricycle.

She abhorred bikes and speed and danger. Everything about Scott represented exactly what she wanted to avoid, but there was no denying she'd been unfair snapping at him the way she did. Swallowing her pride, she shook her head. *Idiot woman.*

When he came back, she'd apologize and endeavor to shake off her constant inability to prevent her mouth from running at ninety miles an hour whenever something unnerved her. Animosity between her and Scott could only be detrimental to Belle. She had to do her best to give Belle her father. She and Scott had covered little ground, and it was four days before Christmas. All of a sudden, she wanted nothing more than to be at home holding her baby.

Carrie stared across the street, simultaneously willing Scott closer and wanting to delay his return.

Any fool who looked into eyes as telling as Scott Walker's could see he had understanding and pride. Worse, Carrie sensed an innate dependability, which was ridiculous and disconcerting, considering how little she knew about him.

Pulling back her shoulders, she forced a smile when he stopped in front of her. "Thanks for abandoning the bike. I shouldn't have snapped at you. You had no way of knowing how my husband was killed."

His gaze lingered a moment at her lips, before he nodded. "Apology accepted." He gestured along the street. "Shall we?"

Carrie nodded. "Sure."

They fell into step side-by-side, and Carrie was instantly too aware of his height and stature. She stared resolutely forward, ignoring the rush of attraction that washed over her once again.

After a few moments, he cleared his throat. "I meant what I said yesterday. I've not shared with anyone else what I shared with you."

She swallowed, her heart pumping. *Why is he going there?* "Whether or not that's true—"

"It's true." His gaze pinned hers.

"Fine, but yesterday when you kissed me—"

"It was a moment of madness, and entirely my fault. It won't happen again…unless you want it to."

She snapped her gaze to his. "I won't." *Yeah, right.*

He smiled. "Fine, but there's nothing about three years ago…or yesterday, that I regret." His voice was low and somber. "What I'll regret is if we can't talk today."

Her shoulders slumped as the tension left her body. "Same here."

His jaw tightened. "Then we're halfway there."

Halfway where? Why did he seem so settled about all this when she was a bundle of nerves? It should be him floundering around, unsure of what happened next, not her.

She glanced at him. "Do you know anywhere private we can talk? I get the impression Templeton's residents like to be in other people's business. I'd much prefer us to be alone."

"We could head to the beach. It's a nice day and they have a hut down there that sells coffee and hot chocolate." He turned and met her eyes. "I know a spot where no one will find us."

The insinuation in his tone stoked her irritation. "I bet you do. I'm sure you know plenty of places to take women so you're alone with them."

He lifted his shoulders. "Maybe I do."

Feeling foolish and immature, Carrie ignored the tension that scored like sharpened claws across her shoulders and smiled. "I'm not afraid of you, Scott."

He frowned. "You say that as though I'd like you to be."

"You seem more self-assured than yesterday."

"And that worries you."

It was a statement rather than a question and the confidence in his tone sent Carrie's apprehension soaring. "What's changed?"

He halted and looked directly into her eyes. "If I have a child, I want to know everything about her. This stopped being about you and me the moment Belle entered the equation."

Dread knotted Carrie's stomach. "Meaning?"

"Meaning it's her at the forefront of my mind right now. Nothing else."

He turned and continued walking, leaving Carrie momentarily paralyzed. What the hell did he mean by that? Blinking, she hurried forward and fell into step beside him, her nerves stretched to breaking. They walked in silence. The street was busy with parents and children and people laden with bags and boxes decorated in festive reds and greens. The scene provided a picturesque and welcome excuse not to talk. Every now and then she stole a glance at Scott, expecting his jaw to be set and his brow furrowed as it had been for most of the time they'd been in each other's company. Instead he was smiling softly.

Does he know something I don't? Why is he so happy all of a sudden?

They left the sidewalk and joined the boardwalk. Scott extended his arm to encompass the sand that stretched over a mile each way. "Welcome to Cowden Beach."

Carrie turned to her first sight of the Cove's sands since she'd arrived. She smiled. "It's gorgeous. The last time I was here I was in a bikini and slathered in sunscreen, but even in December it looks amazing."

She met his gaze. His cheeks were flushed and his eyes were toe-curling and sexily dark.

She frowned. "What?"

"Nothing." He shook his head and looked to the refreshment hut farther along the beach. "Coffee or chocolate?"

"Hot chocolate would be great."

"Good choice. Bart's cabin is by no means Marian's bakery, but he still makes a great hot chocolate. Follow me."

They descended the sand-covered steps onto the beach and when he put a hand to her elbow, Carrie pretended not to notice. Once they were on the sand and his hand didn't move, she continued to ignore it. They approached a hut painted in a faded pink that Carrie imagined was once bright red. It appeared to act as a beacon to any beach dwellers and the line was four or five people deep.

At last, he released her elbow and nodded toward the ocean. "Enjoy the view. I'll be right back."

He left her alone and she ran her gaze appreciatively over his strong, broad back hidden under leather, down to his taut butt and thighs in blue denim. She sighed and dragged her gaze to the blue-gray ocean in the distance, inhaling the salty air and drawing on her emotional armor for what was sure to be one of the hardest conversations of her life.

She would be entirely honest and answer Scott's questions as fully as possible. He kept their agreed meeting and was clearly willing to listen. The question was, where and how to start?

His apparent new state of mind indicated he had things he wanted to share too, but God only knew what he could possibly have to say to make him so damn cheerful. If he thought he got to decide what happened from there on in, he had a shock coming. Belle was her child…and would remain solely hers until she got to know Scott and his intentions.

She glanced toward the hut. He chatted with a man she assumed was Bart, laughing and smiling; the scene was entirely too reminiscent of the first time she'd seen Scott chatting with a bartender on that fateful night they met. She turned back to the ocean and toyed with her wedding band. His comment about Belle being at the forefront of his mind was worrying. Did he mean to claim joint custody? Would this turn into a battle she hadn't anticipated rather than the possible reunion she stupidly came here to explore?

Carrie pressed a hand to the nerves jumping in her stomach and prayed she and Scott quickly found their way to a mutually satisfying agreement. If the tension simmering beneath the surface flared between them again, it would end in certain disaster.

Belle's disaster.

There couldn't be a time when Carrie stood in front of her daughter and was forced to confess it was her failed relationship with Scott that had robbed his presence from Belle's life. If anything happened between her and Scott and it didn't work out…

When Scott turned and walked toward her, Carrie straightened her spine.

"Here you go."

He held out a steaming paper cup and she smiled. "Thanks."

"Why don't we find a sheltered spot on the rocks? I wouldn't have thought anybody would be around there this time of year."

They walked the short distance to a black, gray and brown tumble of rocks that stretched tens of feet from the sand to the bottom of a huge hill dotted with houses high above the beach. He led her to a rock smoothed flat and shiny by years of the tide's assault. He shrugged out of his jacket, folded it and put it on the rock. He sat beside it and patted the jacket, his blue eyes steady on hers. "Take a seat."

She smiled at his show of chivalry. "Thank you."

She settled on his jacket and lifted the cup to her lips. Silence came down between them and Carrie slowly counted to ten, knowing she should be the one to start the conversation. She sipped her drink and then held it in her lap. "I'm sorry it took me so long to come here."

She could practically feel his gaze boring into her temple and she dragged her study from the horizon to his eyes. They were somber but calm, and a relieved breath whispered from between her lips. "I was wrong to keep Belle from you."

"Tell me about your husband."

She stiffened. "What?"

The skin at his neck moved as he swallowed. "Your husband is as much a part of this as you, Belle or me. I see that now." He briefly closed his eyes before opening them. "It was a shock, learning you got married."

She looked away. "Why?"

"It was something you said to me…that first night."

Had parts of their brief conversation ebbed back

and forth in his memory as they had in hers? Had he replayed their words and touches as she had? She inhaled a shaky breath. "What did I say?"

"You asked me to make love to you and then leave."

She nodded as the smell of the hotel room—of him—crashed into her senses. "Yes."

"You said you had things you wanted, things you needed to do."

She faced him and his gaze met hers.

"You said you couldn't give or promise me anything."

"I couldn't."

"Yet you got married."

Their eyes locked for a long moment before Carrie faced the ocean. "I loved him."

"You could've loved me."

Her heart twisted. Why was he doing this? She shook her head, her defenses slamming into place. "Neither of us knows that."

Silence.

He would not make her feel bad or fully responsible for never returning to Templeton after that week. She turned. "You were there too, Scott. You said you didn't want a relationship. That you had enough stress in your life. How was I supposed to imagine for one minute you wanted me…let alone Belle?"

His jaw tightened. "Well, I lied. I lied for my

own protection. I didn't have a clue what was happening when I was in bed with you. From the moment I saw you, touched you, I thought my head would explode. The minute you walked into the garage yesterday..." He swiped his hand over his face.

Panic hurtled through her. She couldn't deny her body yearned to be against his in that moment—couldn't deny she wanted to kiss him and experience the all-powerful sensation that heated her heart and soul when she was with him before, but things were so different then.

She took a sip of her drink. "Everything's changed. I'm a mum now. A widow. I don't believe your life hasn't changed or moved on, either. It's impossible. I've already heard about your reputation with women, and I've barely been here two days. You've hardly been waiting for me to come back." She shook her head. "Don't paint me as the one entirely to blame that we're in this situation. You could have found me, too."

Their eyes locked and Carrie's heart beat fast from the frustration in his eyes. God, even in anger he was handsome. She looked away. "A child changes everything."

"I know that."

"Good."

Carrie stared into the depths of her cup, her body aching for him and who they were that night.

Free and young; passionate and entirely alone. To be looked at the way Scott had looked at her, his eyes wide with passion and desire, would be flattering to any woman, but when the man was as strong, masculine and self-assured as him, it was cruelly irresistible. She met his eyes. "That week was about sex, having a good time and enjoying ourselves. Sex is easy. Raising a child is anything but easy."

"That doesn't mean I couldn't have loved you."

Perspiration burst icy-cold on her nape. *God, he means it. He really thinks he could've loved me.* Why couldn't she fight the feeling of missed chances? That all along she was destined to be with this man? Gerard was so good to her, yet her pull to Scott was still there and as strong as ever.

She inhaled a shaky breath. "You don't know that any more than I do. You won't make me feel guilty for leaving when I thought our time together was nothing more than a fling for either of us. I wanted a career. That was all that mattered. I wanted a career even once I found out I was pregnant. I didn't plan to fall in love with Gerard. It happened. I didn't deceive you." Carrie tilted her chin, owning the moment and all the fear she still carried about their time together. "As far as I knew, you were a player, and I was okay with that. The trouble we have now is, it seems you still are and I don't want that around Belle."

His burning hot-blue gaze lingered on hers, before he shook his head and lifted his steaming cup to his lips. Carrie stared at his neck as the stubbled skin shifted and moved as he drank. Her heart raced and her hands trembled around her own cup. "I think it would be better if we just spoke about what's best for her, don't you?"

He lowered his cup and stared ahead, a muscle leaping in his jaw.

The tension stretched.

He cleared his throat. "This won't work if we don't fill in the gaps."

She turned. His eyes were dark with determination. "What gaps?"

"Belle came before you married, right?"

"Yes. She was a few months old."

"So why you didn't come back when you found out you were pregnant? Why didn't you at least give me the chance to be there?"

Fire flashed in his gaze. He was rightly confused and angry. She blew out a breath and slumped her shoulders. "I can't change my feelings, my thoughts or my actions. I've apologized, but I can't keep apologizing. What happens now should be your only concern. Nothing else."

"Well, I'm sorry, but I don't take things at face value. I need to know it all, not just the bits you'd already decided to tell me when you came here."

Irritation seeped in and her spine turned rigid.

"She's yours. If you don't trust me, then we'll do a DNA test."

"Trust?" He shook his head. "Don't you think we're a million miles away from trust right now?"

He might as well have slapped her. "I made a mistake, but I am trustworthy. I stand by people. I make decisions and stick to them. You have no right to make a judgment about me when I'm here to put things right."

"No? What else am I supposed to do? God, Carrie, I'm reeling here."

Their gazes locked and her breasts rose and fell in sync with his chest. If he didn't want to know Belle, that was fine. She'd done her part by coming here and there was no way she'd go through this agony a second time if he changed his mind about meeting Belle in the future.

Every thread of her many fears about returning to Templeton clung like tendrils of seaweed around her heart. Why couldn't he accept her truth when she'd told him this was all about ridding herself of her mistakes so she could move on?

"What is it you want me to tell you exactly?" She stared at his hardened profile. "My relationships after I left here have nothing to do with you being Belle's father."

He looked at her. "I want to know what led you to marry some guy and let him bring my daughter up as his before trying to contact me."

Her heart beat fast and her mind spun. *Answer him. Tell him.*

Because I was scared I'd always loved you and I've lived a lie for the last three years. Because my daughter would one day know I slept with her father and then ran for the hills. Because even though I loved my dead husband, he never made me feel an ounce of the passion you do....

"Because I can't stand the guilt anymore," she blurted. "Life can change in a heartbeat and too many heartbeats have passed without you knowing Belle or her knowing you. God damn it, Scott, you don't need to tell me how selfish or stupid I was to keep her from you."

His gaze dropped from her eyes to her mouth and Carrie inched back. How dare he do that hungry, heavy-lidded thing with his eyes—something she found so damn hard to resist. This wasn't supposed to be happening. *She* was supposed to be the one in control.

CHAPTER SIX

MIXED FEELINGS OF fear and longing rushed through Scott as he stared at Carrie's flushed face. Her huge brown eyes were wide with honesty and apprehension. She flicked out her tongue to wet her lips and his chest constricted. God, he wanted to kiss her so badly, but to do so again would be stupid. She still wore her wedding band, was still grieving.

He shot his gaze to the horizon, battling his need to take her in his arms and instead forced his focus one hundred percent on the sole reason he wanted to meet her today. His child. "You weren't selfish or stupid keeping Belle from me. You did what you thought was right." He sipped his lukewarm coffee to ease his dry throat and lifted his gaze to hers. "You might as well accept I won't walk away from her once I know for sure she's mine."

Her gaze darted over his face, uncertainty showing in her eyes. She exhaled. "Good, but this is going to take time. I don't know you."

"Do you want to?"

Her attention dropped to his lips. "Yes."

Scott ran his gaze over her eyes, to her hair, to the soft, feminine curve of her neck, and smiled. "Good. Then we have somewhere to start." He drew in a long breath. "If I wasn't so scared of falling in love with a kid I've never seen, I'd ask to see a picture of her."

She smiled and her eyes softened with undeniable pride, as shiny and tempting as melted chocolate. She reached for her bag. "I have several in my purse if you—"

He shot out his hand and covered hers. "Not yet. I need to know…"

"That she's really yours." She eased her hand from his. "I understand."

He stared deep into her eyes. A perpetual awareness he wasn't ready to be a father, and the fear he wouldn't go the distance if he was, edged into his conscience. "Do you?"

She nodded and moved her hand from her bag, curling her fingers around the edge of the rock beneath her. "Of course."

Guilt pressed down on him and Scott steadfastly pushed it away. "You're leaving sooner rather than later. How are we supposed to do this?"

"One day at a time. You have a beautiful two-year-old girl who is your spitting image. We have to try to make this right. For her."

Scott inhaled with unexpected pride. "She really looks like me?"

"Yes." She laughed. "She even acts like you. She's a fiery pain in the butt eighty percent of the time."

He lifted his eyebrow. "And the other twenty?"

"She's kind, funny…" A faint blush darkened her cheeks. "And has a smile that will undoubtedly lead the opposite sex into all sorts of trouble in the future."

Once again, longing for this gorgeous, sexy woman who'd given birth to his child took off before Scott had a chance in hell of catching it. He needed to taste her. Feel her smooth, silky lips against his. As foolish as it was, the desire was far too strong to resist. He leaned toward her slowly, giving her a chance to move back. She stared at him, her eyes wide. He gently brushed his lips over hers before pulling back. He swallowed. "I'm glad you came back, Carrie."

She shivered. "Me, too."

He glanced along the beach. "We should go. You're getting cold."

She touched his arm. "Scott?"

"Hmm?"

"I know you want answers, but the honest truth is I made some selfish decisions for my own protection…and then Belle's. When you walked into the bar that night…" She shook her head. "I had to go with you, and to this day, I have never done anything like what we did again. It's not who I am, and it scared me to death."

He clenched his jaw. "But you're glad you found me again? Glad I was here when you came looking?"

She nodded. "Yes."

He slid his hand over her clenched fist, resting on her thigh. She moved to pull away and he tightened his grip. Trepidation, fear and desire stormed in her dark brown eyes. He smiled softly. "Whether you like it or not, I could read you like a book as soon as I met you and I can now. It's in your eyes, Carrie. You're battling this tension between us as much as I am. We're strangers...but we're not. I've got no idea where to go from here, but we'll work it out."

She hitched her shoulders. "I came to Templeton to tell you about Belle and you're right, we shouldn't be thinking about us in all this. We can't make any mistakes. Belle is too important to me."

Determination hummed as the protectiveness and need to provide for his family hurtled through him. He needed to be there for his daughter, the same as he did for his family. "I get the feeling you thought this entire trip through on your terms only."

She pulled her hand from his. "That's not fair."

He lifted an eyebrow. "Can you honestly say you

thought long and hard about how I'd feel when you came back and told me about Belle?"

Her eyes flashed with defensiveness. "It's taken me three years to get here. How can you say I haven't thought about this? Maybe I didn't consider your feelings too deeply because I didn't think for one minute you'd have any. Maybe there was a chance you might care about Belle, but not about me…and definitely not about us."

"Then you were wrong, weren't you?" Tension burned hot and heavy between them, despite the frigid air. "I have commitments here I won't walk away from. People relying on me to always be here. Whatever happens next is going to be as difficult on them as it is for me. You need to know that."

She pushed to her feet. "Okay, well, now I know."

She averted her gaze to the promenade in the distance. He turned to the ocean. Stalemate. Frustration pumped through him. His mother and his sisters were all the commitment he could handle. What if two more people in his heart were two people too many and he ended up failing one, or maybe all of them?

The proof of the possibility showed in the sickness in his gut and the dryness in his throat. What if he let Carrie down like his father had his mother? God, what if he let Belle down and she was forced to be responsible for Carrie like he was for his mother and sisters?

"We should go."

Her voice cut through his unwelcome thoughts and he turned around. She stared at him, her eyes big and brown, and her blond hair shining like spun gold in the sun. She was beautiful, and all he wanted to do was make the anguish in her gaze disappear. Even now, his attraction to Carrie was out of his control. His body quivered with the effort it took not to take off her coat and whatever she wore underneath, so he could smooth his hands over her skin once more. He wanted her weight against him and her heat straddled over his groin and her lips on his.

His desire for her was raw and animalistic.

She was back and he was still completely messed up about her and now their child too. He concentrated on a couple walking hand-in-hand along the shore and shook his head. "And to think I only wandered into the bar that night for a quick beer."

Silence.

He looked at her. Her eyes were bright with tears. She tipped her head back and laughed so infectiously Scott laughed, too.

"What? It's the truth."

"Can we please put that time behind us now?" She grinned. "Those weren't the actions of sensible parents. They were the actions of lust-fuelled maniacs. Come on, it's cold. Let's go inside somewhere."

Their eyes locked for a moment before their smiles slowly dissolved. Scott exhaled. "Can I just ask you one more thing?"

Her gaze shadowed with wariness once again. It had felt so good to laugh with her. To see her smile when so far nothing but fear and worry had been present on her face whenever she looked at him. Yet he couldn't let their conversation go without asking this one final thing.

"So your husband…Gerard…did he think the baby was his at first?"

She shook her head. "No. I've known him for years. We dated on and off. I told him about you, about Templeton, and he still wanted the baby and me. We married a few months after Belle was born. He was a good man, Scott. He loved Belle and he loved me."

The honesty in her eyes was clear. She wasn't a bad person. She fell in love…Scott swallowed. Just not with him. Time stood still even as the world continued to turn. Who was he to say things could've worked out between them? What could he have given her and a child when his anger about his father's abandonment was a hell of a lot deeper back then than it was even now?

She was a mother. A mother who loved her child…who loved *his* child.

The gathering breeze whipped her long hair about her face and, instinctively, he lifted his hand and brushed it back, its soft floral scent whispering into his nostrils.

She stilled.

He pretended not to notice. "You're beautiful, Carrie."

"Scott, please."

He dragged his gaze from hers and looked toward the promenade running the length of the beach as ominous gray clouds gathered in the distance. "Why don't we head back to town and grab a bite at Marian's? I missed breakfast and I don't think very well on an empty stomach."

She followed his gaze, uncertainty etched on her face. "Is there somewhere else we can go?"

His smile faltered. Nick. He'd harassed her at Marian's and it had clearly shaken her. Scott scowled. His friend would damn well apologize to her sooner rather than later. Either that, or he'd drag him through a brick wall. "Sure, but there's nowhere that serves pancakes like Marian."

"Okay." Her chest rose as she inhaled a shaky breath. "Marian's it is, then."

He grasped her hand and she stiffened for a millisecond before her hand relaxed in his and he led her from the beach. They had a baby together and, in time, he would learn to curb the urge to yank Carrie's curvaceous, sexy body to his and step up to what he really needed to do. Provide for his child and her mother.

Once or twice as they covered the distance from the rocks to the promenade, she tugged her hand slightly in his but he didn't let go. He understood her hesitation, but the lack of conviction in her attempt to instill distance didn't merit releasing her, and no part of him wanted to surrender the feel of her hand in his.

The circumstances of their reunion were beyond painful. His emotions, and hers, were raw. They reached the promenade and this time her tug was succinct and their hands parted. Scott glanced at her, but her expression was a mask as she stared at the shop facades on the other side of the street.

He had to be stronger than this. He couldn't lose his head—or heart. He had to think of his mother—if she had a grandchild and he messed this up, she'd never forgive him.

They walked on in silence for a few steps before Carrie gasped and drew to a stop outside the shop beside them. "Wow, look at this. Belle would love this place. We have to go in."

Scott inwardly groaned, grappling to find an excuse why he couldn't follow her into the brightly decorated toyshop. He didn't want Carrie to go in there and come face to face with a part of his past that refused to be put to rest.

The shop was a little girl's paradise. The lattice window coerced passersby inside with bright, sparkly pinks and reds, dolls and ribbons, satin-covered boxes and glittering costume jewelry. The knickknacks and dressing-up clothes apparently tipped a wink at every female in town, judging by the frequency the shop door opened and closed, welcoming and dispersing chattering females, old and young, with or without kids.

Carrie turned, her smile wide. "Can we go in? I won't be long."

He shrugged, feigning indifference. "Sure. I'm right behind you."

Taking a deep breath, Scott braced himself for the onslaught of the shop's owner and followed Carrie inside.

CHAPTER SEVEN

CARRIE'S HEART TWISTED with longing for her absent daughter as she walked into the richly decorated, winter wonderland store. The soft ringing of sleigh bells and giggling children sounded from concealed speakers as customers browsed the shelves or stood in line at the counter. The atmosphere was festive and friendly. People smiled and laughed as calls of "Merry Christmas" and "Season's Greetings" floated throughout the small, intimate shop.

She wandered around, picking up and replacing glistening tree ornaments, candles of every shape and size, entirely aware of the enforced distance Scott had instilled for the first time since they'd sat so close together at the beach. The hand-holding, the brush of his lips, so different than the hunger of the night before, had crawled under her skin and revealed a softer side to the man she was only just beginning to know. Now he loitered near the door, casting surreptitious glances toward the woman behind the counter, his face a mask of distaste.

Carrie looked from Scott to the woman again.

She was about Carrie's height, slim with dark, curly hair that tumbled past her shoulders. She was dressed in an elf outfit that might be deemed a little risqué for a kids' toyshop, considering the degree of her visible cleavage. The customers she served laughed and smiled with her as her wide, bright eyes sparkled.

Carrie shot another glance at Scott. Seemingly oblivious to her study, he shook his head and turned to stare out the glass-paneled door behind him. Carrie frowned. Was the woman an ex? The apprehension on his face would suggest so—purposefully avoiding eye contact, aloof and awkward, no matter how he tried to hide his discomfort. An entirely unexpected and unwanted twinge of jealously threatened and Carrie shoved it aside. None of her business. Yet her habitual curiosity failed to diminish even when she selected a beautiful doll from the display in front of her. Its eyes were the same bright blue as Belle's and her hair the same ebony black. She'd love it. Smiling, Carrie joined the queue and waited to be served.

The woman behind the counter handed a bag with a huge teddy bear wearing a Santa hat to a waiting customer and, as she did, glanced toward the shop door. Carrie waited for the woman's reaction. This was possibly the first time she'd seen Scott since they'd entered the shop. Her cleavage visibly heaved, her eyes widened and her cheeks flushed scarlet as she grinned. Carrie glanced over her shoulder at Scott and flinched at his unexpected glare.

"What?" she mouthed, feigning innocence.

He tilted his head toward the door, indicating he wanted to leave. Carrie held the doll aloft. He glanced from the door to the counter before raising his hand in a gesture of surrender. Interesting. At the beach, he'd insisted on knowing about Gerard. Did his need to know have anything to do with this woman? Carrie would've bet her life's savings she was about to come face-to-face with one of Scott's lovers.

She turned and met the steady stare of the woman behind the counter. The appraisal she gave Carrie was decidedly chillier than the one she'd given Scott. She blinked and her bright wide-eyed, "friendly shopkeeper" welcome miraculously reappeared.

Carrie resisted the urge to shiver. "Hi. Just this, please."

The woman smiled, her straight, white teeth glowing beneath the string of bright, icicle-shaped lanterns above her. "Isn't she beautiful?" She reached beneath the counter and brought out a roll of pearlescent blue wrapping paper, the exact shade of the doll's eyes and dress. Carrie held back a grimace. No matter how much she might have fallen in love with the toyshop's Christmas ambiance, the atmosphere around this woman was just too squeaky clean to be authentic.

Carrie glanced over her shoulder toward Scott as she spoke, unable to resist checking if he watched them. "She's gorgeous. I wish I could afford to buy the whole collection."

Scott scowled, his gaze firmly fixed on the woman serving her.

"So, did my eyes deceive me or did you come in with Scottie? He's standing at that door like he's going to bolt any minute." The woman laughed, the sound high and ultra-feminine, her fingers a blur as she measured and cut a length of paper with a pair of sparkling silver scissors. "The question is whether he's desperate to run from me, you or the other females in the store."

Carrie stared at the woman's bowed head. "He's showing me around town. I'm visiting for a few days."

"Is this your first time in Templeton?" Her gaze darted over Carrie's shoulder toward the door and back again.

"Second. I was here a few of summers ago. I'm not sure if the Cove looks more beautiful in winter or summer."

"Well, there's no better person to show you around than Scottie." She lifted a box from the shelf behind her before drawing out a huge bag of shredded paper. "I hope he didn't pick you up as you were walking along the street minding your own business. Scott Walker is a man who likes the ladies…at least for a while." She met Carrie's eyes, her gaze blue and cold. "But you look the type of woman to handle him."

"I'm not sure he needs handling any more than anyone else does." Carrie's stomach knotted with annoyance, but she kept her smile firmly in place. "He's been nothing but a gentleman."

She laughed. "Oh, he's a gentleman. That's not even up for debate." She nestled the doll into the paper-filled box and replaced the lid.

Carrie frowned, curiosity gathering momentum as the woman wrapped and taped the box with lightning speed, completing her task with a knotted blue satin bow and a flourish.

"There you go." She grinned. "Enjoy."

Carrie stared at the box in disbelief. It would've taken her over an hour to achieve the same flamboyant and utterly beautiful package. "Wow, thank you. My daughter is going to be beside herself when she sees this. She won't even care what's inside."

The woman stiffened. "Your daughter?"

Her gaze was so intense, Carrie fought the urge to step back as wariness skittered over her skin. "Yes, she's not with me. My parents are looking after her for a few days."

She glanced toward the door once more, her smile unsteady. "How lovely. How old is she?"

"Two."

The woman continued to stare in Scott's direction for so long, Carrie turned. He pushed away from the wall and strolled slowly toward her. Carrie turned back to the counter and the woman's gaze shot to hers, her smile wide and steady once more. "Well, that's just lovely. If you find yourself at a loose end while you're here, I shut up shop every night at six if you want to meet for a drink or dinner. You'll find everyone in Templeton really friendly."

Carrie cleared her throat. "That's kind of you. Thank you, but I won't be in town—"

"My name's Amanda. Amanda Arnold." She thrust out her hand, seemingly oblivious to the growing number of customers waiting in line. "I'll be here whenever you want to pop in. Are you staying at one of the bed-and-breakfasts? Aren't they to die for? So beautiful inside and out."

"I'm staying at the Christie."

"Ooh, even better."

Carrie sensed Scott behind her just as his fingers gripped her elbow. "Are you ready to go?" His voice was a low rumble.

Carrie turned. He fixed his eyes on hers, his jaw a hard line. Fighting the trepidation that furled inside her, Carrie nodded. "Sure." She faced Amanda. "Nice to meet you."

Amanda beamed. "You, too."

Carrie picked up her package and she and Scott walked back through the shop in silence, his grip firm on her elbow. He opened the door and stood back, letting her go out ahead of him. The air was bitingly cold after the warmth of the shop and Carrie sucked in a breath. "Wow, it's getting colder. We might have snow later. That would be kind of nice before Christmas."

Silence.

Questions danced and burned on her tongue, but there was no way she was going to ask Scott who Amanda was to him. The one thing she was sure of, she was *something* to him. She studied his masklike face. "You okay?"

He stared at a spot over her head. "Fine."

"Are you sure?"

"Yes." His eyes met hers. "Did you get everything you wanted in there?"

She lifted an eyebrow. "I didn't get the impression you wanted me to spend time browsing." She lifted the package. "I got this for Belle, but maybe I'll go back and have another look around before I leave."

He snorted and glowered at the shop window. "Yeah? Well, maybe you should consider full body armor next time." A muscle quivered at his jaw.

Swallowing down further questions, Carrie glanced left and right along the high street. It had gotten a whole lot busier in the fifteen minutes they'd been in Amanda's shop. "So, Marian's?"

"Yes. Let's get out of here."

When he stalked away, Carrie let him go. She shot a final glance toward the shop window and started when she looked into Amanda's cold eyes as she stood, her hands fisted on her slender hips, on the other side of the glass. Carrie smiled and waved. Amanda returned the wave…but a smile from her appeared a stretch too far.

JUST AS HE pushed open the door of Marian's Bonniest Bakery, the first spits of sleet dashed Scott's face. He stepped inside and held the door open for Carrie. Feeling like a damn idiot for walking away from her, he tried to relax the muscles in his face and neck—and damn near trembled from the effort. Amanda Arnold. Her final words of their last conversation over two months before echoed in his head. "Next week or next year, you'll regret the day you walked away from my son, Scott Walker."

The woman was a man-eater and had more than the proverbial screw loose. Something he discovered a little too late—after becoming embroiled in her life and that of her seven-year-old son. He closed his eyes. God only knew how the poor kid would find a way to cut the apron strings when they were practically tied around his neck...

The click of Carrie's heels snapped Scott's eyes open and he pulled back his shoulders. Now there was every possibility he was a father and he couldn't deny the gut-wrenching fear slipping through him. Time and again, he'd made mistakes with Amanda's son...time and again, she'd told him he had no clue about kids or what they needed. How the hell was he supposed to convince Carrie he was a good bet for Belle when he didn't believe it himself? As much as his father's absence had affected his family, he also knew being a dad meant more than living under the same roof and financially providing for them. If he was going to be the father Belle deserved, he had to put his heart and soul into every moment he spent with her. He knew this, but the perpetual fear of failing lingered deep inside. What choice did he have but to take a leap of faith to know if he was good enough? Was that fair to Belle—or even Carrie?

She stepped into the bakery and stopped directly in front of him, her intelligent gaze locked on his. "Didn't realize how much of a hurry you're in when you're hungry."

He shrugged, shoving away the insecurity and urge to put distance between him and Carrie and all she represented. He would not walk away from this woman. Not this time. "A man's got to eat."

She moved past him and into the bakery, by-passing the counter and heading straight for one of the booths at the far end of the shop. He closed the door. The moment Carrie walked into Amanda's shop, protectiveness had unfurled inside him. Protectiveness and fear that Amanda would finish whatever developed between him and Carrie before it even started.

Dating Amanda had been a mistake, but a night out drinking and brooding over money could lead a man to make dire mistakes. After kissing her outside The Oceanside, he'd felt duty bound to ask her out again. The date had gone well, so there was another date…and another. When she'd taken to dropping her son at the garage almost every other evening so Scott could "bond with him" while she worked or caught up on paperwork, Scott began to feel an inkling of fondness for the kid. When she began dropping him off with a list of criticisms and mistakes he made whenever he was with Rhys, her sense of entitlement had seemed a step too far. Not to mention the added weight it gave to what Scott already suspected—he wasn't cut out to be a dad any more than his own father.

So he'd called it off. Months ago. Yet Amanda continued to have trouble understanding his point of view…and he didn't think she'd mind telling Carrie all about how he wronged Amanda and her little boy. He had a feeling she'd want further vengeance after a single glimpse at Carrie's gorgeous face and sexy figure.

Cursing, he headed for the counter. He glanced across the bakery toward Carrie and their eyes met. He lifted his head as a way of asking her if she was okay. She smiled softly and nodded. He released his held breath and faced front. So far, so good. The last thing he needed was Carrie thinking he'd tossed Amanda and her son aside when deep inside he still had no idea how he really felt about the potential of Belle being his.

He might have as little as twenty-four hours with Carrie before she disappeared again to spend Christmas with Belle. He understood her need to be with her daughter and wouldn't try to stop Carrie leaving, but he didn't doubt for one minute if she suspected he would turn his back on Belle, he'd never see Carrie or the little girl again.

He had to figure out a way of ensuring she understood it was Amanda's words rather than her son's presence that so quickly felt like a squeezing hand around Scott's throat. The suffocation he'd felt had been about Amanda, not the boy.

Self-doubt ricocheted inside him and Scott glanced toward Carrie a second time. Her determination to tell him he was a father had only provoked his attraction toward her further. She was strong, committed and independent. All the things he craved in a woman and had yet to find before or after her. She was still in Templeton, despite his less than amicable reaction…and Nick's blunt and cold welcome. She didn't spook easily and that was more important to him than she could ever know.

Yet, right now, Belle was his priority. He refused to get emotionally involved with Carrie until he knew for sure the little girl was his. What was to say Carrie wanted him anyway? She'd said nothing about trying again. In fact, she'd made it pretty damn clear she was there for Belle and Belle only.

Scott clenched his jaw and moved forward in the line. He wanted a life partner who could handle his family, his baggage and his messed-up resentment toward his dad—and he couldn't help thinking no woman had come closer to being the right one than Carrie.

Yet, whether he liked it or not, he couldn't ignore her husband had been a stand-up guy…and Carrie still wore his ring.

Scott shifted from one foot to the other. The long queue ahead of him hadn't moved. Marian whirled back and forth, harassment showing in her red face. Scott left the line. Marian would send him away anyway if she spotted him waiting—either that, or get him kneading dough. She held no qualms with making her regulars wait if they were under the age of thirty-five. To quote her, "Kids your age can wait without risk of your knees giving out or your incontinence pants leaking."

Forcing a smile, Scott slid into the seat opposite Carrie. She'd removed her coat and faced the window, her long, thick hair a blanket of wheat down her back. Thinly disguised apprehension showed in her pallor and stiff shoulders. His smile faltered. "What's wrong?"

Her smile was too immediate and too wide to be sincere. "Nothing." She glanced at the empty table. "No pancakes?"

Hating that he didn't have the words or actions to comfort her when his mind and heart were in such a mess, Scott nodded toward the queue. "I might as well rest my legs considering the time it's going to take to get to the front of that lot."

She glanced at the counter and flashed him a smile before gazing through the window once more. The atmosphere intensified with unspoken words. It was clear she'd seen enough at the toyshop to understand he and Amanda had history. He swallowed against the bitter taste that coated his throat.

What could he really tell her? How time and again he avoided relationships? How the weight of responsibility pressed down on him more often than it lifted him? She would hate him before he'd had the chance to figure out what to do about her, Belle or anything else.

He had to fix this atmosphere threatening to obliterate the gentle whispers of trust beginning to develop between them. If the child was his and he ran at the first hurdle...

He took a deep breath. "Amanda's my ex."

She turned, her eyebrow lifted and a soft glint of teasing sparkled in her eyes. "Ah."

Shifting in his seat, Scott glanced toward the window. "It ended badly and—"

"Was the decision yours or hers?"

"What?"

"To end it."

"Mine."

"Right."

He frowned. "What?"

"So now you're going to say she's the mad-bitch psycho ex and not to listen to anything she has to say, right?"

"No."

She raised her eyebrows but said nothing.

"Fine, maybe I was. The point is, don't judge me on it not working out with her, okay? She has a son. A little boy. I don't want you thinking it was because of the kid that I walked. It wasn't."

Her smile stayed in place but Scott saw the subtle shift in her gaze—teasing to careful consideration.

She glanced down at her hands folded on the

table. "So do you want to tell me your side of what happened? Or shall I wait to hear hers?"

Defensiveness slithered over his shoulders and his gut tightened. "I'm on my way to where I want to be in this world, Carrie. I have plans…"

"Plans that don't include a woman who could mess that up…especially a woman with a child."

"I didn't say that."

"Then what are you saying?" Her cheeks darkened and her gaze flashed with impatience. "I gave you my truth, Scott, now give me yours."

"She wanted more. All the time. She's selfish, demanding and vain. I don't have time for a woman like that. It wasn't all about the boy." He reached over and covered her hands with his, unsure who he was trying to convince more, Carrie or himself. "None of this is easy for me. You've told me I have a daughter and it's like I've taken a bullet to the chest. A relationship, kids…I just don't know if I'm ready for it yet."

"We don't always get to choose when these things happen."

He tightened his grip on her hands. "I know. The moment I laid eyes on you, I would've done anything to get to know you better, to have you stay with me and not leave, but I know how things can change. I know how easily people can leave and never come back—"

"Which will always be entirely out of your control. It's the same for everyone, Scott. That's life. What is it you're really trying to tell me? Just say it. I'm big girl."

He ran his gaze over her face and took a deep breath. "My father ran out on us a long time ago, said he couldn't handle it anymore."

"It?"

Scott clenched his jaw. "Marriage. Kids. Responsibility." He glanced around the bakery. "So it all came down to me, or rather I made it come down to me."

She frowned. "And I should be worried about that?"

"No…you should be worried that time and again I fear how much of him is in me."

"Oh." She pulled her hands from his and crossed her arms. "Well, I appreciate your honesty."

You've lost her. You've lost her big time. "But I haven't gone anywhere yet. Maybe I never will."

"Maybe you won't, but that's not enough for me to introduce you to our daughter, especially when you could one day leave and never see her again. I'd rather she never met you at all."

"Carrie—"

"I don't know what else you expect me to say."

He swiped his hand over his face. "I just need to have everything in place. Know that I have everything set up to be a good man, husband and father before I make that sort of commitment to anyone." He forced his eyes to hers. "And I don't have everything in place. Not yet."

Silence.

She pursed her lips and the noise and chatter all around them grew in volume as he counted the seconds. He'd given her his truth. He'd said the words out loud and now the ball was in her court. He might just have made the biggest mistake of his life, but he refused to lie to her, or make out he was someone different. He held his breath and waited for Carrie to jump to her feet and bolt from the bakery. If she did, he wouldn't let her get very far. If he had a kid, she had no right to tell him that and then disappear again. No right at all.

She smiled softly and her shoulders drooped. "Thank you. For telling me the truth. You were right about what you said at the beach, too."

He waited. Which part? He'd said way too much.

She blew out a breath. "I should've thought long and hard about how I'd feel if someone turned up and told me I was parent to a two-year-old I knew nothing about. I'm not asking you for anything. That's not what this is about. I just wanted you to know about Belle, that's all."

Relief she was still sitting and hadn't run re-laxed his shoulders. He smiled. "Then tell me about her."

She grinned. "She's beautiful…"

He kept his eyes on her face, but her words faded into the background as the magnitude of trouble he was in crashed into his heart. Carrie's eyes were alight as she chatted about Belle, her voice full of pride and the odd bout of vicious possession he recognized in his mother. His smile was locked in place, his heart beating like a freight train. They had a child together. A child Carrie was so certain was his, she'd willingly do a DNA test.

Hope and pride bloomed within him, only to be whipped away by insecurity and the overwhelming need to run as she continued to give him a seemingly second-by-second account of his daughter's life. Scott inhaled a deep breath. The one thing he couldn't change, or fight, was the fact Carrie affected him. He couldn't explain what it was, or even why this seemingly normal woman seemed so extraordinary to him. Yet, the same hot, molten need to have her in his bed…and in his life still ran through him as it had before.

"So that's it. That's your daughter in a nutshell."

Her laugh cut through his fearful contemplation. Her eyes searched his, her cheeks flushed and her lips pulled wide by the breadth of her smile.

Taking a deep breath, he reached for her hand. "Will you stay awhile longer?" The words tripped from his tongue like water. So smoothly, he wasn't certain he'd actually said them.

Her hand stiffened and she frowned. "What?"

"Stay. Just until Christmas Eve. I want to get to know you before Belle comes into the equation. Everything is moving so fast and I want to spend some time. Just you and me."

She shook her head, disappointment showing in her gaze. "Belle is what this is all about, Scott. Don't you get that?"

"I do, but is a few days too much to ask? I need time to get my head around this and I don't want you to leave. Not yet." Fire churned and scorched inside him. His feelings for her grew stronger every time she was near.

He'd be a fool to brush them aside a second time.

"Scott…I have to be with Belle on Christmas. Staying here isn't an option." She slid her hand from his and closed her eyes. When she raised her hands to her face, her fingers trembled. "You have no right to ask me to stay."

His gaze hovered on her wedding band and he closed his eyes. "Maybe I haven't, but please, stay until Christmas Eve. After that, you leave in time to spend Christmas with Belle. I need this, Carrie. To get my head straight."

She dropped her hands. "You just told me you're not sure you're ready. You can't expect me to stay here, at Christmas, with the risk that you might turn around and decide you're not cut out to be a daddy after all."

"But—"

"No. I won't do it."

"I won't let you walk away a second time."

Her angry gaze darted over his face. "Let me? That isn't your choice to make. You call me after Christmas, in the New Year, whenever, but there is no way I'm staying while you figure out what you want."

She pushed to her feet and Scott gripped her wrist, his heart hammering and his head whirling with the myriad of unwanted emotions rushing through him. He clenched his jaw. "Don't go."

"Let go of me." She snatched her arm from his fingers. "I don't want to regret coming here, Scott. I have a home and a little girl waiting for me. I'm sorry." Her pretty porcelain skin shone pink at her cheeks and neck.

Frustration mixed with desperation. Dented pride mixed with his stupid lust for this woman with the thick, blond hair and eyes like melted chocolate. "God damn it, Carrie, so I've got standards of who I want to be as a dad. Standards that are pretty damn high. Is that so wrong? Or would you prefer some two-bit daddy for Belle? It might take me a while to get there, but I know one thing for certain, if there's anyone I'll reach those standards for, it's you."

She opened her mouth as if to say something and then snapped it closed. She shook her head and slid from the booth. Turning away from him, she jabbed her arms into her coat and yanked the belt at her waist so tightly Scott flinched. She hitched her bag onto her shoulder and shot her gaze to his. "Goodbye, Scott."

Turning, she stormed away from him, sashaying through the tables and tens of people filling the bakery. It was a miracle she didn't barrel anyone over as though they were little more than pins at a bowling alley. Scott closed his eyes, dropped his head to the table and welcomed the pain.

CHAPTER EIGHT

BURNING WITH ANGER and frustration, Carrie strode along High Street. She passed the shops with their merry, twinkling facades and headed for God only knew where. Scott's words reverberated in her mind, making it more and more difficult to breathe against the ice-cold wind that whipped around her.

What was she supposed to do with the confession that seemed to spew so easily from his mouth? He wasn't sure if he was cut out to be a dad yet, but he wanted to try? Because of her? The guy was insane. Did she really think she'd let him anywhere near Belle with such a flimsy resume?

Why had she thought coming to Templeton to find him was the right thing to do for Belle? What more did she need than a strong, steady mother who had all the love in the world to give her? Just because Carrie couldn't imagine a life without her father didn't mean Belle needed one who might or might not be there in two years, twelve years or twenty-four.

Gerard's sensibility and strength poured into

Carrie's heart. His committed writing schedule and time-management reminded her of the things they had in common. The virtues that provided her daughter a steady life to aspire to. Virtues Carrie clung to in a steadfast attempt to avoid the yearning for excitement that resided just beneath the surface of her skin; the craving Scott ignited so easily—and so clearly lived by.

Carrie narrowed her eyes. She'd learned her lesson, and throwing caution to the wind once had allowed a storm to blow in and turn her life upside down. She refused to let Scott be a tornado in her life a second time.

Her parents had stood by her, never demanding answers about her week with Scott. They'd cared for and loved Belle so Carrie could continue to work until she could afford a place of her own and child care. *She* didn't need Scott. Didn't he understand that? It was all about Belle.

Scott didn't understand anything. No one did until they had a child and their entire world was tipped on its axis, ruled by deep, unconditional love. Scott didn't seem to have any idea what his life would be like next week, month or year. She did. She would be caring about her daughter's heart and welfare. Period.

Well, there was no way she'd let his bright blue eyes and occasional sexy smile smash her reality to smithereens and blind her with an idyllic,

movie-like scenario that was illusory and dangerous. Dangerous to Belle and her.

She might have thought of Scott before and during her marriage; was reminded of him every time
she looked at her daughter; but that didn't mean
she'd let him close enough to waver her decision-
making.

Carrie hurried blindly forward with no clue
where she was going or what to do next. She
walked along the promenade, farther and farther
from the center of Templeton, oblivious to the distance she covered or her surroundings until the
sight of a holiday park ahead snagged her attention. Carrie stared through the open gates, her eyes
widening with surprise.

The Good Time Holiday Park was lit up in all its
glory. Fairy lights blinked beneath the eaves and
around the door of the reception building, while
an eighties' Christmas hit rang out from what Carrie assumed was some kind of clubhouse. Beyond
that, the roofs of rows and rows of mobile homes
stretched into the distance.

She glanced behind her. How far had she
walked? She had no idea this place existed. Then
again, she and her friends hadn't ventured farther
than the town center three years ago. Bars, the
beach and good restaurants had been the order of
the weekend.

She wouldn't have thought holiday parks would

be open right before Christmas, but this one was alive with laughter from the people bustling to and fro around the reception area and clubhouse.

The shouts of good cheer and shrieks of enjoyment twisted her stomach with regret. Family holidays had been something she and Gerard talked about often, but one never came to pass before he was killed. Her conscience might have forced her to come to Templeton, but Carrie couldn't deny part of her was curious to find out if Scott was a different man than she'd assumed he was years before. Hadn't she secretly hoped he wasn't a player, but a man capable of family parties, holidays and school plays? That kind of life, that kind of family, was what Carrie wanted for Belle more than anything in the world.

Isn't it what I want for myself too?

She approached a bench opposite the Good Time Holiday Park and sat, staring up at its brightly painted sign. Until she'd looked into Scott's eyes again, the fear of facing a future alone with her daughter had been a phenomenon Carrie hadn't considered—she'd thought she and Belle would be just fine on their own.

Now her mind and heart reeled with an overwhelming sense of loss. However, as much as she hated the inexplicable but very real sadness that Scott wouldn't be a part of his daughter's life, she also recognized that she hadn't gotten to her position at work or raised her daughter or succeeded in other areas of her life with Scott by her side. It was time to go home.

She closed her eyes and dropped her head back against the bench. So why did her heart feel so damn heavy? Why did her eyes burn with unshed tears?

Because despite his failings, Scott evoked strong feelings of destiny in her.

Her body traitorously yearned for him even if she'd purposely put her heart under lock and key. The bursts of lust that heated her blood were exciting, no matter how adulterous they felt to Gerard's memory.

Wasn't that another reason for her blank refusal to stay here a few days longer? Because she didn't really have the strength to resist her physical want of him for another few days while they talked and spent time together? If he made another move to kiss her...

"Goddamn it. Why is this so hard?"

Carrie inhaled a long breath and when she exhaled, the air turned white in front of her mouth. She shivered. She'd chosen Christmas as the right time to come to Templeton so she could start the New Year afresh. She was a fool. Whether it was Christmas, Easter, the height of summer or the beginning of fall, new beginnings began regardless of the season.

Christmas just made failure cut that much deeper.

"Are you all right?"

Carrie snapped her eyes open. The woman standing to the side of her was wrapped in a chestnut wool coat the exact shade of her thick, long and very enviable hair. Carrie forced a smile and sat up straight. "I'm fine. I'm just—"

"Freezing yourself to the bench? It's beginning to snow." The woman held out her hand and soft white flakes drifted to her leather-gloved palm. "I love winter." She glanced toward the park gates and grimaced. "Not that I should, considering I run a holiday park."

"It's yours?"

The woman laughed, the sound warm. "Not mine, exactly. I'm Angela Taylor, the manager. I came outside for a breather. The Christmas visitors are equally as boisterous as a group of twenty-somethings on spring break."

Carrie smiled. "Would it make you want to slap me if I said I was finding their boisterous good time entirely comforting?"

Her eyes turned somber before they softened and she smiled again. "Are you okay? Do you want to come in for a while? We've got a mean coffee machine in the reception."

The gentle concern in her eyes made Carrie slump her shoulders. "I'm hiding."

"I thought as much." Angela's smile dissolved. "Is there anything I can do?"

Carrie's cheeks warmed. "Is it really that obvious?"

"Only to someone who recognizes the anxiety on your face...the hunch of your shoulders." She looked around. "Are you out here alone?"

"Yes, but that's exactly how I want it for a while."

"I see." Her gaze zeroed in on Carrie's and intensified as she lowered onto the bench. "Feel free to tell me to mind my own business but if you need some help—"

"I'm fine."

Angela lifted her eyebrow. "And someone who's fine chooses to sit alone outside a holiday park a few days before Christmas until they're trembling with cold?"

Carrie laughed. "Maybe."

She tilted her head toward the park. "Come inside. We can have hot chocolate. I promise not to ask any questions."

Despite Angela's kindness, Carrie's need to maintain distance between her and the residents of Templeton rose once more. She forced her necessary boundaries into their somewhat wobbly position. "If it's all the same to you—"

"I'm not nosing into your business, I'm just offering a friendly shoulder...or not. The hot chocolate is still up for grabs either way."

Carrie studied Angela from beneath lowered lashes. Her worldly-wise gaze screamed of experience. Instinctively, Carrie sensed Angela knew she struggled with the choice of whether to fight or flee. She drew in a long breath and exhaled. "Can I ask you something?"

Angela nodded. "Sure."

"Have you ever been faced with a situation where you have absolutely no idea of the right thing to do?"

Angela's breath puffed out in front of her as she blew out a sigh. "Now there's a question." She glanced toward the gates of the holiday park, her expression growing guarded. She sighed. "We all have moments like that. You have to listen to that little voice deep inside. For better or worse, it's rarely wrong."

Carrie nodded, her gaze resting on the holiday-makers whooping and laughing within the gates of the park. "Someone has asked me to do something that I feel as though I owe him to do, but…"

"Is this a friend? Boyfriend?"

Carrie met her eyes and grimaced. "Neither. More of a long-ago lover and father of my child."

Angela sucked in a breath through clenched teeth. "Ah."

"It's such a mess and I came here thinking I had everything worked out. I couldn't have been more wrong and now I'm worried about making things worse."

"Do you like him?"

Carrie smiled wryly. "Yes. I probably like him too much."

"Can you trust him?"

Carrie frowned and turned to face her. "I don't even know him. Not really."

"Hmm…and what is your gut telling you?"

Carrie considered the question. How could Scott not be trustworthy after his clear commitment to his family? He might have gone from one woman to the other, but that was all she had to criticize. He'd been honest and caring of her. He'd listened and given her his truth. "I can trust him."

"Then unless the guy is asking you to do something immoral or illegal, I think you should consider doing whatever he's asking." Angela smiled. "Look, a lot of things have happened to me and the most important thing I've learned is sometimes we have to take a leap of faith and not cut people off because we're worried what may or may not happen."

If there's anyone I will reach those standards for, it's you. Scott's words resounded in Carrie's head.

"I have to get this right for my daughter. If it was just about me…"

"You'd do whatever he's asking in a heartbeat?" Angela raised an eyebrow, her eyes teasing.

Carrie laughed as the truth of Angela's insinuation hit home. "Maybe. It's complicated. My feelings for him seem to be based on little more than the overwhelming desire to jump the man."

Angela laughed. "Is that so bad?"

Carrie sighed. "It is when I've only just told him he has a daughter despite her being three this coming April."

Angela winced. "Oh."

"Exactly."

"Come on. It's freezing out here." Angela stood and held out her hand. "This calls for more hot chocolate than our machine can hold, but I've got access to a bar full of wine if need be. Let's go inside and, between us, we'll figure out what your next move should be."

Carrie stood and smiled. "Okay. Why not? I was thinking of leaving tonight and never coming back. Never speaking to him again, but now..."

"Now what?"

"Now I'm wondering whether to give him a chance. He really hasn't done anything wrong. Neither of us has."

Angela grinned. "Good. Come on. Have a drink with me and then go get your man."

Carrie's stomach knotted as Angela led her into the park and through the bustling area in front of the reception building. *Go get my man? Scott Walker is so not my man right now.*

People were out in droves delighting in the first snowfall of winter. A lump caught in Carrie's throat as she absorbed the awed expressions of mothers with their children and grandparents arm in arm. Her heart kicked painfully. God, she wanted that. She wanted a family. She had to try again with Scott. As much for herself as for Belle. Gerard wanted them to be happy and happiness came through trust, commitment and tenacity.

What would it say about her and everything Gerard had taught her if she walked away through fear of the future? Life was too short to waste it.

The shriek of a little girl drew Carrie to an abrupt halt, her heart stuttering. A young father ahead of them tossed his toddler daughter onto his shoulders and she giggled with delight. She stuck out her tongue to catch the snowflakes while her father marched up and down in the mode of a soldier on duty outside Buckingham Palace.

"That. Right there. That's what matters."

"I couldn't agree more." Angela cleared her throat. "Nothing is more important than a girl—or woman—feeling secure. Nothing in the world."

The hairs at Carrie's nape rose. Scott hadn't said no to Belle. He hadn't said no to trying. He'd asked her to stay; to spend some time. He hadn't demanded a DNA test, but he did deserve one. If there was the smallest chance of Scott being in Belle's life, it was Carrie's duty as her mother to ensure it happened.

Unless Scott gave her just cause to think he might harm Belle emotionally, physically or mentally, she wouldn't walk away.

She faced Angela. "Do you mind if we get that drink another time?"

She smiled. "Somewhere you need to be?"

"I need to talk to him. I walked away too easily."

Angela nodded. "Then go."

Carrie squeezed her arm. "Thanks for listening. Maybe we can catch up again before I leave?"

"Sure. I'd like that." Angela winked. "I want to know how things turn out. Good luck."

SCOTT STARED THROUGH the bakery window, his ass cheeks numb from the length of time he'd been sitting immobile. Why had he told Carrie he'd try to change for her? What did he expect to happen? A woman as determined and passionate as Carrie had no facet in her person that showed she'd wait for him to make up his mind whether it was possible for him to be a father. Why should he expect her to?

He dropped his head back against the seat and groaned. Why the hell had he just blurted it out when he asked her to stay? Carrie didn't know him. He could be a head case for all she knew.

He should've approached the whole thing differently. Maybe taken her somewhere fun for the afternoon? Showed her he was capable of laughter and good times as much as he was brooding and walking away from past lovers?

If Carrie had avoided coming to Templeton because she feared what would happen when they came face to face again, he had more than likely sent her to packing her suitcase. What woman would say yes to staying in a strange town so close to Christmas knowing only a man with a reputation like his? An undeserved reputation he couldn't have cared less about—until Carrie.

He clenched his jaw. Whatever mistake he might have made asking her to stay, he wasn't wrong in saying they needed to get to know each other a little better before Belle was brought into the equation.

During the years he'd thought about Carrie, he'd wondered countless times if their time together had become a fantasy in his head—and the reality was if Carrie reappeared they'd both get seriously burned. He'd been worried about his heart and this whole time Carrie had been worried about their child.

"God damn it." Scott squeezed his eyes shut. He couldn't commit to moving toward a relationship with the daughter he was yet to meet when he was nowhere near ready. He had plans to see through before his life was ready for a little girl who deserved a good and present dad.

He needed to make sure his mother had somewhere nice of her own to live. He needed to get the second garage up and running and turning a profit. He needed to refurbish his three-bedroom bachelor pad and fill it with at least something appealing to a woman. He opened his eyes as self-loathing furled inside him.

He couldn't take the risk of committing only to buckle under the pressure and walk away further down the line. He couldn't risk being shown as the same man as his father...

He stared across the bakery at Marian.

She'd come to Templeton knowing no one but George, the man she loved, but was now an important part of the whole community. She blended into her new role of wife and became a mother to nearly everyone in town. Despite having no children, she held a maternal instinct nobody could dispute. Who was to say he didn't hold the same untapped capabilities to be a good father to Belle?

He snatched his gaze to the window. Who was he kidding? What had he ever done to show he could care for a child? Care for a woman for an infinite amount of time?

His history with women held the tangible proof he turned his back the moment things got tough as far as relationships were concerned. His business was thriving. He was a hard worker…but couldn't deal with emotional strains and fallouts outside of his mother and sisters. Four upset females was enough for any man to take…or at least it had been for his father.

What did Scott being a hard worker count for if eventually he upped and left, giving little more than a child-support check to Carrie until Belle hit the grand old, government-decided age of eighteen? He and his sisters passed that age a long time ago, but each of them still thought and talked about their absent father as though they would've liked the guy to stick around. Kids grew into adults, yet their childhoods shaped everything…

The snow falling outside the window came down heavier. People rushed by the bakery, pulling up their collars and bracing their bodies against the gathering storm. He should move. Get out of there. Go to the garage and pound on some metal for a while. Anger and resentment against his father built inside him like planks on a burning pyre. Memories of his mother crying and wailing, screaming and blaming. Over and over, he told himself he wasn't his father, yet here he was, part of him undeniably terrified Belle was his.

"Well, then, Mr. Walker, where have you been hiding yourself these past weeks, huh?" Marian's booming voice to the side of him cut through Scott's reverie.

He battled his scowl into submission and forced a smile. "Busy avoiding the Christmas madness as I do every year."

Marian rolled her eyes. "I should bang your and George's heads together. Now you've finished that car of his, I wake every morning expecting to see tire marks on the driveway where he's skipped out of town as quick as lightning. I know he's got a bee in his bonnet about Christmas because of that ex-wife of his, but still, Christmas is Christmas."

She slid into the opposite seat and Scott struggled not to fidget under her scrutiny. "So…" She leaned her forearms on the table and linked her fingers. "What's the deal between you and the latest pretty young thing to stroll into the Cove and cause a ruckus?"

Scott struggled to keep his smile in place as his hackles quivered under the scent of unwanted questions. "Nothing."

Marian's bark of laughter bounced from the windowpane and hit him straight between the eyes. He closed them. "What?"

"You and her had a thing, didn't you? There's no chance of you letting a girl who looks like that breeze in and out of town without trying your luck for a little up-and-personal time."

Scott snapped his eyes open. "What's that supposed to mean?"

Marian grinned. "You know exactly what it means."

Heat pinched his face as irritation swept through him. "Doesn't it count for anything that the girls I've dated still talk to me?" He scowled. "So I slept with a few of them, that doesn't make me some kind of jackass when they were willing participants. I'm getting sick to death of—"

"Whoa, she's certainly more than nothing to you, isn't she?" Marian laughed. "Never seen you so riled up by a bit of teasing. You like her, huh? You like her a lot."

Scott opened his mouth and then snapped it shut. Giving Marian any more to go on than what she'd already concluded was lethal. The woman could run with a theory regardless of the facts… and, more often than not, landed scarily close to the truth.

She stared through the window. "Did she tell you Nick took twelve chunks out of her in here the other day?" She shook her head. "How I didn't throttle the boy, I'll never know."

"He told me. I kind of did some throttling of my own so don't worry about it."

She frowned. "You boys didn't fight, did you? No woman is worth friends like you two falling out over."

Scott sighed. He wasn't happy how things still were between him and Nick. He should go see him sooner rather than later. "We'll figure it out."

"Make sure you do. Come on then, out with it. What does she want?"

"Like I said—"

"Nothing, right?"

He lifted his eyebrows and a couple of seconds passed before Marian raised her hands in defeat. "Fine. Your business is your own, but that girl has the look of a mother about her. I'm no Einstein, but I know people. It doesn't take a mathematician to add things up."

Scott held her gaze. "She's a friend. That's all you need to know."

"It's all I need to know, but it's not all I *want* to know." She took his hand and held it. "Talk to me, honey."

Words bit and burned his tongue. "I can't."

Marian smiled, her gaze soft with compassion. "Sure you can. I won't judge, you know that. I want to help you. How about you and George have a poker night at our place tonight? I'll get you boys some beers and those disgusting fat cigars you like to pretend you know how to smoke."

Scott smiled. "We don't smoke them, we just hold them because it makes us look good."

Marian's smile dissolved. "*You* look good. My

George looks like a bad impersonation of George Burns in his heyday."

Scott laughed and drew his hand from her grasp. He shut his eyes. "God, what a mess."

"What is?"

He met her steady gaze, took a breath and released it. "Fine. If I tell you what I'm thinking right now, you can give me advice, but you don't tell anyone what I told you."

"Cross my heart." She licked her finger and swiped it over her chest.

"I had a thing with Carrie a few summers ago—"

"You had sex."

Scott rolled his eyes. "Yes."

"Go on."

"And she's back, and the way I feel about her is as strong as ever."

"You want her back in your bed."

Scott frowned. "You don't think that little of me, surely?"

Marian raised her eyebrows, a glint of pride shining softly in their depths. "Are you saying there's a chance you want more than that?"

The mess of emotions that had raced around him ever since Carrie left the bakery hitched up a notch. He slumped back in the seat. "I don't know what I want."

"Didn't it occur to you that one day a woman

would walk into your life and make the famous Walker love machine retire his rubbers?"

Scott glared. "Thanks for the support."

She reached for his hand lying on the table and squeezed. "Oh, honey, I'm teasing, just trying to make you smile."

Scott shook his head. "Every instinct in my body wants Carrie to stay here, but those feelings aren't enough. I don't know her any more than she knows me. There's a child slap bang in the middle of the confusion—"

Marian's smile vanished. "Oh, Scottie. Did you get that girl pregnant?"

Scott stared, inwardly cursing his stupidity. How could he tell Marian he was a father before he told his mother? "No."

She narrowed her eyes and studied him for a long—long—time, her gaze alight with knowing as he struggled not to flee from the bakery. He waited. And waited.

Marian cleared her throat. "Go on."

"Look, forget I said anything." He moved to stand. "I've got things I should—"

"Sit."

Feeling like an idiot when her voice boomed so suddenly the guy at the next table splashed his black coffee on the table, Scott closed his eyes. "Marian—"

"So there's a child too. What did you say to her

to make her leave like her ass was on fire? You don't hurt women on purpose. I know that as well as I know my George likes his briefs good and tight so his bits aren't flailing around."

Scott squeezed his eyes shut against the image and blew out a breath. "I said I'd try to do whatever it took to please her. As soon as the words were out of my mouth, she ran for the hills…or at least the hotel." He opened his eyes. "I don't blame her. My arrogance makes me want to throw up."

"Hmm." She stared at him a few moments longer before sliding from the booth. "It was the *try* that did it."

He frowned. "What else was I supposed to say? How can I promise her anything?"

She fisted her hands on her hips and shot him a glare that would've felled a lesser man. "You can't, but you didn't have to say *try*. Don't you men ever learn anything about the female race? *I'll try* is worse than *I can't*. Means we haven't got a damn thing to hang our hats on. Now, you sit there and have a little think about what you're going to do to fix this. I assume you want to fix it?"

He opened his mouth to respond, but Marian hadn't finished.

"'Course you do, so I'll grab you a coffee to go with your brooding. If you're lucky, I'll spend some time mulling over your stupidity too." She turned and walked toward the counter just as the bakery door swung open beside her. She drew to an abrupt halt. "Well, lookey here."

Scott's heart leaped into his throat as Carrie stepped inside, shaking snowflakes from her gorgeous hair and reminding him of a model in a shampoo commercial. She looked up and started when she met Marian's gaze. "Marian."

Marian crossed her arms. "Carrie."

Scott's mouth drained dry. *Leave her be, Marian. Leave her be.*

Carrie glanced around her as if seeking escape before she faced Marian again. "Is everything all right?"

"I like you. No idea why, but I do." Marian jerked her head in Scott's direction. "He's over there where you left him. Be gentle with him. There aren't many women who walk out on him. He's kind of sore you did."

Goddamn it. Scott cleared his throat. "I can hear you, you know."

Carrie snapped her head in his direction, but he focused his glare on Marian.

She lifted her shoulders. "So? You think I wouldn't whip your pants down and slap your damn ass in front of this girl? Get on with it, both of you. I'm not as young as I used to be. I haven't got time for hand-holding."

She stormed toward the counter, leaving Carrie

standing in the same spot. Scott stood and waved toward the table. "Shall we try again?"

The furrowing at her brow and the doubt in Carrie's big, brown eyes showed her hesitation, but she came closer. She stopped directly in front of him and tipped her head back to meet his eyes. "I shouldn't have skipped out on you before."

He ran his gaze over her beautiful face, somehow getting sidetracked around her mouth. "Yes, you should. I shouldn't have asked you to stay like that. It's too soon, but I'm glad you're here now." He curled his hands into fists as his fingers itched to take hers.

She slid into the booth. "We need to sort this out once and for all."

CHAPTER NINE

CARRIE INHALED A strengthening breath and concentrated on keeping her cool even when, instead
of taking the opposite seat, Scott slid in beside
her. She needed the table between them, because
now all she could think about was his proximity
and his musky scent. She had to find a quick and
painless way to move forward, had to find a so-
lution to everything that prevented her daughter
from having two parents in her life like any child
deserved.

She squeezed her eyes shut. "I'll stay for another
couple of days, but then I have to go home. I can't
stay here for Christmas."

The soft whisper of his exhalation drifted over
her folded hands on the table. "Thank you."

She swallowed, wanting the words she needed
to say out of her body as soon as possible. "You
have your life, and I have mine." She opened her
eyes. "Neither of us has to change our plans because I've told you about Belle. You can still do
what you want to do."

His eyes ever so slightly darkened. "If I'm a father, it changes everything."

Be strong, Carrie. Lay down the ground rules. "I disagree." She straightened her spine. "I get it, Scott. Truly. I understand you think knowing about Belle means you have to change your entire life, but that's not true."

"That's not what I'm—"

"Let me just say this, please."

He closed his eyes and she took that as permission to continue. She inhaled a deep breath. "I like, and appreciate, how you think so seriously about what you should to do and how to do it, but I'm not asking you to change your plans overnight. This is going to take time. I *want* it to take time. Belle doesn't need to know about you yet. You can go on with your life and when the time's right, I'll tell her about you."

Silence.

Carrie swallowed against the dryness in her throat. When she'd been standing outside the holiday park, with the decision to see her mission through to the end burning like a flame inside her, she'd thought her words would be strong and clear, delivered with a conviction he couldn't argue with. Yet now, her stomach trembled with nerves and her hands longed to take his.

Why did he make her feel so torn and her reasoning unfair? Belle was hers. He had no obligation to her unless he wanted one. "I'm not saying that to be cruel, you know." She sighed. "I've looked after her the last year without a partner beside me. She'll be okay…whatever you decide."

His continuing silence made her fear she had driven a bigger wedge between them, but she wouldn't falter. She had come to Templeton and achieved what she came to do—the gates were open and Scott could step through them whenever he was ready. As long as he realized the hinges wouldn't creak back and forth on a whim.

He slowly opened his eyes and Carrie stiffened. His gaze was fiery hot once again and his jaw had hardened to granite. "So, just like that, the problem's fixed?"

Irritation threatened and Carrie struggled to fight it. "I don't know what else to say. I'm trying to be reasonable. I'm trying to think of a way forward."

His gaze bored into hers. "We'll spend some time together these next few days and before you leave, we'll have worked out what happens after that, together. No more decision-making without me, Carrie. I want to work through this together. As Belle's parents, because that's exactly what we are for the rest of our lives, whether you want that or not."

Belle's parents. For the rest of their lives. Her heart stumbled and her stomach flipped over. It shamed her how amazing it felt to hear him say that, not just for Belle, but for her too. Her gaze wandered to his mouth and lingered there…traveled lower to stare at the hollow at the base of his neck. His strength and integrity floated toward her and she inhaled, fighting the rush of need that swept through her core.

How I am supposed to stop this overwhelming need to see him naked whenever he talks as though he cares about me? Cares about Belle? How can I keep my head straight when all I can think about is his body on mine and the two of us tumbling and laughing beneath warm bed sheets?

He smiled, his gaze softening. "I want to get to know you before I know Belle. I want to know your likes and dislikes, what makes you happy, your goals and aspirations…don't you want to know the same about me? These next few days will be good for us."

The lowered tone of his voice quivered over the surface of her skin, sparking the air around them with awareness and bringing sex closer and closer to the forefront of her mind. Once again, her gaze dropped to his mouth. "Okay."

He grinned and she looked up to meet his eyes—her heart hitched. His gaze was on her mouth too. She wet her bottom lip and his eyes ever so slightly widened before he met her gaze. "I'm going to show you how good Templeton can be."

Stop this. Stop it now. She shifted in her seat and cleared her throat, looking toward the bakery counter. "Good." She faced him and arched an eyebrow. "Maybe one of Marian's pancakes would start things off the right way."

A couple of heartbeats passed before he touched her arm. "Do you skate?"

Carrie stiffened. "What?"

He grinned. "Do you skate?"

She frowned. "A little." She glanced past him toward the window and the ice rink in the center of the town square in the distance. "You're not thinking—"

"Yep...and after we've done a few circuits, you can consider whether or not you'd let me introduce you to my family before you leave."

She froze as dread dropped into her stomach. "Your family? Don't you think it's a bit soon to—"

"My family means a lot to me and, whether it's ideal or not, they're a part of this." His eyes softened. "Belle will have a new grandma and aunts. I can't shut them out of this. I *won't* shut them out of this."

Words escaped her as trepidation whispered over the surface of her skin. He was right. This was about so much more than her, Scott and Belle. Belle would have a new extended family. A soft whisper of joy filled Carrie's heart, even as her worry heightened.

He inhaled a shaky breath and released it. "I'm a bigger part of my family's well-being than I'd like sometimes, but that's the way it's been for years." He smiled. "They're a pain in the ass from time to time, but they've got a lot of love to give a little girl—and you."

She forced a smile even as uncertainty lingered. A family. A real bona fide maternal and paternal family for her little girl. Carrie exhaled. She had to walk this path with Scott, had to embrace the chance for her baby to be surrounded by as many people as possible who loved her. "Okay…but one step at a time. This is about your relationship with Belle, before anyone else's."

"Of course." He slid his hand along her forearm and took her hand. "Thank you."

Their eyes locked for a moment, before a movement to her side caught Carrie's attention and she looked up, snatching her hand from Scott's fingers.

A waitress stood there, holding a tray laden with coffee cups and pastries. She smiled. "Two coffees and two honeycomb muffins. Marian said to bring them over."

"Thanks, Stacy."

She plonked the tray on the table and the crockery clattered. "You're welcome. If you need anything else, just holler."

When she'd left them alone, Scott pushed Carrie's latte toward her and she clasped her hands around it without looking up. "I want a family for Belle, Scott." She pushed some hair behind her ear, her hand trembling. "Someone more than me. When Gerard was killed, it woke me up to reality." She met his eyes. "Life is unpredictable and, for the most part, painful. If anything should happen to me…"

"Hey." He cupped his hand to her jaw. "Don't think like that. You're going to be around a long time, okay?"

Tears burned and she nodded, forcing a smile. "Okay."

She lifted her face and his hand slipped away as she picked up her coffee. His words clutched around her heart and the promise in his gaze made the urge to kiss him barrel through her once again.

She stared into the milky-brown depths of her cup. "You're her father. The sooner we get a DNA test done, the better. I hate the way you keep saying *if* you're her daddy." She swallowed. "Although, I understand how you would need proof, considering I practically dragged you out of the bar that night."

He smiled. "I was there too, you know. I could've stopped what was happening—"

"Could you?"

Their eyes locked. Heat rose and lingered. The intense heat in his gaze, the light flush at his cheeks told her all she needed to know. He was there and he was trying his hardest. There was nothing more she could expect or ask. Her body ached to move toward him—on him. A strange peace eased the tension in her Carrie's neck and shoulders and she arched toward him. *Trust him.* As though drawn by an invisible force, he leaned closer too, his wide, muscular shoulders strong and unyielding as he stole his hand onto her arm...

"Hello, big brother."

He snatched his hand from her arm with lightning speed and they snapped their heads up in unison. A stunning, dark-haired, blue-eyed woman who looked far too much like Scott smiled directly at Carrie, her eyes glinting with undisguised glee. "And who might this be?"

Carrie looked to Scott.

He closed his eyes. "What are you doing here?"

"Is that any way to talk to your favorite sister?" She grinned.

Carrie couldn't move. His sister? How did she deal with this? How did *they* deal with this? Apprehension rolled like a wave into her stomach and stayed there. Take control. Carrie forced a smile and offered her hand. "Nice to meet you. Carrie Jameson."

"Well, it's nice to meet you too, Carrie Jameson. I'm Bianca Walker, Scott's sister."

Still smiling, Carrie eased her hand from his

sister's and faced Scott. "I'm going to go back to the hotel. Call me later."

He glanced at his sister. "Carrie, will you just hold on a minute?"

She widened her eyes hoping he understood her leaving was not up for debate. "Can I get out, please?"

He briefly closed his eyes, frustration show-ing in his raised shoulders before he slid from the booth and stood. "I'll call you."

Carrie smiled and exited the booth. "Great."

Entirely too aware of his sister's curious glances between the two of them, Carrie lifted her coat from the back of the booth and hitched her bag onto her shoulder. She nodded to Bianca, her smile firmly in place, even though her insides were a mess. So much for her control from there on in; control flew straight out the door the minute his sister opened it. "It was nice meeting you."

Bianca beamed, delight gleaming in her bright blue eyes. "You too."

"Carrie." Scott's voice was low, commanding… determined. "Don't leave."

She felt claustrophobic as his gaze locked on hers and she glanced toward his sister. "I have to."

"No, you don't." He snapped his gaze to Bianca. "Go grab a coffee or whatever it is you came in here for."

Bianca narrowed her eyes and lifted her chin. "When I'm ready."

Scott glared and crossed his arms. "Now, Bianca."

Carrie pulled herself up to her full five feet seven inches, sensing if she didn't stand up to Bianca now, there was every possibility she'd be mincemeat the next time they met. The tense atmosphere grew in strength as the three of them stood in a circle. Finally, Bianca threw her hands up in surrender. "Fine."

She flounced toward the counter and Carrie turned to Scott. "I don't want to talk about Belle in front of your sister. I'm nowhere near ready for that. Not yet."

His eyes stormed with frustration. "Believe me, neither am I."

"Then call me when you can."

When she moved to walk away, he gripped her elbow. "I'm going to speak to the local doctor and ask him to hurry through a DNA test."

Carrie nodded. "Okay."

"Once…" He glanced toward the counter, color darkening his cheeks. "Once that part is done, we'll know where we stand."

She followed his gaze toward the counter, where Bianca was in deep conversation with the waitress who'd brought them their coffees. Bianca and the waitress looked over, curiosity etched on their faces. Swallowing against the weight of their judgment, Carrie faced Scott. "You have friends and family here, I don't. I don't want this turning into a witch-hunt. You need to speak to your sister. Tell her who I am if you have to, because I won't have people making me out to be a villain."

"I won't let that happen."

She tilted her head toward the counter where Bianca and the waitress watched them. "Do you really think you have a choice?"

He glanced over her shoulder. "I'm my own man, Carrie. I do what I want, when I want. You have to meet me halfway and let me deal with my family as I see fit." His gaze bored into hers, determination turning them the darkest blue. "Just trust me, okay? Let me deal with my mum and sisters."

She lifted her chin. "I want to leave by Christmas Eve. I won't spend Christmas Day without Belle."

"I know."

Before Carrie could say anything else, Bianca strode on high heels toward them, her mouth stretched into a wide smile and her intelligent gaze piqued with intense interest. "What did I miss?"

Scott faced her. "Nothing. Carrie's leaving."

Bianca pouted. "There's no need to hurry off on my account." Her gaze ran over Carrie's hair. "It's been a while since I've managed to pin down one of my brother's conquests."

Irritation burned behind Carrie's ribcage. "I am

not one of your brother's conquests. I'm someone he met for the briefest time and we've been thrown back together…possibly again, for the briefest time. Goodbye."

With the weight of their stares on her back, Carrie whirled around and left Scott with his sister, wondering whether the steam pouring from her ears was actually visible. The careful calculation in his sister's gaze was surely just a taster of the animosity Carrie could be exposed to in this town. The feeling of being entirely alone amongst a jungle of potential danger and threat shivered through her.

She flung open the bakery door and inhaled mouthfuls of dense sea air as though starved of oxygen. She was here and she would fight for Belle's right to know her father, whatever the external obstacles. She looked to the sky. The gunmetal rainclouds of earlier had cleared, leaving the sky the same azure blue it had been upon her waking that morning. She smiled triumphantly. All would be well now she and Scott had met halfway. She didn't doubt his ability to fight right alongside her once he knew for sure Belle was his.

Feeling stronger than she'd felt since arriving in the Cove, Carrie rammed her arms into the sleeves of her coat and purposely scanned the road. Her plan to get in and out of Templeton within a day, two at the most, had failed dismally. Wariness and suspicion had ebbed and flowed in her veins when Carrie looked into Bianca's eyes; the woman had smiled, but her steely gaze left Carrie in no doubt just what trouble Scott's sister could cause if she put her mind to it.

Carrie breathed deep. Yet, Bianca didn't frighten her any more than Scott's friend Nick had. Their hostility was a spark to her determination and would do nothing but push Carrie forward with more energy than ever.

She jogged across the street and hurried toward the Christie Hotel. She was a stranger in a town where everyone knew everyone's business. She'd do well to remember that and be on guard. Even though Marian had been friendly enough, that didn't mean anyone else would be...or even that Marian wouldn't jump sides once she discovered Carrie had given birth to Scott's baby and neglected to tell him he was a father for almost three years.

Staying here to be bullied and judged wasn't an option.

She might want something more to happen between her and Scott—even if it had felt entirely physical at the bakery—but she would not allow him to skew her vision of what she wanted for Belle. If she and Scott made some small steps toward a resolution, that would be enough.

With each passing hour she spent in the Cove, it

seemed Scott was deemed Templeton property by the women in town. As far as she knew, she could remain a nobody in the eyes of a closed community for weeks, months and years. She wasn't a nobody. She was Belle's mother and the sooner Scott and everyone in town appreciated that, the better.

She purposefully marched onward. The first step was a DNA test. Once Scott had the black and white proof he needed, Carrie would insist he make a decision to either be a father, or not. Either way, come hell or high water, she wouldn't expose her daughter to one iota of hurt from a man or a town they barely knew.

When she decided to come to Templeton, no part of her had considered Scott's wider circle. The unit had been her, Belle and Scott. Now, though, it was abundantly clear Carrie was alone in her endeavors. Yes, her mother had offered to come to Templeton as moral support, but Carrie wouldn't let that happen unless it was absolutely necessary—she refused to risk exposing the people she loved to dangers she hadn't yet identified.

CHAPTER TEN

SCOTT STARED AT the bakery door and tried to get a grip on his anger. His sister's perfume wafted over him as she squeezed past him into the booth. This was just the beginning. If Bianca suspected Carrie meant more to him than any other woman he'd dated, all hell would break loose. He couldn't allow her the tiniest access to the mess of feelings battering around inside him before he'd had time to examine them.

He inhaled a long breath and turned.

Bianca, eyes wide with expectancy, casually leaned back and crossed her arms. "Well, she's all kinds of pretty, isn't she?"

He slid into the booth opposite her and leaned forward, pushing his and Carrie's cold coffees and pastries to the side...disastrous breakfast number two. He glared. "Listen to me. I want you to stay away from her. Who she is, why she's here, is none of your concern until I say it is. I don't want her becoming a family problem, okay?"

She smiled, her eyes shining with excitement.

"Is she the reason Mum pushed us out of the house this morning?"

"Bianca, I'm warning you—"

"What?" She raised her hands in mock surrender. "I'm just interested, that's all. If you want to keep the blonde your little secret, who am I to interfere."

"She's not my little secret. Like Carrie said, she probably won't be here more than another day or two. It's nothing." His gut clenched at the blatant lie. Carrie was already so much more than she was the first time around. He still wanted her... still wanted to feel her skin and warmth; to see the revealed, animalistic side of her he'd only known behind a closed bedroom door, but the fervor in her eyes whenever she spoke of Belle added so much more...

Scott swallowed. He couldn't go there. He could not imagine Carrie as a mother and still expect to think straight and have his wits about him. He had to think of her as a woman he once knew until he was sure the child was his. To start to care for Carrie and then have it turn out she lied about Belle...

"Hello? Earth to Scott."

Scott snapped his gaze to his sister's. "What?"

Bianca lifted an eyebrow. "So she's nothing? I don't think so."

Scott glared. "I didn't say she was nothing, I said *it* was nothing. Us. Me and her. There's nothing going on."

Her gaze turned somber and she reached across the table to cover his hand with hers. "I'm only trying to break through a little here, Scottie. You haven't been right for the last couple of days. Is it just the blonde? Or is something else going on?"

"Her name's Carrie." He glanced around the bakery, a preferable option than looking into his sister's astute gaze. "She's just visiting a while and then going home."

"So work's okay?"

He faced her. "Yes. Why wouldn't it be?"

"Because this is the second day in a row the place has been shut up, that's why." She slid her hand from his and picked up her coffee. "I can't remember the last time you weren't working. If it's not the blonde…Carrie, I thought something else might be bothering you. Nick said—"

"Nick said nothing." He glared. "It's Christmas. Maybe I want some time off."

She huffed out a laugh. "Now I'm really worried."

"Look, can you just give me some space? I don't need you, Mum, Ella or Lucy getting involved right now, okay? It's Christmas. Go shop, go out with your work friends, decorate the damn Christmas tree. Come Christmas day, I'll be sitting around the table with you as usual."

"And will Carrie be joining us?" She stared, her eyes wide with feigned innocence.

"No."

They locked gazes. Scott glared until Bianca put down her coffee cup with a clatter of china. "Fine."

"Are we done here?"

She recrossed her arms. "Not by a long shot, but I'll let it go for now."

"Good."

Pressure bore down on Scott's chest as he glowered at his sister. He wanted to get the hell out of there and get to the doctor's office. The sooner he found out if a DNA test was possible before Christmas, the sooner his mind—and heart—would know for sure whether or not he was a daddy.

"I've got somewhere I need to be. If there's nothing else—"

"I think Mum's heard from Dad."

He froze, every nerve ending screeching to high alert. "What?"

Her cheeks flushed. "She's more agitated than normal. I think something's going on. I might be way off the mark, but I've got a funny feeling he's contacted her. If he has, we have to do something." The previous curiosity and scheming vanished from Bianca's eyes, leaving behind the younger-sister "help me" look Scott knew so well.

He tightened his jaw. "Why would you think that?"

"I don't know. Call it instinct. Haven't you noticed the change in her recently? She's... almost chirpy."

"Mum doesn't do chirpy."

Bianca lifted her eyebrow. "No? Then what about the new lipstick she's wearing and…" She shook her head. "She bought jeans, Scottie. *Jeans.*"

Scott frowned. Had she?

Bianca sniffed. "Well, that's just typical for a man not to notice a change in what a woman is wearing."

Scott bit back a smile. He always noticed what Carrie wore. Always. "You're jumping to conclusions. What possible reason could he have to contact her now? It's been ten years."

"As far as we know."

Tension knotted his shoulders. "Meaning?"

"How do we really know anything about him? For all any of us knows, he could contact Mum whenever he wants something." She locked her gaze on his, her cheeks flushed. "You're not at home much to keep an eye on her, are you? You're either at the garage, with the boys or off chasing a skirt most of the time."

Anger simmered and he glared. "If you really think that, why are you here?"

Her shoulders slumped and she closed her eyes. "Sorry."

Inwardly cursing, Scott sighed and touched her hand. "What's happened to make you worried enough to tell me about this now? It has to be more than the lipstick and new jeans."

Bianca opened her eyes. "It's something Mum said on the phone earlier."

Unease rippled through Scott's blood as he waited.

"She asked me if I think you're getting itchy feet like Dad. Then she asked me why men think they can come and go as they please. Ruin people's lives and laugh as they do it."

Scott shrugged. "She always talks like that."

"This was different. Something's not right. Why would she ask that?" Her gaze bored into his. "Are you leaving? Is it because of this Carrie woman turning up?"

Scott blew out a breath as the familiar feeling of suffocation flowed through him. "I'm not going anywhere, so leave Carrie out of it."

"Are you sure about that?"

He glared. "Yes, I'm sure. How could I leave even if I wanted to?"

"Why are you snapping at me?"

He gripped his coffee cup. "Because sometimes, it gets a little much that a man of my age and means can't take a damn shower without his mother or sisters wondering why. Even if I wanted to leave, I wouldn't. Until I know Mum's happy and looked after, I've no choice but to stick around."

She narrowed her eyes and the silence stretched as Scott's habitual guilt of splintering under his obligations sucked the air from his lungs. He squeezed his eyes shut and Carrie's face appeared behind his closed lids. "You've got nothing to worry about, okay?"

Bianca sighed. "So you'll talk to Mum? Make sure everything's okay?"

He opened his eyes. "Yes."

"Promise?"

"Yes, Bianca, I promise. Leave it with me." *What the hell's going on here? First I find out I might have a child, and now Dad could be sniffing around again after a ten-year absence?* "I'll talk to her." He slid out of the booth, tossing a ten-pound note on the table. "See you later."

"But—"

Leaving Bianca calling after him, Scott strode from the bakery and along the High Street. His mind buzzed with the possibility of his father coming back into their lives at any given moment. A possibility he hadn't considered for years, since he put that painful and pointless want in a box in the very dark, dangerous shadow of his psyche.

Over my dead body will the man turn up and spew over the successes I've made for myself or destroy the happiness I've ensured for Mum.

Scott marched toward the garage. He needed to get on his bike and get something concrete done with at least one aspect of his life that was under his control, and then he'd speak to his mum. He broke into a jog and made his way back toward the Christie Hotel, where he'd left his bike what felt like eons ago.

SCOTT SOON REALIZED trying to make his way to the reception desk at the doctor's office on the twenty-first of December was as bad as facing the prospect of shopping for his female-heavy family. After a twenty-minute wait, he was finally next in line and immediately swapped his scowl for his very best smile when the attractive middle-aged receptionist faced him.

"Good…" He glanced at his watch. "Afternoon, Julie."

Her face broke with a wide smile. "Hi, Scott. How's your mum?"

Pushing Bianca's suspicions about their father returning out of his mind, Scott raised his eyebrows. "Well, she has a baking list about a mile long in preparation for Christmas, so she's in her element. How's Connor?"

"Just great. Wanting Mark and me to buy him a car for Christmas…" She sniffed. "I swear the kid will never stop believing money grows on trees in our backyard." She rolled her eyes. "Are you looking for an appointment? Unless it's an emergency, you'll have to wait until the New Year."

"Um…I was hoping for a quick word with

Kevin." He glanced behind him. "I assume he's back to back today, tomorrow and the next day?"

She nodded. "Yes, yes and yes."

"Could you maybe ask him to call me? It's medical…and it's a kind of an emergency."

She lifted an eyebrow, her dark eyes glinting kindly. "The kind of emergency that doesn't need to take place in a doctor's office, I assume?"

"Something like that."

"You boys. You, Nick and Kevin will never change. Thick as thieves." She picked up a pen. "What's the message?"

"Tell him I'll be at his place about seven tonight. If there's a problem, he can call me."

She scribbled down a note and dotted the paper with a firm pop of her pen. "Consider it done."

Scott grinned. "Thanks, Julie. You're a star."

"That's what they all say."

He was about to turn away when his friend and doctor, Kevin Blake, strode into the reception area. "Julie, could you possibly call Mrs. Warren and ask if she can come in to discuss these blood test results sooner rather than later?"

Scott waited for his flushed-faced, spiky-haired friend to notice him.

Julie scribbled a note. "Sure. You have someone here to see you."

Kevin frowned. "I have lots of people here to see me."

Julie tilted her head in Scott's direction. Kevin looked up and his frown was replaced with a surprised smile. "Hey, what are you doing here?" Concern immediately furrowed his brow. "Something wrong?"

Scott glanced around for a second time, all too aware of listening ears and watching eyes. "Sort of."

Kevin lifted his eyebrow. "Sort of? As in this is something Nick can't help with?"

"Not right now, no."

Kevin ran his gaze over Scott's face, scrutinizing him in the way only a doctor could. Scott shifted from one foot to the other. "It can wait until tonight if you fancy me bringing over a pizza and a couple of beers later?"

After another long moment of study, Kevin nodded. "Hmm. Okay, you're on." He looked past Scott to the ever-growing line behind him. "Come round at eight. I should be finished by then...I hope."

"No problem. See you then. Good seeing you again, Julie."

Scott exited the doctor's office in the mode of a gladiator running a gauntlet. He reached the parking lot and headed for his bike, pulling his cell from the inside pocket of his jacket. His thumb hovered over the speed dial for Carrie. He wanted to speak to her, hear her voice and know she was okay. He wanted to make sure she hadn't hotfooted it out of town after Bianca's appearance....

He cursed and shoved it back into his pocket.

He needed to give her some space. God knows, he sometimes bent under the pressure surrounding him from every corner. Why should Carrie be any different? He'd call her tomorrow when she'd had time to process everything they discussed as well as being thrust into his sister's intense spotlight. He clenched his jaw. Some time apart would be good for them to gain some perspective.

Scott buckled his helmet beneath his chin and straddled his bike. He turned the ignition, and the powerful engine roared to life, rumbling through him and matching the adrenaline pumping through his blood. He needed some distraction, a few hours' headspace, before he told one of his best friends he needed him to perform and hurry through a DNA test.

He glanced toward the doctor's office. There was no way in hell Kevin would do anything until he had some answers to his non-doctorly and doctorly questions. Scott's gut tightened. It had always been the three of them, Scott, Nick and Kevin, for the last two decades, and the notion of leaving Nick out of the loop ate at Scott's gut. How had three childhood best friends remained so close, despite one growing up to be a mechanic, one a DJ and the other a doctor? Scott smiled. It made no sense, but the number of times he'd been grateful for his buddies was endless.

He pulled out of the parking lot. He needed to go see Nick and put an end to the tension between them—which would be easily done if his friend was prepared to apologize to Carrie. If he wasn't, Scott had no idea how their argument would pan out.

As he rode toward the garage, the streets passed in a blur of people. The light snow that continued to fall barely touched his visor before being snatched away again by the wind. Images of Carrie mixed with his intense attraction toward her, tormenting his mind as he endeavored to focus on the road.

Minutes later, Scott pulled into the garage lot and cut the engine. Parking his bike, he pulled off his helmet. Nick leaned against the iron doors, his jacket collar drawn up around his jaw and a beanie shoved down over his ears, his gaze unmoving as he stared directly at Scott. He slowly pushed away from the wall and crossed his arms. "You certainly like to keep a man waiting. I've been here for over an hour."

Scott exhaled. When you had known someone as long as they'd known each other, you learned to read a friend's body language—Nick's screamed of "let's get this over and done with," with a hefty dose of "I still don't think I did anything wrong."

Walking forward, Scott raised his hand. "Good to see you, man."

The two of them clutched hands before Scott released him and approached the doors. "Come on, I need caffeine. It's been a long day."

Nick laughed. "You know it's only one-thirty, right?"

Scott glanced over his shoulder. "Feels like bloody midnight."

They climbed the steps to his office and Scott flicked on the overhead lights. Dumping his helmet on his desk, Scott walked to a small side sink and filled the electric kettle. Switching it on, he took a moment to contemplate his next words before turning around and facing his best friend. He leaned against the counter and crossed his arms. "I'm in deep shit."

Nick slowly removed his hat and fisted it in his hand. "I know."

Scott tensed. "You know?"

"I knew the minute I met Blondie at the bakery. She's the hottest, fiery-tempered, brown-eyed piece of ass I've seen around these parts for a long while. You were in deep shit from the moment you laid eyes on her three years ago."

Scott grinned and shook his head. "You're unbelievable."

"What? I'm telling you, man, it's lucky for you I go for brunettes."

Scott lifted an eyebrow. "Or what? I wouldn't stand a chance?"

Nick shrugged. "Your words, not mine."

Laughing, Scott turned to the kettle as it whistled to a boil. "So I guess sending you off to her hotel for a groveling apology is out of the question in case you decide you prefer blondes after all."

"Never gonna happen."

Scott's smile dissolved. He kept his back to his friend and inhaled. "The apology or the hitting on her?"

"Both."

Scott's blood heated dangerously as he turned around. "You were out of line."

"Was I? You just said you're in deep shit. I saw it coming the minute you called me and told me she was back."

"Why are you doing this?"

"Doing what? Looking out for you? Come on, Scott. Is it that easy to forget it was me who picked you up last time?"

"And you think I'm going to put myself through that again?"

"Isn't that exactly what you're doing?" Nick shook his head. "It was me who watched you go from a guy who did his work and then had some fun to someone who went after women as though he had a limp dick. Sure, things have picked up with you as far as women are concerned but, God, you were stonewalled by her, man. Why are you letting her do the same thing again?"

Irritation hummed in Scott's gut like acid. "Can you really say you're happy dating a different woman every week? That's where you want to be?"

Nick lifted his shoulders, his cheeks darkening. "Sure, it is. What's not to like?"

"Bullshit. You and I both know it's a waste of time and, more often than not, more trouble than it's worth. I like Carrie. I like her a lot and if I had to choose her over every woman I've dated in the last three years, she'd be the hands-down winner. Don't tell me if a woman came along and grabbed a hold of you so damn hard it knocked you sideways, you'd let her walk away to go and find someone else."

Nick's jaw tightened. "I wouldn't know 'cause it hasn't happened."

Scott glared. "Well, who says it isn't happening to me?"

Nick raised his eyebrows and Scott fought not to turn away as he let the thought of being with Carrie slip into his heart…just to see how it felt for a while. "Why can't you apologize to Carrie and let me see what happens between me and her, huh?"

Nick planted his clenched fists on his hips. "So she's back for good? She feels the same way about you and wants to set up home in Templeton?"

Scott clenched his jaw. Once again, Carrie intended disappearing. Would she be back in the New Year? Only time would tell. "Not exactly."

"Jesus, man." Nick paced to the windows at the rear of the office and back again. "Then why the hell are you giving me the brunt of your bad-ass temper instead of her? What is it I've actually done wrong here?"

"Carrie and I haven't discussed *us* yet. So having you get in her face won't help things if we do decide…" Scott clenched his jaw, unable to say the words and regret them if either he or Carrie couldn't hack a relationship. He stared as his respect for Nick and his burning desire for Carrie gathered in a fireball in his chest. "You shouldn't have spoken to her the way you did. Since when do you go after women like a jackass?"

"Until you can make me understand why that woman has such a hold over you, I'll carry on being a jackass. So you need to either explain it to me or I walk out of here until you get your head straight."

Squeezing his eyes shut, Scott tipped his head back and took some strengthening breaths in a bid to slow his heart rate. He calmed down and opened his eyes. "If I tell you something, you have to promise you're not going to freak out or do a damn thing about it. You're going to trust me to deal with this my way. The same way I deal with anything that affects my family. Deal?"

"She's not your family."

"I know that. I'm just saying."

"You're saying she matters as much to you as your mum and sisters?"

"Of course not." Yet, the strength of Scott's feelings for Carrie smacked him hard in the center of his chest. It was crazy when Nick said it out loud, but maybe right now Carrie was as important as his family. Who was to say, in time, she wouldn't always be? From the moment Scott first saw her, his entire world shifted and now there was Belle, too.

He blew out a breath. "She's special, Nick. Really special. I'm sorry if you can't accept that, but that's the way it is. I've spent my whole life either picking up my father's mess when he was here, or clearing it up since he's gone. She does something to me I can't explain. She makes it go away. But at the same time I can't help thinking what the hell can I offer her? I won't leave Mum and let her believe her son is no better than her husband, so I'm stuck in Templeton whatever happens."

Nick's eyes widened. "Are you serious?"

"Yes."

"I don't know which is more insane. That you'd even think about leaving the Cove for this woman, or that you're stuck here out of some irrational duty to your mum."

"What other alternative is there? I can't see a way to pursue whatever the hell I'm feeling for Carrie without someone getting hurt. I can't promise her anything. I don't *want* to promise her anything."

"And why should you? Come on, Scott, we're who we are. You and me are guys who like our freedom, man."

Scott stared at his friend. Nick was right. That's exactly who Scott was and how he felt…until he learned he could have a child out there somewhere. He swallowed. He wouldn't bail out on Belle. No way, no how. As for Carrie…they came as a package. A broken family wasn't something he wanted for his child and he'd do his damnedest to make sure he and Carrie gave it their best shot.

Nick shook his head and sighed. "I don't know what the hell we're arguing about. I did you a favor telling her off. Hopefully, she'll get the message and disappear and then you won't have a dilemma on your hands, will you?"

"It's not as simple as that."

"The hell it's not."

"There's someone else involved."

Nick frowned. "Who are you talking about? Me?" He laughed. "Believe me, if you want me to leave it alone, I will."

"It's not you."

"Then who?"

Scott looked to the ceiling. The two sides of his internal battle were becoming bloodier and bloodier. "I can't believe I'm telling you this."

"Hey."

Scott dropped his chin and met Nick's steady gaze.

Nick raised his hands in a gesture of surrender. "I'm your friend. Just tell me."

"You're going to let me deal with this my way?"

"For Christ…" Nick briefly closed his eyes and opened them again. "Yes. Scott's honor."

Incapable of even a glimmer of a smile, Scott drew in a shaky breath. "Carrie came back because she had a baby. My baby."

Silence.

The seconds ticked by and Scott held himself rigid, waiting for the explosion. He stared in morbid fascination as Nick's face paled before turning a worrying color of gray. Two heartbeats passed and a flush of bright red lit his entire face and most of his scalp visible through his blond hair.

"Are you freaking kidding me? And you believe her? Please tell me you haven't signed over your life savings to some unknown bank account in her name or something stupid like that. You have, haven't you? You've given her money."

Scott glared, anger and frustration roaring through his blood as Nick continued his rant.

"Don't you dare take this on face value, man. I get that you feel responsible for your mum and sisters. I was there when your dad left you with next to nothing, but bloody hell, you don't know this woman."

Scott's simmering temper snapped. "Do you think I'm an idiot? I'm getting a DNA test, but I fell for Carrie the minute I saw her. I fell and I fell hard. I won't ignore her now she's back. Especially if somewhere out there I have a child."

Nick's chest rose and fell. "Listen to me—"

Scott raised his hand. "Don't paint me as a sap waiting to be walked all over, Nick. Don't do that. I care about people. I care about you, Kevin and my damn family. I care about half the people in the Cove, and I'll do everything in my power to protect all of you. That doesn't mean I'll be played for an idiot by anyone, including Carrie."

The atmosphere pulsed around them, matching the blood pumping in his ears. He would not let Nick do this. Nick was a player. A man yet to fall for anyone or anything. He was independent, a carefree bachelor who made the most of his position as a DJ to pick up and enjoy the women who idolized him. Scott loved him, but Nick knew shit about providing for people who needed you to do just that.

Nick's heavy exhalation rasped through the silence. "Holy shit."

"Yeah, holy shit." Scott dropped into the chair behind his desk and cradled his head in his hands. "I finally thought I knew how to make myself happy in Templeton. Finally accepted making a life in the Cove wouldn't be so bad." He lifted his head and swiped his hand over his face. "I thought buying a second garage, earning a shitload of money and providing for Mum would be enough. That I'd eventually meet a girl, fall in love, the whole thing…"

Nick stared, his gaze steady as he slowly nodded. "But…"

"But now Carrie's back, I want to explore if she and I are a possibility, but Templeton's too small for a woman like her. She should have the whole damn world at her feet."

"God, you've got it bad, man, but you're jumping way ahead."

"Maybe. Maybe not." Scott inhaled a long breath. "Me and Carrie are different people. What do I know about raising kids? More than that, do I want to know right now? God, this thinking is entirely my dad's fault and if I saw the man now, I'd show him exactly what he's done to me."

"He's done nothing to you unless you let him." Nick came forward and planted his hands on the desk, his gaze trained on Scott's. "First of all, we need to find out if this baby is yours. After that, we'll deal with the rest, okay?"

"*We'll* deal with the rest?"

Nick shrugged. "You really think I'm going to sit back and not help you fix your happily-ever-after? If this girl's gotten a hold of you, you have to work this out." His eyes glinted with mischief. "So…I assume you've called the most intelligent out of the three stooges?"

Scott's shoulders came down from around his earlobes and he smiled. "I'm going to Kevin's tonight."

Nick straightened and grinned. "Then we'd better get extra pizza and beer, hadn't we?"

Scott laughed as the weight of his burden lifted from his shoulders and split three ways. "Sounds like a plan."

Nick gave a curt nod. "Good. Now pour me some coffee. I need time to think."

Shaking his head, Scott turned back to the kettle, his heart pumping. It was as though a switch had been flipped inside him and, feeling Nick's support, Scott was now entirely committed to finding a way to convince Carrie he'd be there for her and Belle. More than that, he wanted free of the damaging, burning resentment that tainted his life, his mother's and sisters'.

He spooned instant coffee grounds into mugs, his hand trembling. If what Bianca suspected was true and his father intended on worming his way back into their lives, Scott would be there to give him the welcome back of a lifetime. Jacob Walker would not have a second chance to break his mother's heart and hurt her children. This time around, Scott was a man, maybe even a father...and not a kid of nineteen who knew jack shit about real life and the choices a man could, or should, make.

CHAPTER ELEVEN

CARRIE GLANCED SURREPTITIOUSLY around the hotel dining room. A chilled glass of white wine perspired alongside the tips of her right hand, while the fingers of her left rolled and released the corner of the linen napkin the waiter had drawn across her lap a half hour before.

She'd made it through her appetizer.

I can do this. I'm a young, independent woman and mother. I don't need company at dinner. I don't need Scott here with me. All I need is to know I have Belle waiting for me at home.

When her feet itched to move and her brain told her to stand up and leave the dining room, Carrie picked up her wineglass. She took a deep, fortifying gulp and replaced it on the table, steadfastly ignoring the way the liquid trembled.

The dining room was full of holidaying couples and big groups enjoying the start of the holiday season. Baubles sparkled, candles flickered and the enormous Christmas tree, eclipsing the corner of the room, claimed focal prominence. Christmas anthems played cheerfully, muted only by the various British accents that mixed and rose as joviality increased and the alcohol flowed. Yet, with each passing minute, the loneliness and pining for Belle gripped harder around Carrie's heart. The more she fought it, the more she edged toward the easiest option of leaving the table and going to her room.

Two days. She had two days to get through before her final deadline to Scott of Christmas Eve. If she gave up now and went home, he'd have the ammunition to use one day that could potentially cause an irreparable split between her and Belle. There was no guarantee that now Scott knew Belle existed, he wouldn't track his daughter down in the future—or that Belle wouldn't make it her mission to find him. If that happened and Scott told Belle it was her mother's fault their relationship never stood the smallest chance of blossoming, Carrie would be the villain in Belle's eyes. No one else.

"Hey, I found you."

Carrie jumped so high, her thighs knocked the table, sending cutlery clattering and her wineglass wobbling. She reached out to steady it and looked up into Amanda Arnold's smiling face.

Oh, God. What's she doing here? Carrie's stomach tightened as she forced a smile. "Amanda. What are you—"

"You've been on my mind all day." Amanda

laughed as she slid into the seat on the opposite side of Carrie's table. "All I could think was whether Scott would do the right thing and keep you company tonight, or leave you to have dinner all alone in a strange town." She looked down at the place setting for one and tipped her head to the side and pouted. "I guess my supposition was right. He's such a rat bag."

Defensiveness for Scott rose on a hot, pounding wave, pinching Carrie's cheeks. "The subject of dinner was never on the table…so to speak. We're not dating. He's just a friend."

Amanda arched her eyebrow. "Friends don't leave other friends to eat alone while they're visiting. Whatever his excuse, it's unforgivable." She stood and shrugged her coat from her shoulders, revealing a black, second-skin dress and a necklace with a single diamond pendant so big Carrie could only presume it was fake…unless boutique toyshops had a turnover beyond her imagination, of course.

She opened her mouth to say something, anything, to get Amanda to leave, but she was already waving for the attention of a nearby waiter. "Excuse me, waiter?"

Briefly closing her eyes, Carrie took a breath and steeled herself for whatever was coming next. The smartly dressed waiter strode toward the table, his smile ever-ready. He bowed slightly. "Yes, madam?"

Carrie grimaced as Amanda fluttered her eyelashes and coyly ran her peach-painted fingernail along the cuff of his jacket. "Is it possible you could set another place at this table? I would love to join my friend for the main course and dessert. Of course, we'll need a very expensive bottle of wine to accompany our meal, too." She flashed Carrie a wink.

Carrie smiled, the strain of it making her cheek-bones ache.

"Of course, madam. Just one moment, please." The waiter nodded and hurried away.

"There. See? Easy. Now you won't have to endure the humiliation of eating alone." Amanda hung the strap of her bag on the chair before sitting down, smoothing her hands down the bodice of her dress, leaning her elbows on the table and lacing her fingers. "So? How was your day?"

Carrie scowled. "I don't find it humiliating to eat alone. I'm a single parent. It's necessary sometimes. Moreover, I'm a producer and like to people-watch."

"A producer? Wow, how very cosmopolitan."

Cosmopolitan? Carrie gritted her teeth and reached for her glass. The Chablis tasted better and better.

"You know…" Amanda glanced around the

dining room. "I did have an ulterior motive for tracking you down tonight. It wasn't just the fact I was concerned Scott might leave you stranded."

Carrie took a second gulp of wine. *Surprise, surprise.* "Oh?"

"I hate to say this, but I'm concerned you might well be his next target, whether you realize it or not."

"Next target? As in a hunter shooting an innocent doe?" Carrie raised her eyebrows. The wine that sloshed through her inspired her to be naughty or nefarious, she hadn't decided which. "You should give me a little more credit. I'm in Templeton for a reason and intend on being fair and considerate to the person involved for as long as I'm here, and then I'll be on the next train home."

"Fair and considerate to Scott, I presume?" Amanda's bright blue eyes glittered with interest.

Carrie slowly replaced her glass on the table. "Scott and I have things to discuss, yes. In the meantime, I'll enjoy a little time in the Cove, shopping, eating, meeting new people…" *Liar, liar, pants on fire.*

Amanda's eyes widened. "You don't want him, then? You have no romantic interest in Scott? My, my, you should be stuffed and put in the city museum."

The waiter returned and Carrie swallowed the retort that scalded her tongue. *Who the hell does this woman think she is? One thing is for certain, she's got a six-foot, two-inch chip on her shoulder called Scott Walker.*

Amanda's uninvited place at the table was duly set and the waiter produced the wine and food menus with a flourish. Amanda took the menus and perused the choice of food. Carrie watched her from beneath lowered lashes, her mind scrambling how to play out the next hour, or however long she'd be forced to sit and make small talk— although "small talk" was a complete understatement if her suspicions about Amanda's motives were anything to go by.

Amanda smiled and snapped the food menu closed. "Do you know, I've changed my mind. I won't eat after all. I'd just like the wine." She opened the wine menu and glanced over the selection before looking at Carrie. "Any preference?"

Carrie lifted her glass. "The Chablis is highly recommended."

Amanda smiled and snapped the menu shut. "Chablis it is, then."

The waiter bowed. "Thank you, ladies. Your wine and just one order of main course will be with you shortly."

Carrie followed his retreat with her gaze. She needed to take control of this conversation before Amanda got there first. "So, have you lived in Templeton all your life?"

Amanda grinned. "It's no good changing the subject. You and I both know I'm here with your best interests at heart. I don't want to see Scott take down another beautiful woman who could do so much better."

Okay, enough's enough. "Take me down? Amanda, we need to get something straight. I'm not the type of woman to be taken down by anyone." *That's right. You've never succumbed to Scott Walker. Never. Not once.* Carrie swallowed. "I lost my husband last year and I'm getting through it. I have a little girl whom I love dearly and will continue to love for the rest of my life."

"So your daughter isn't Scott's, then?"

Carrie stilled. "No."

Amanda stared, her eyes narrowing. "Hmm."

Carrie took a sip of her wine to ease her arid throat. "I'm a producer on a successful TV show. I don't need a man to change my life. Okay?"

Amanda said nothing, and instead continued to stare at Carrie until she began to feel like an exhibit in a museum.

"What?" Carrie trembled with frustration. She didn't want this woman here. She didn't want to hear what Scott had or hadn't done...or at least, that was what she'd keep telling herself.

Amanda cleared her throat. "It's because of your daughter that I felt duty-bound to find you, you know."

Carrie's stomach tightened. "Why?"

"Because I'm a mother too, Carrie."

"And?"

"And I cannot advise you strongly enough to enjoy this evening and then get the first train out of here in the morning."

Carrie's irritation bloomed into a simmering anger. "Why?"

Two spots of color darkened Amanda's cheeks and she gripped Carrie's hand where it lay on the tabletop. "All I'm saying is Scott Walker is a womanizer. You don't want to go falling for the man when you have a child to consider. I did. It got me in a mess that led to my darling little boy wondering why his new daddy had disappeared."

Nausea rose bitter in Carrie's throat. "His new—"

"Yes. Scott treated my boy like a prince. What did he think would happen if he walked away?"

"He wouldn't just walk away without good reason." *He treated your little boy like a prince, huh?* Carrie bit back her smile. Amanda had inadvertently given Scott a brownie point.

Amanda arched an eyebrow. "You know that for sure? You've known Scott for so long you can vouch for his stand-up character?"

Unease raised the hairs at Carrie's nape. She didn't know Scott at all. Not really. Doubt about Belle's biological father, and who he was, rippled through her once again. How was she to ever know for sure she was doing the right thing by being here? Carrie clenched her jaw. She could not let Amanda have the upper hand. *All I need to know about Scott—the stuff that matters—I'll learn.* "I know enough that it would surprise me if he walked away without so much as a backward glance from anyone. Child or no child." The passion and reverence in her words tore at Carrie's heart. She wanted, desperately, to believe Scott would be good to Belle…for the rest of her life.

Amanda's eyes glinted with malice. "Then tell me why walking away was exactly what he did."

Carrie eased her hand from Amanda's and leaned back in her chair. She carefully considered the woman in front of her, using her every intuition to conjure up an accurate assessment of Amanda's intentions before she drew Carrie unwittingly into something she wanted no part of. "I won't sit here and let you bad-mouth him. As far as I'm concerned, Scott deserves my judgment based on what I know, not what I hear."

The waiter reappeared with their wine and Carrie gratefully took the time to gather her temper. She had to keep her cool and not let Amanda see how her suggestion Scott had no consideration for anyone but himself rankled.

Maybe it would be a blessing if Amanda provided evidence to back up her claim against

Scott…thus confirming Carrie's fears Amanda's spiteful allegations were true. If he was a womanizing, noncommittal waste of time, then it would make everything simpler. One, Carrie could leave the Cove guilt-free once she'd given him a chance; and two, her entire being would stop humming with the need to find out if they were ever to make love again, and have him take her in the same powerful and magical way he had before.

Carrie cursed her lustful thoughts, but how was she to fight her attraction to him when so far Scott had been attentive, considerate and willing to listen to her? Hadn't he offered to try and do whatever he could to meet Carrie's standards and his own? What more could she have hoped for?

Amanda's derision of him had to be unjustified. How could a man committed to his family, who ran his own business, lack in the steadfast ability to see things through to the end? Carrie had seen the anguish her returning to Templeton had brought him. Everything showed so clearly in his dark blue eyes. Deep down, she sensed that not knowing whether he could be a good father pulled on his every emotion. Could she show him he could? Carrie swallowed. Surely it wasn't her job to show him. Her heart ached with sadness. He needed to know it himself.

With their glasses filled, the waiter carefully

placed the bottle into a wine chiller he'd brought to the table. He bowed and left her and Amanda alone. Carrie took a sip of wine and met Amanda's expectant gaze.

Amanda smiled. "Are you all right? You were miles away."

Carrie replaced her glass on the table, her armor stealing over her shoulders and straightening her spine. "How long did you and Scott date?"

Surprise flickered through Amanda's gaze before she blinked and it was replaced with superiority. She lifted her chin. "Two months. Why?"

Two months? Carrie's stomach knotted with a sensation that felt too much like misplaced envy. The thought of Amanda having night after night with Scott made her time with him either pathetic or precious. She had no way of knowing which. She nodded. "Two months exclusively?"

Amanda flushed. "Of course."

"He never cheated on you? Stood you up? Lied to you?"

Her color darkened. "No, he just walked away."

Satisfaction—and relief—furled in Carrie's stomach. Amanda's deepening blush told her Scott had remained faithful until the end. "You're telling me nothing that makes him a womanizer. In fact, you're not telling me anything that makes me less likely to trust him than I do now."

Amanda's eyes lit with cunning. "So you do want more than friendship with him?"

"I didn't say that." Carrie cursed the heat that pinched her cheeks.

Amanda smiled. "You didn't have to. I know what Scott is to women."

"And what's that exactly?"

"Someone none of us will ever have forever."

Carrie's food arrived and with a final loaded glare at her companion, she focused on her plate of spaghetti carbonara, which now looked as appealing as a plate of malnourished eels. She picked up her fork and twirled it into the pasta. "Let's talk about something else. Your shop, for instance. It's beautiful."

Silence.

Carrie looked up. Amanda watched her, her gaze determined. "I bet you and he had a long-distance relationship of some sort and now you've turned up at the Cove, he's dumped you, right?"

"What?"

"That's why you're in the hotel, eating alone."

Carrie laid down her fork, her stomach burning with acidic vengeance. "I could call him right now and he'd be here. It was me who walked away from him this afternoon."

Amanda's eyes grew wide with childlike excitement. "Call him now and ask him to come."

"No." *This woman is crazy.* Crazy because of

what Scott did to her? Carrie held Amanda's un-relenting gaze. No matter how much Amanda might have shaken her trust in Scott, it was nothing compared to the mammoth distrust she had in Amanda.

"Prove me wrong, Carrie. I'd welcome it."

Temper snapping, Carrie whipped her clutch from the table and extracted her phone. Cursing the tremor in her fingers, she called Scott's number and waited. The tone continued to ring as Amanda's smile spread wider. Voice mail kicked in and Carrie snapped the phone shut. The last thing she needed to hear was Scott's voice. It would only weaken her defenses.

"No answer." She shoved the phone back into her bag.

Amanda stood. "You know where to find me if you want to talk."

Carrie stared. "You're leaving?"

"I've seen and heard enough." Amanda smiled. "Enjoy the wine. I'll pay for it on the way out. Night, night."

Carrie glowered after Amanda until she left the dining room. Once she'd gone, Carrie whipped the bottle of Chablis from the cooler.

Damn her insinuations. Damn her for making me doubt Scott when I so badly want to trust him. Damn her for having had two months with a man I've never forgotten. Not for a single day.

CARRIE MARCHED TO her hotel room and used the keycard to open the door. Stepping inside, she flicked on the lights and slipped her stilettos from her feet, welcoming the depth of the carpet as it cocooned her toes. She walked farther into the room, tossed her clutch onto the bed and collapsed face first onto the mattress, not caring that her silk dress would be little more than a crumpled dish-rag by morning.

Her meal had probably been delicious but her mouth was coated with distaste after Amanda's performance. The woman clearly had a screw loose and Carrie had to find a way to delete her insinuations about Scott from her mind. Amanda's entire diatribe stank to high heaven of jealousy and dented ego. She hardly looked brokenhearted, with her impeccable clothes, hair and makeup. If anything, Amanda looked well and truly insane.

Carrie glanced at her watch. It was barely nine but nothing felt more appealing than getting into her pajamas and making a cup of tea to drink in bed. Maybe the TV would distract her from the myriad of thoughts and worries bouncing around in her head. Pushing from the bed, she slipped her dress from her shoulders, letting it pool on the floor before reaching for the TV remote. She pointed it at the TV and the screen flickered to life.

Nothing like a period drama to ground a girl in reality.

Dressed in her underwear, she grabbed the kettle from a tray on the dresser and walked into the bathroom to fill it. She caught her reflection in the mirror and slowly lowered the kettle to the sink. Her skin looked tired and drawn and she had black circles under her eyes. She tugged at her cheeks. God, the emotional strain of her mission was making her resemble a zombie. The sooner she and Scott got a DNA test done the better.

The ringing of her cell phone in the bedroom snapped her gaze to the door. Scott.

Her stomach executed a loop-the-loop as she hurried from the bathroom. She pulled the cell from her clutch, and a funny sensation skittered across her heart when she saw her intuition about the caller had been right. She pressed the talk button. "Scott?"

"Hi. I've got a missed call from you. Everything okay?"

The low rumble of male voices in the background filtered down the line and Carrie pulled back her shoulders. She didn't want anyone else knowing their business. "Sure. It was nothing. I didn't mean to disturb your evening."

"You're not. Why did you call?"

"I don't want to talk about it if you have company. Why don't we meet somewhere tomorrow?"

"Hold on." The background noises slowly faded

and then there was the click of a door closing. "I'm in the bathroom. What's wrong?"

She dropped onto the bed, her head falling back against the pillows. "You didn't have to leave your friends."

"I wanted to. Talk to me."

Carrie squeezed her eyes shut. The low, masculine and caring tone of his voice seeped into her ear and spread over her body in a soothing and heated mist. Loneliness and confusion rose and enveloped her in silent yearning for him. Just one more night together would be all she needed to sate the erotic thoughts that chased through her mind. Just one night would give her the evidence she needed to accept what they had before could never be resurrected. If he had been in the room with her, Carrie would have put all the distrust and insecurity that lay between them to one side...just for a while.

She snapped her eyes wide open and forced her heart into submission. "I had an unexpected companion at dinner. She challenged me to call you."

"She?"

"Amanda."

The silence stretched for a second or two until he took a sharp breath. "Whatever she said, ignore it."

"Believe me, I am. But you've certainly made yourself an enemy in her."

"I know, but whatever I say to the woman, nothing changes. I didn't walk out on her the way she tells everyone I did. I tried my best, but it didn't work out. She didn't stop criticizing me."

"About what?"

"About her son, Rhys. That's part of the reason I'm shot through a loop now I know I could have a child of my own. Amanda got inside my head, Carrie."

"And made you think you weren't cut out to be a parent?" Carrie frowned. "You know she's kind of crazy, right?"

He laughed softly but Carrie sensed his insecurity. It was on the tip of her tongue to ask him to come to the hotel. The reasoning shamed her… for it had nothing to do with their daughter and everything to do with the sensations rolling over her body in undulating waves. "Scott—"

"I need to see you."

She stiffened. "Now?"

"Now. It's important. I'd rather not wait until the morning. Shall I meet you somewhere?"

Carrie sat up and looked about the room and then down at her state of undress. "What do you want to talk about that can't wait?" *Please say you can wait so I can rid myself of this stupid, lonesome desire before I see you.* "Has something happened?"

"I've…" He exhaled. "I've got a friend who's a doctor. He's willing to rush through a DNA test."

Her heart thumped hard and her libido instantly cooled as though his words were ice-cold water he'd poured down the telephone line. "Right."

"Do you have something of Belle's with you?"

She looked toward the end of the bed where Belle's toy dog lay looking lost and forlorn. She picked it up, pressed it to her face and inhaled. "Yes."

"My friend said we need a single hair of Belle's, that's all."

"Right." Blinking back tears that Belle's paternity had come to this, Carrie plucked one of Belle's black curls from the dog's fluffy back. "No problem."

"Can we come to the hotel now?"

She stilled. "Both of you?"

"I'm sorry, but Kevin needs to do this ASAP. If he takes the swabs from us tonight and bags Belle's hair, he can get it all couriered to the lab first thing in the morning." He exhaled. "He thinks if he pulls in a favor, we could have the results as soon as tomorrow evening. I need to know, Carrie. The sooner the better."

She squeezed her eyes shut. "Okay. I'm in room six-forty. I'll see you soon."

"Great…and, Carrie, everything's going to work out. I want this. I want our baby."

The line went dead and Carrie dropped the phone to the bed as unexpected sadness washed over her. *He might want our baby, but not once has he mentioned wanting me.* She swallowed. *If he only wants a relationship with Belle, then that's fine. I'd much prefer that to having him want me just because I'm her mother.*

Standing on trembling legs, she walked in a dazed state into the bathroom. When she looked at her reflection, her skin was as pale as porcelain, and her heart beat a dreaded tattoo in her ears. She strained to think of a moment when Scott mentioned wanting to see whatever it was between her and him reconciled, for them to give their relationship a chance. Nothing but his mention of doing whatever he could for Belle bounced around in Carrie's head.

She gripped the sink and prayed that her instinct she was meant to come to Templeton, was meant to find Scott Walker again, was the best course of action rather than a mission created through her own stupidity. She lifted her chin and stared into the mirror. He wouldn't take her baby and leave her out in the cold. He wouldn't do that. Would he?

CHAPTER TWELVE

SCOTT STEPPED OUT of the elevator on The Christie's sixth floor and headed straight for Carrie's room, leaving Kevin to follow. Tension rippled through every muscle in his body—damn, it was as if he'd discovered muscles he never knew he had. He set his jaw, every nerve in his body screaming with apprehension.

"You ready for this?"

The somber tone of Kevin's voice brought Scott to an abrupt halt. He turned and blew out a breath. "As I'll ever be. I have to know for sure one way or another."

Kevin looked along the corridor. "And if you're the father, then what?"

"Then it'll be time for me to meet my daughter."

"Just like that."

"No, not just like that." Scott frowned. "This is insane, but the one thing I know for sure amidst all this crazy is I won't turn my back on my kid. Ever." Protectiveness rolled through him as Scott stared along the corridor. "Nor Carrie...if she wants me."

Kevin raised an eyebrow. "So you're seeing the kid and her as a package, huh? You want to be with her?"

Scott nodded. "But I've no idea if she wants me and her to be a part of this."

Kevin shook his head. "You need to take this slow and steady. Don't rush into anything. You've not been in a relationship for any amount of time before and I've been a doctor long enough to know a child changes everything."

Scott faced him, passion for Carrie and Belle heating his blood. "I've never stopped wondering where Carrie is and who she's with. If I'm Belle's dad, it proves it's meant to be the real deal between us. I'm sure of it."

For a long moment, Kevin said nothing and Scott resisted the urge to turn away from his friend's assessing gaze. Finally, Kevin smiled and slapped his hand on Scott's shoulder. "Fine. Then let's do this."

Nerves jumping, Scott led the way to room six-forty. He glanced once more at Kevin before raising his hand and rapping his knuckles against the door. Each second felt like a minute until the door softly clicked open.

Neither Scott nor Carrie moved or spoke. She appraised him from head to toe and he did the same to her. His dick twitched awake. Even dressed in sweat pants and a plain navy-blue T-shirt, with her face devoid of makeup and her hair tied into a knot on top of her head, she looked amazing—and sexy as hell. He languidly slid his gaze over her covered breasts and lower to her bare feet with scarlet-painted toenails. He met her eyes. They were full of caution, but still Scott wondered how the hell a woman could look more beautiful each time you saw her.

She stepped back and waved them inside. "Sorry. Come in."

Fighting the need to pull her into his arms, strip her naked and feast on every inch of her exquisite body, Scott stepped inside the room and smiled. "Thanks. This is my friend Kevin."

"Hi." She smiled before pushing the door closed. "Go on through."

Scott walked into the small but tidy hotel room. Her things were laid out on the dresser and he ran his gaze over everything as though seeking some small insight into this woman he knew nothing about, but wanted to know everything.

"Can I get you some tea or coffee? Water?" Carrie's voice filled the room, breaking the silence.

Scott shook his head. "I'm good."

She looked to Kevin. "Anything?"

Kevin smiled. "I'm fine." He placed his brief-case on the single bed. "Why don't we get the hard bit out the way so you two can breathe a little easier. It's starting to feel like the walls are closing in on us." He laughed.

Scott looked at Carrie. Her smile wobbled and her eyes were impossibly wide when she looked at him. He winked, hoping to pacify the open guardedness in her gaze but instead she snapped her gaze to Kevin. Unease knotted Scott's stomach and his smile dissolved. The tension coming from her was palpable.

Clearing his throat, Scott spoke to Kevin's turned back as he extracted various plastic bags and swabs from his briefcase. "Who do you want first?"

Carrie brushed past him. "Could I go first?"

Kevin straightened. "Sure. I just need to take a swab from the inside of your cheek. It's quick and painless."

She nodded and stepped forward. Scott shifted from one foot to the other as Kevin held the swab and Carrie opened her mouth. Kevin was clearly trying to put Carrie at ease by saying the procedure was painless, but there was nothing painless about any of this. The entire thing was as painful as anything Scott could imagine.

"All done." Kevin smiled at Carrie before turning to Scott. "You're up."

Scott stepped forward. As Kevin scraped the wand over the inside of his cheek, Scott was aware of Carrie resolutely studying a hideous watercolor of drab blues and greens above the bed.

His heart kicked. Could she not even bear to look at him? Did she hate him for putting her through this and not taking her word Belle was his? He hoped she understood having it confirmed in black and white was the best way forward for both of them. This way, Belle's paternity could never be questioned in the future—by anyone. Including his overprotective, nosy sisters or even Belle herself.

"All done." Kevin pulled the swab from Scott's mouth and dropped it into a plastic bag. He sealed it and placed it next to Carrie's.

The tension grew as Kevin took a pen from inside his jacket, labeled the samples and organized them in his briefcase. Scott stared at Carrie until she turned to face him. Their eyes locked and Scott's heart picked up speed. He longed to hold her, to take away the anxiety in her gaze…

Kevin cleared his throat and Scott snatched his gaze to his friend.

Kevin frowned as he looked at Carrie. "Scott said you have something with your daughter's hair on it?"

"Yes." She uncrossed her arms and swept across the room to a chair in the corner. She picked up what looked like a well-loved toy dog and thrust it toward Kevin. "There are quite a few of my daughter's curls on there." She laughed, the high-pitched sound revealing her nervousness.

Scott kept his gaze on her profile as Carrie re-crossed her arms and focused on Kevin. He took some tweezers from an open box on the bed and carefully removed three or four of Belle's stray hairs from the toy and placed them in another plastic bag and sealed it. He handed the toy back to Carrie. "That's it." He labeled the bag.

She clutched the dog to her chest and nodded curtly. "Good. So you think you'll have the results as soon as tomorrow?"

"I certainly don't want to promise anything, but I'll do my best." Kevin glanced at Scott. "He's calling in a favor from me, and I'll do the same with a friend at the lab. As soon as they come through, I'll ring Scott and then you can both come to my office. Okay?"

"Great. Thank you." She spun away and bus-ied herself propping the toy this way and that on the bed.

Silently cursing his helplessness, Scott turned to Kevin as tension once again permeated the room. "Okay, well, there's nothing else to do but wait until tomorrow, then."

Kevin gave him a loaded stare before turning and packing up his briefcase. "If you two want to chat some more, I'll get out of here and get these results couriered overnight. They'll be at the lab first thing."

Half expecting Carrie to protest his staying, Scott hid his surprise when she remained static and quiet, her feet seemingly glued to the carpet.

Kevin lifted his briefcase and smiled at Carrie. "See you tomorrow."

She smiled as she rolled back and forth on the balls on her feet. "See you tomorrow."

"I'll walk you out." Scott placed his hand on Kevin's shoulder and steered him toward the door. He opened it and faced his friend. "I'll wait by the phone for your call."

Kevin glanced over his shoulder into the room. "She's a beauty," he whispered. "But this is complicated. I know what you said about you two being together, but just don't do anything stupid like falling headfirst in love with her. As much as you think you know her, you don't. At all."

Scott clenched his jaw and held Kevin's gaze.

Kevin shook his head. "Fine. Do what you have to do."

"See you tomorrow, Kev." Scott closed the door, his heart pumping.

He and Carrie were finally and completely alone. No risk of interruptions. No risk of someone overhearing them. His body came alive with adrenaline as his mind soared with good and bad opportunities of the sexual kind. He turned back into the room.

Carrie stood exactly where he'd left her, her arms tightly crossed, her chin lifted and her steady gaze trained on him. "So, that's it, then. Tomorrow you'll know Belle is yours."

"Yes." He nodded, trying to figure out the look in her eyes. She looked anxious, yet determined. Scared, yet poised. Her body was rigid with tension. "What is it, Carrie? What do you want to say?"

"I love her more than life itself, Scott. Promise me you'll never try to take her from me."

Disbelief rocketed through his body and pushed the breath out of his lungs. "You think me capable of taking your daughter? Carrie…" He closed the space between them in two long strides and gently eased her arms uncrossed. He gripped her hands, willing her to believe his next words. "I would never do that to you. Ever. You look at me now and believe that. You have to." He shook his head, his gaze boring into hers. "I will never hurt you."

Her eyes were wide as her gaze darted over his face to linger at his mouth. After a long moment, she shook her head and glared. "I have no reason to trust you on that."

Scott stared and slowly narrowed his eyes. "What's happened, Carrie?"

"What do you mean?"

"You're different. Angry. Distrustful. What have I, or someone else, done to make you wary of me? I thought...I thought things were going pretty well between us."

She glanced past him before meeting his eyes once more. "If you don't want me and only Belle, that's fine. Maybe I shouldn't have come here to see..." She closed her eyes.

Scott frowned. "Come here to see what?" He touched his finger to her chin and she opened her eyes. "Carrie? You shouldn't have come here to see what?"

She stared deep into his eyes, her gaze determined. "I shouldn't have come here to see whether or not there would be anything between us. I should've just come for Belle."

Scott's heart kicked. "You came here for me, too?"

She lifted her chin from his hand, her gaze dropping to his mouth. "I didn't say that."

She wanted him. She wanted him as he wanted her. "Carrie." Desire for her swept through his body and Scott took her hand, lifting it to his lips. "I thought about you all the time. I wondered...I tormented myself with what you were or weren't doing. I'm glad you're here. Really glad."

Her gaze bored into his as though searching for his sincerity. Scott stared straight back, his spine rigid. To have her reject him now...

She wet her lips. "I need to know you want to see what could happen between us because you like me…not because I'm Belle's mum."

He smiled and stepped closer. He smoothed his thumb over her bottom lip. "I wanted you before Belle and I want you now. How can you not know that?"

She briefly closed her eyes, her cheeks reddening.

He might have gone a small way to easing her fears with words, but now all he wanted to do was relax her with the physical. Hold her, touch her, show her how everything was going to be all right as he softly caressed her body and kissed her lips. Exhaling, he glanced toward the mini-bar in the corner of the room. "I'd kill for a drink."

"What?"

He met her eyes. "I need a drink. Would you join me?"

She stared, indecision storming in her wide, beautifully brown eyes. A few seconds passed and a soft smile curved her lips. "Sounds good to me." She walked to the mini-bar, opened it and cruelly leaned over, perking her perfect, curvaceous butt right in front of him. "Red wine? Or something stronger?"

"Red wine's perfect."

She extracted the mini bottles of wine, and the door softly clunked closed. Throwing him a soft smile, she padded toward the bathroom, reemerging with two plastic tumblers. She held them aloft with the bottles. "Classy, huh?"

He laughed. "I'm game if you are."

She came closer and turned away to put everything on the dressing table. Scott stared at her turned back at she opened the wine and poured their drinks. The sight of her shapely neck was enough to turn him on, let alone thoughts of what she wore under her clothes. He clenched his jaw, his body humming with desire. He had to touch her, had to kiss her again. The anticipation and need of wanting her was messing with his head and he wanted it gone. If their lovemaking wasn't as hot and passionately mind-blowing as it was before, then at least he'd know his yearning was one-sided and start learning a way to deal with it.

"Here." She held out one of the tumblers. "Cheers."

"Cheers." Scott clinked his drink to hers and drank deeply.

She took a delicate mouthful, her eyes on his above the rim.

He had no idea who moved first. It could have been him or her, but in the next second, they were kissing. She tasted like the sweetest treat a man could want—dark chocolate mixed with a hint of alcohol, warm and comforting. Her scent teased his nostrils…musky and welcoming, like a cinnamon-filled room when you come in from the cold. His mind and senses filled with her as Carrie's tongue met his and she softly whimpered into his mouth.

He moved his head to kiss her deeper, to take more of her flavor. His free hand clutched her waist, but he wanted more. Pulling back, he looked at her. Her eyes were hooded with desire; dark and intensely sexy. Her cheeks were flushed and her mouth ajar as if she tasted something soft and delicious. He eased her drink from her hand and placed his and hers on the table by the bed.

"God, Carrie." He stepped toward her. "I want to make love to you. I have to. Please."

With her gaze locked on his, she remained sexily silent, the glint in her eyes telling him everything he needed to hear. Slowly, she stepped back and Scott's heart plummeted when her gaze fell to her left hand. She slowly turned her wedding band, only once glancing at him before focusing her attention back to her finger. Drawing off the ring, she exhaled a shuddering breath and carefully placed it on the dresser.

Scott held his breath and waited. His heart pounded. This was entirely her decision to make. She looked at him and he exhaled. Her eyes were dark with certainty and intention. She gripped the hem of her T-shirt and whipped it over her head before tugging at the string of her jogging bottoms. She shimmied them over her hips and kicked them to the side. She wore nothing but a black satin bra and panties. His cock hardened.

She stepped toward him, her gaze steady on his. "I have no idea why I'm doing this, but I know I want to more than anything." She closed her eyes and drew in a shaky breath before opening them again. "You…" She shook her head. "You are…."

He lunged forward and covered her mouth with his. She didn't need to say anything else because he understood her. She wanted him with the same inexplicable, passionate yearning with which he wanted her. They were meant to be together, making love at every opportunity. He was meant to care for her, love her, bring her pleasure and soothe any pain he couldn't stand the thought of her having to ever endure. He was meant to be hers.

CARRIE TREMBLED AS her entire body was overcome with arousal, and her heart with liberty coated with delicate, fearful permission. Her happiness was strong, if her motivation still unclear.

Her fingers ached to touch every part of Scott's body. Her center throbbed with the need to feel him deep inside her. Her heart beat with want and need for a man who'd never fully left her consciousness in three whole years. Maybe, just maybe, they could have sex this one time and then know they were never meant to be. Maybe she would touch him and he'd touch her and the need would be sated...

Laughter rang in her stupid head as she clasped her hand to the back of his strong, masculine neck and pulled his face to hers. Their lips met and he lifted her into his arms. She locked her ankles at the base of his spine and he held her there. His body was solid, his stance firm, making her feel feather-light in his embrace. Her femininity soared and her body came alive as though it had lain dormant since she was last in his arms.

She ran her hands over the hardened ridges of his shoulders then lower to grip biceps wider than the span of her hands. He was brick swathed in silk; every muscle hard, every vein large and engorged with hot male blood. Carrie kissed him deeper as her body screamed for his touch. With their lips devouring, taking and branding, he carried her backwards and then lowered her to the bed.

Their eyes locked as he stood at the edge of the bed and pulled his shirt over his head. Next he yanked open his belt and unbuttoned his jeans, pausing to draw a wallet from his back pocket. He pushed the jeans down his thighs and her heart hammered as her gaze fell to the erection tenting his boxers. She trembled with impatience, her nipples tightening and her core growing warm with wetness.

He removed a foil packet from his wallet and put it atop the bedside table. He met her eyes, silently asking the question. Do we do this or not? Do you want me like I want you? She nodded, excitement soaring through her blood on a hot, heady wave of certainty.

Smiling softly, he relaxed his shoulders and kicked off his shoes, leaning down to tug off his socks. Carrie licked her lips as he finally got rid of his jeans and came toward her. He crawled onto the bed and laid his huge, muscled bulk next to hers. Achingly slowly, he trailed his fingers down the side of her face to her neck, his gaze following their journey. She screwed her fingers into the bed covers. She was little more than a weakened slave and he her master. The thrill of having a man as quietly strong as Scott admire her in the way he was turned her body and heart to putty in his hands.

His fingers reached the curve of her breasts and he snapped open the front fastener on her bra. He leaned over and took one peaked nipple into his mouth. She sucked in air between clenched teeth and closed her eyes, moving her hand to caress his smooth, broad back. She clung to him as he sucked and teased, his hand gliding down over her belly to trace the line of her panties.

The agony was excruciating but she didn't ask him to stop, sadistically wanting the pleasure/pain of his lovemaking to stretch for as long as they could make it last. Back and forth he brushed those teasing fingers…

"Look at me, Carrie."

She opened her heavy lids.

He stared deep into her eyes, his blue gaze dark with desire and his jaw set. "You're beautiful. You're sexy…and tonight, you're mine."

She nodded. "Yes."

There was no finesse in the hungry jab of his hand into her panties and over her clitoris. Her body screamed with pleasure and she cried out as she gripped his neck, pulling him down and hungrily claiming his mouth. He massaged her, slipped his fingers deep into her wetness and sweet joy swelled in her heart that he now knew what he did to her. The shame she'd anticipated, the nerves she'd expected, didn't show up and she didn't care to ask why.

Scott was all she could think of.

He pleasured her until her body climbed toward the place she wanted to be with him buried deep inside her. Blindly, she reached for the condom packet and ripped it open.

"Here, let me touch you." Her words were jerky and demanding, illustrating her need and desperation.

He eased away from her and she reached for him. Trailing her nails down his chest, over his navel and the line of dark hair to his boxers. Together, they eased them off and she caressed the length of his erection. He was just as she remembered and her body trembled at the thought of what was to come. She cupped and teased his tightened balls and upward to massage his penis.

"Carrie…"

Smiling softly, she lifted her head and they kissed. Their tongues strained and battled as she sheathed him. His thumb ran over her nipple, heightening her arousal and fuelling her desire. He eased her back and then moved over her. She opened her legs wide and he slid one hand beneath her waist, hitching her closer, and with a final, loving gaze, at last, he entered her.

"Oh, God…" She sighed, her mouth dropping open.

In and out gently then a possessive thrust. Over and over, he brought her closer…then drew her back. She whimpered and clasped her hands to his taut ass, taking over and pushing him to do her bidding. She lifted her legs and he slid deeper until the rising heat of the building sensations sent her need into overdrive.

She couldn't have imagined their lovemaking being any more sensual. He took her as she wanted. His thrusts, powerful and meaningful, given with love and attention. She couldn't hold back anymore and dug her nails into his shoulders as her orgasm crashed through her body, sending delicious tremors of pure pleasure pulsing from her toes to her scalp.

His shoulders stiffened and then his breath left his lungs as he shuddered, taking his pleasure and hers. On and on, the tremors rolled through them, uniting them in a mist of passion that made her want to cry out loud. Slowly, they came back down to earth and Carrie smiled. He met her smile and leaned in to kiss her. Carrie closed her eyes as reality tiptoed back in and whispered into her ear what she already knew. One summer's night three years ago, her soul mate walked into a bar and she immediately fell in love.

CHAPTER THIRTEEN

SCOTT PUT HIS key in the lock of his front door. It was 2 a.m. and every part of his body was alive with a feeling as terrifying as it was amazing. He and Carrie had broken the barrier. Scott smiled. Thank God her need matched his. When she removed her wedding band…

He took a deep breath and exhaled. The same terrifying feeling he was falling in love with her was happening all over again, but this time he was ready and willing to accept it. The only fear that tainted the certainty edged with illicit excitement at the prospect of a future with Carrie was he still didn't know for sure Belle was his. Scott smiled. Yes, he did. He knew without any test results.

He trusted Carrie more than he'd ever trusted anyone. Wasn't that enough to know it was right they were together?

His smile faltered as he closed the door and hung his keys on a hook beside him. With no idea whether her wedding band had gone back on her finger the minute he left her hotel room, his insecurity was hard to handle, but Scott was determined to fight for Carrie's love and trust and would make whatever changes he had to make to ensure that happened.

He shrugged out of his leather jacket and slung it on the banister before moving along the hallway, praying his mum and youngest sister were asleep. If they were still up, there would most definitely be questions.

He and Carrie had made love twice, lapsing into whispered conversations and laughter in between. If the DNA test came back negative...he shook his head. He couldn't go there. He was falling for her and the thought she could've lied to him, or come back to Templeton for something more than his right to know about his daughter, lingered on his heart like a bruise.

Scott resolutely shook off his negativity and strained his ears to any sounds coming from the living room or kitchen. Nothing. Humming softly, he strolled into the living room and his heart stopped. His mother was hunched in her armchair.

"Mum? What are you doing sitting in the dark?" He strode forward and flicked on the lamp beside her, casting her frozen face in an amber glow. "Mum?" She flicked her gaze to his and her unspent tears glimmered in the semi-darkness. Scott inwardly cursed. What now? Why couldn't his happiness, his lack of worry, ease for just a few hours? "Mum?"

She blinked and her face broke with a soft smile. "You're back."

He frowned and glanced around the room as though looking for an explanation that could send his usually vibrant, active mother into this coma-like state. "Has something happened?"

"No. Everything's fine."

He looked deep into her eyes. "Talk to me. Everything's not fine."

"Where have you been, sweetheart?"

"Mum, what's wrong?"

"Have you been with that girl? The blonde, as Bianca calls her."

"Yes, but I don't want to talk about Carrie right now—"

"Carrie. Pretty name for a girl I hear is pretty damn beautiful."

Scott narrowed his gaze. "Stop avoiding the subject. What's happened? Why are you sitting alone in the dark?" He glanced toward the open door. "Isn't Lucy here?"

"She's in her room and asleep, I hope." She cupped her hand to his jaw. "It's nothing for you to worry about. Go to bed, I'll be up shortly."

Scott took her hand from his face and pressed a kiss to her palm. Still grasping her hand, he slid onto the chair beside her. "Nice try. Spill. Now."

She opened her mouth, most likely to protest, but then snapped it shut. She closed her eyes and slumped against the cushions at her back. "I don't want to talk about it."

"Why?"

"Because it's late and I don't need you telling me off."

"Telling you off? Since when do I tell you off?"

"You will if I tell you this."

Unease lifted the hairs at the back of Scott's neck as Bianca's concern at the bakery hurtled through him. "Is this about Dad?"

His mother flinched. "What?"

"It is, isn't it?" He tightened his jaw. "Has he been bothering you?"

"No." She snatched her gaze from his to glare at the blackened TV. "I'm big enough to take care of myself, thank you very much."

Taking a deep breath to calm his simmering temper, Scott closed his eyes. "Then if it's not him—"

"It is him, but that doesn't make this your business. Not yet."

He opened his eyes as dread, anger and revulsion knotted his stomach. "Mum—"

Her gaze hardened. "I'm not an idiot or too weak to deal with a man I've been married to for close on forty years. I don't need your involvement in what goes on between us. If, or when I do, I'll let you know."

Scott pushed to his feet and his hand trembled

when he pushed it into his hair and held it there. He stared down at his mother, protectiveness forming a rock in the center of his chest. "You might still be married to him, but you haven't seen him for ten of those forty years. What's he done now? What does he want?"

"He hasn't done anything."

"Then what—"

"He wants to come visit for Christmas." She closed her eyes and turned her face to the TV a second time. "He says it's time he made up for the mistakes he's made. He wants another chance." She looked at him. "From all of us."

Scott huffed out a laugh as his temper gathered strength. "Are you serious?"

"We've been..." She looked at him from beneath lowered lashes. "We've been talking over the last few weeks and—"

"Wait." He widened his eyes. "You've been talking to him for *weeks?*"

She lifted her chin, her gaze determined. "Yes."

"How is that possible?"

"You don't understand."

"No, Mum, I don't, so you need to explain it to me." He snatched his hand from his hair and curled it into a fist at his side. "Because right now, I want to go out that door and find him. Find him and tell him to disappear back to wherever the hell he came from."

"You've never loved anyone apart from me and your sisters, Scottie." His mother's voice was soft with concern rather than accusation. "You can't possibly understand this."

Carrie shot into his mind and he closed his eyes. His father's disrespect toward his mother over the years could not compare to something so fresh, new and exciting beginning between him and Carrie. Maybe he didn't know about long-lasting love, but he knew about caring for people.

He fisted his hands on his hips and tipped his head back to stare at the ceiling. "So because I've never been in love or married, I'm expected to roll out the red carpet for the man who walked out on my mother and sisters and now decides he wants to make up for things." He met her sad gaze and slumped his shoulders. "That's just ridiculous, Mum and you know it."

She shook her head, a lone tear slipping down her cheek. "I'm sorry."

Scott dropped to his haunches in front of her, taking her hands in his. "Sorry for what? What have you told him?"

She shook her head. "Nothing."

"Then there's no harm done."

She eased one hand from his and swiped at her face, her gaze burning with determination once more. "I will continue to speak to him. This is my decision to make, not yours."

Frustration burst like wildfire in his chest and he stood. "So you're actually going to let the man stick his cheating, abandoning feet under the table this Christmas? You've worried about me ending up like him in the past and I truly believed it was for fear of losing me the way you did him. But maybe all along you were angry the bastard had yet to crawl his way back here."

"Don't you talk to me that way." His mother pushed to her feet and pointed her finger. "I'm your mother, and who I do and don't cook for on Christmas is up to me."

"Really?"

"Yes, really."

Scott scowled, his mind racing and his heart hurting for the potential heartbreak that could befall his mother a second time if she let his father back into her life. He loved her so much. Over his dead body would he let her be blindsided by a man who caused her so much pain and worry—and could easily do so again. "I can't let you do this, Mum. I won't."

"Let me do what exactly? Live my life? Make my own decisions?"

"This isn't a good decision. Look what you're doing already. The man has been calling, writing or whatever, and now you're sitting alone, in the dark, at two in the morning worrying and fretting.

He's no good and deep down, you know that and don't need me to tell you. Have you told Bianca?"

Her cheeks reddened. "Not yet."

"Good. We need to talk about this as a family."

"No."

Scott stared at her. "No?"

"You're my children and I love you, but you're grown. What I do now is up to me."

Anger pulsed through him. His father already had his mother caught in his snare. Somehow, unbeknownst to Scott, the spider had wound its web and caught her while his children carried on with their lives, oblivious to what he was doing. Scott concentrated on cooling his need to punch the wall. He had to play this nice and steady or risk sending his mother running into her husband's arms. He raised his hands in surrender. "Fine. If you want to see him, I can't stop you, but you can't bring him here and expect us all to welcome him with open arms. You tell him I don't want him here and I very much doubt the girls will, either. Do you even know what he wants after all this time?"

"He wants us."

"Us? He has no idea who we are anymore."

"Then we should let him find out. Dads are only human, Scottie. They make mistakes." She smiled wryly. "Admittedly, most of them don't make mistakes that run ten years, but they do make mistakes that hurt and change their children. You're not a daddy yet, but one day, I hope you will be and then you'll know." She frowned, her eyes pleading with him. "You'll know what it's like to have your little girl or boy look at you as though you're their entire world and how scary it is day after day doing your best not to let them down."

The secret of his child—of Belle—fell like lead into his stomach and stayed there. Within hours he could be a father to a little girl he'd yet to meet. Would he let her down in the years to come too?

He swiped his hand over his face. "Fine. Do what you have to do, but Bianca, Ella and Lucy have a right to know what's going on, and they have a right to refuse to see him, too."

"You can't hold on to this forever. Your resentment toward your father will destroy you in the end. No good comes from holding grudges."

Scott stared. "I get he's human, but I really can't see my feelings about the man changing."

"Would you not even try if I asked you to?"

Her eyes pleaded with him and Scott's anger deepened that already his father had pushed the beginnings of a wedge between him and his mum. He closed his eyes. "In time…who knows, but that's the best I can do right now."

Relief relaxed her rigid body and she sat back in her chair. When she looked at him, her gaze was softer but marred with anxiety. "We've been exchanging texts and phone calls for a while, and he swears he's changed. He wants my forgiveness for the cheating and ultimately leaving us. I'm old, sweetheart."

"What do you mean old? Since when have you cared about a number?" He smiled in an effort to ease his disquiet. "You often act, think and look younger than most women my age."

She smiled softly. "Nice try."

He came toward her and bent down on his haunches, taking her hands in his. He stared straight into her eyes, trying his best to figure out what this was really about. "What are you scared of? Why are you really considering starting something with him again?"

Her gaze ran over his face. "I've been selfish letting you look after me and your sisters for so long. I shouldn't have come to rely on you like I have. I live in your house, I interfere—"

"You care. There's a difference." He lifted her hands to his mouth and kissed her knuckles. Carrie and Belle edged into his conscience once more. "Things change, I get that. Maybe one day I won't always be here. Is that what this is about?"

His mother studied him. "Bianca told me about this Carrie. She thinks you could be in a whole lot of love trouble. Her words, not mine."

God, if only you knew how much trouble. He

smiled. "It's nothing I can't handle and it's nothing that should make you think you have to run straight back into Dad's arms so you won't be alone. That's what this is really about, isn't it? You think I could fall in love and leave you."

Her cheeks darkened. "You're not responsible for me."

"Yes, I am. You don't need him, Mum. You have me."

"Scott—"

"If I were to ever leave Templeton, I wouldn't move to the other side of the world. I can be here whenever you need me." He rose to his feet, still clasping her hands. "Come on. Go to bed. Think about what I've said and we can talk in the morning at a better hour than 2 a.m., okay?"

She sighed and stood, bringing her arms around him in an embrace. "You're a good boy, but this is my decision. If you really don't want your dad here on Christmas, then I'll tell him that but I'm not making any promises I won't see him in the New Year."

Fear clutched like talons in Scott's gut as he pressed a kiss to his mother's temple. "Just think about this very carefully. You don't need Dad to fix your worries. He's the last person to rely on."

She lifted her hand to his cheek. "I love you, Scottie. Night, love."

Scott pursed his lips as she left the room, her

slippered feet brushing the carpet and her shoulders slumped. Guilt twisted in his chest as the reality of his mother's fears hit home. Hadn't he said to Nick that Carrie wouldn't come to the Cove? That he had no right to even ask her? If Kevin delivered, tomorrow Scott would know for sure if he was Belle's father. If he was, he wanted both the child and Carrie close. He wanted to be a part of their lives. Every day. Scott closed his eyes. Would he ever find the determination to move away from Templeton after his family had endured his father's abandonment?

For the first time in his life, Scott questioned his ability and need to stay static. Maybe it was time he moved forward and put his father's actions in the past where they belonged, once and for all. He wanted to explore a future with Carrie and Belle; wanted to be there for them as much as he was for his mum and sisters.

He sucked in a breath as the breadth of the push and pull inside him hit full-force. The certainty he wasn't ready to be a dad had somehow disappeared when he wasn't looking, and now undeniable hope Belle was his simmered deep in his soul.

He could've stayed with Carrie in her hotel room for hours, their arms and legs entwined, their bodies joined as one. His doubt of her telling the truth about Belle dissipated with each second they were together.

From the moment she walked into his garage, he felt connected to Carrie…now the lust was beginning to give way to something a whole lot deeper.

CHAPTER FOURTEEN

AFTER HER THIRD cup of coffee in a small cafe, Carrie walked across town toward the library, buzzing from caffeine and laden with bags of Christmas gifts she couldn't afford. Passing the day while waiting for DNA results initiated frivolous spending. She looked to the heavy gray-white clouds and predicted further snowfall by the evening. She smiled. Waking to glistening whiteness in the morning would only add to her festive feeling. Her steps were lighter and her heart happier than it had been for a long time. The shadow of Scott's caresses lingered on her skin and his kisses smoldered like a brand on her lips.

She might be feeling better now, but she hadn't slept entirely peacefully the night before. When Scott left her room, she dozed and then woke a couple of hours later. An hour-long marathon of tossing and turning under a blanket of guilt ensued. She'd slipped her wedding band back on her finger and removed it again more times than she could count.

Maybe Gerard wouldn't have wanted her to

spend the rest of her days alone and lonely, but she couldn't imagine he'd want her tumbling under the sheets the way she had with Scott, either. Yet she'd waited to regret making love with Scott, had waited to start beating herself up for being so impulsive again…but hours later, remorse was yet to surface.

To say she felt sorry about even a second of her actions would be a lie. The moment had felt utterly right. Being in Scott's arms and surrendering to the powerful feelings she had harbored for years, despite her love for Gerard, had brought moments of pure joy she'd never forget, whatever the future held. They were Belle's parents. They'd made a beautiful child together. Their reunion was bittersweet, and Carrie prayed Gerard looked down and gave his blessing.

She blinked back tears and lifted her chin.

Today was a new day and she'd wait for Scott's call telling her when to meet him at the doctor's office. She pressed her hand to her stomach. In the meantime, she'd go and spend some time at the local library.

As Carrie strolled along the street, she couldn't help but notice the sidelong glances of several people, teemed with the blatant stares of others. She swallowed and pretended not to notice. Templeton was most definitely a small town and, as much as she'd enjoyed the hen weekend, it was a place she wouldn't want to raise Belle. The feeling it gave her was that of a closed community—one in which outsiders would never truly be welcome.

She stared down one particularly openly hostile-looking woman about her age as unease niggled inside her. Could this be another of Scott's lovers? Carrie snatched her gaze away.

It was more than Amanda insinuating Scott's womanizing that made Carrie worry she'd be a fool to trust her instinct that she meant more to him than the others. Even though her heart longed to explore what burned between them. She was independent before Belle and she was independent now. Gerard had been her partner, not her savior. She'd fallen in love and welcomed him into her heart. She hadn't been with him because she needed him. She'd loved him—and now everything in her heart told her she had fallen for Scott, too.

She marched on, confidence increasing her pace. Marian and Angela were the only two people in Templeton who'd made her waver against the feeling of a lingering phantom waiting in the wings to lynch her in this sleepy seaside town, and maybe their kindness should be at the forefront of her mind today when Scott knew for sure Belle was his.

Yet, for all her best intentions, Carrie couldn't help but worry what mutually agreeable arrangement she and Scott would come up with in regard to Belle and her best interests. For a time, she'd been only too willing to imagine a scenario where Scott was the bad guy and she was the good mum who'd done the decent thing and tried to connect with him. What she envisioned hadn't happened at all.

Scott not only wanted to see Belle, he'd made love to her mother like he wanted to do it again and again. There had been no running for cover or shirking his responsibilities. No nonchalance or doubt in the way he'd touched and talked with Carrie into the early hours. But where did they truly go from here?

She inwardly chastised herself. She was thinking too deeply, too fast. They needed to get Christmas done with their own families and then decide their relationship in the New Year. For now, all she wanted was to get to know Scott better and tell him everything he wanted to know about the daughter he never knew he had.

Life changed in a heartbeat—and it had a habit of happening to her more than most because of her impulsive decision-making. She refused to make another mistake. Whatever happened between her and Scott, romance or friendship, it had to be for keeps for Belle's sake. There could be no in-between if she had any chance of protecting her from further heartbreak after already losing the only father she'd ever known.

The town's ice rink came into view and Carrie's worries scattered. "Wow."

Having only seen the rink from a distance, she felt the true magic of it clearly needed to be seen up close. Smiling, she hitched her bag higher onto her shoulder and walked nearer, sliding her forearms onto the barrier running around its circumference. It was barely midday but the winter sun shone brightly, its beams dancing and playing on the surface of the ice and in the eyes of the children skating.

The pay booth in the corner was beautifully decorated in glittering golds and greens, and a gorgeous line of bells edged its eaves. Carrie smiled, her heart warm. Despite her internal worries, she couldn't deny the beauty of Templeton, whether in winter or summer.

The smiles on the children's faces and the delight of their mothers as they skated or called to them from behind the barrier brought Belle deeper and deeper into Carrie's heart and mind. *I miss you, baby.*

Tears burned and Carrie hastily wiped them away just as her cell phone rang from inside her bag. She quickly extracted it and looked at the display. Michaela. Carrie grinned and pressed the talk button. "Hey, you."

"Hi, yourself. Are you okay? You sound awfully pleased to hear from me."

"I'm good. Right now I'm watching someone else's kids having the time of their lives on the most beautiful ice rink."

"How lovely."

"It is and it's making me think of Belle and how much I want to be with her. Have you seen Mum?"

"Yes, and Belle's fine. I saw them in town yesterday and Belle is being spoiled rotten. Stop worrying about her and tell me what's happening with Mr. Sexiness instead."

Carrie grinned, despite the immediate knotting of her stomach as Scott's face filled her mind's eye. "Do you have to call him that?"

"Why not? I bet he hasn't changed a bit."

"Well, he's certainly still gorgeous..." She glanced over her shoulder and lowered her voice. "And pretty amazing in bed."

Michaela squealed. "You haven't!"

"I have." Carrie squeezed her eyes shut. "I think I love him, Michaela. I think I always have."

"Oh, Carrie. That is so amazing. I'm happy for you, really I am. And he knows about Belle?"

"Uh-huh." Carrie exhaled. "We're picking up the DNA results later today and then the whole what happens next begins."

"You had a test?"

"It's a long story." Carrie stared out across the

rink, her gaze falling on a young girl with dark hair, a little older than Belle. "One I can't go into now."

"But everything is going as you hoped?"

The unsettling feeling Carrie had of not belonging slipped over her once more before she could stop it. She silently admonished herself. Why was she fighting the kindness of the good people she'd met in this small, picturesque town? Why was was she forcing herself to reject them for fear of what it would do to her if Scott turned out to be someone so different than who she hoped?

Michaela cleared her throat. "Carrie? Are you still there?"

"I'm here."

"Uh-oh. What's wrong?"

Carrie sighed. "Nothing. Something. Oh, I don't know." She closed her eyes and pressed her fingers into the pulse of a headache at her temple. "Scott really belongs here."

"And?"

"And if we're going to give us a try, I'm going to have to ask him to leave at some point."

"If he loves you, he'll move wherever he has to be."

"Maybe."

"Listen, I know you. You wouldn't have let him get close enough to…you know, if you thought he'd bail. What's going on? Don't you trust him?"

Carrie opened her eyes and stared once more at the laughing families ahead of her. Light snowflakes had started to fall and the children's faces were brighter than ever as they cheered and whooped in welcome of a white Christmas. "It's not about trust."

"What is it about?"

"I didn't come here because I need his help with Belle. I've got that covered. But…"

"But what?"

Carrie closed her eyes again. "If it's possible, I think Belle will love Scott more than I do. Now I'm with him again, it feels so right. Have you ever known a guy to mention his family unless he was in something for the long haul?"

Michaela laughed. "No way."

"Exactly. Scott's more of a father than he realizes, before he's even sure Belle is his."

"And that's great. Carrie, don't beat yourself up over the past. I can hear it in your voice. Maybe you made a mistake by not coming back to the Cove to find Scott when you found out you were pregnant, but at the end of the day, no one got hurt by you not coming. You did what you thought was best at the time. Did you lie to Gerard at any point about Scott? Deny you had feelings for him? That the night was a mistake you'd rather forget?"

Carrie's heart beat faster as the point Michaela made broke through her psyche and filled her soul.

She'd done nothing that couldn't be fixed. She was a human being who sometimes got it wrong. She smiled. "No."

"Did you see, speak or contact Scott during the entirety of your marriage?"

"No."

"So there you go. You're living your life the best way you know how. You still are. We all are."

Carrie shivered as memories of her and Scott's lovemaking whispered through her. "God, the minute I saw him…"

"You were run over by him a second time?"

Carrie smiled. "Exactly."

Michaela laughed. "Then it's just as well you went back."

Carrie looked down at her newly-bared ring finger and her smile faltered. "My husband's dead—"

"Gerard loved you. You made him happy and he died wanting you to be happy. Deep in your heart, you know that, right?"

Carrie's vision blurred. "Yes. Yes, I do."

"Good, because the only unforgivable thing about this entire scenario will be if you don't take this second chance to find out if you're meant to be with a man you fell in love with years ago. I for one, my friend, want to know if love at first sight truly exists."

CHAPTER FIFTEEN

SCOTT GOT OUT of his car outside the town's ice rink and leaned against the hood, his phone in his hand. When he'd called Carrie half an hour before and she asked if he could meet her here, a million questions had been on the tip of his tongue, but he'd kept quiet. He hoped she didn't plan on taking him up on his offer of skating when they were due at the doctor's office in a while. Spinning around on his ass and making a fool of himself had been an option to make her laugh, not to turn up at Kev's battered and bruised and have his friend rib him for the next fortnight.

He glanced toward the rink, lit up like Santa's grotto, and smiled. He could just imagine what Carrie would look like trussed up in that fur-collared coat of hers, her hair loose and sexy down her back and donning professional and very white skates. Yep, the image was pretty damn beautiful.

The trouble niggling him was he wanted to see her there in the spring, summer and autumn too but couldn't expect her to up and leave her job and move Belle from the only home the kid had ever known. The moving would be in his court.

He stuffed his hands into the front pockets of his jeans. If Belle was his, he wouldn't be waiting until spring to see her. Even the thought made his blood hum with frustration. He saw Carrie and his stomach knotted. She walked toward him but her gaze was on the skaters on the rink beside her. A soft smile played on her lips and her eyes were wide with happiness.

Scott straightened and exhaled an appreciative breath through clenched teeth. Her thick, blond hair lay in a single plait over her right breast, her sexy bangs whipping back and forth from the cold breeze. Wearing her fur-collared coat over blue jeans and black patent, high-heeled boots, she looked amazing.

He took a few steps forward, purposefully stuffing his hands deeper into the front pockets of his jeans to prevent himself from grabbing her and feasting on her gorgeous lips. She faced him and her smile widened. "Hi."

He raised his eyebrows. "You do know there's snow on the ground, right?"

She came closer and lifted her shoulders. "Barely a covering. What about it?"

"The heels."

She glanced down at her feet. "Why does it confuse men so much that some women choose to wear heels come hell or high water? It's as though we're a phenomenon to you."

"It's not that. It's dangerous. I don't want you—"

"It makes us feel sexy and confident." She held his gaze for a second before brushing past him to his car. "Thanks for bringing the car instead of your bike."

"The bike's gone as long as you're here."

She halted and turned, her gaze slowly dropping to his mouth. "Thank you."

Scott released his held breath as she faced the car once more and slid into the passenger seat. They were about to receive confirmation of whether Belle was really his...yet all he could think about was how Carrie would look in his bed, naked except for the knee-high boots she wore.

Cursing his libido, he walked around to the driver's side and got in. "So, picking you up here was a surprise. I thought you might want to take me up on my offer to skate."

She glanced through the window at the rink and sighed. "It really is beautiful." She faced him. "There are some nice people in this pretty town, too."

He smiled, a small bolt of hope dashing through him. "We're not too bad once you get to know us."

"Hmm, a few of the residents are okay, I suppose."

He lifted his eyebrow. "Present company included?"

She shrugged. "You're all right."

He laughed and turned the ignition. "Gee, thanks. Okay, you ready for this?"

"Shouldn't it be me asking you that? I didn't need this test, remember? I know you're Belle's dad."

He faced her. "Sorry. I'm an ass…and nervous." He turned to the windshield and put the car into first, exhaling a long breath. "Let's get this over with."

He pressed on the gas and headed toward the outskirts of town and the doctor's office. The low volume of the country rock ballad playing on the radio eased the tension, at least for him. He glanced at Carrie. She stared out the side window, her jaw set. He looked to her hands clenched in her lap. "You okay?"

Her smile was a little too wide to be real. "Absolutely."

"Carrie…"

"I'm fine."

He frowned. "I've been around enough to know 'I'm fine' is a woman's biggest lie. What's wrong?"

She swiveled in her seat and the weight of her stare bore into his temple. "I just hoped the prospect of these results would evoke a more positive statement from you than 'let's get this over with.'"

He glanced at her. "I didn't mean—"

Her eyes flashed with the angry fire he was

coming to know well. "Just because we had sex last night, you don't have to—"

"Hey, I'm here, and when I know Belle's mine, I'll always be here."

Silence.

"I mean it, Carrie. I won't let you or her down."

She turned to the window and Scott focused on the road. God, he had so much to learn about women and thinking before he spoke, and for Carrie, he'd be a more than willing student. He continued to drive to Kevin's office, casting glances at her tense profile and noting the way her leg bounced up and down.

He silently cursed that he was driving. He sensed she needed something more from him, and wished he could put his arms around her. For lack of being able to do anything else, he gripped her hand. Relief flooded through him when she closed her fingers tightly around his.

She glanced at him. "When you know Belle is yours, how are we going to do what's best for her? Not us, her. We can't be stupid or selfish enough to think last night is any sort of proof things could work out between us. We need more than sex. I need more than sex."

He swept his gaze over her beautiful face and his gut tightened. The same conclusion had echoed in his mind and heart countless times since he woke this morning, and he still hadn't found the definitive answer. The lingering threat of his father re-entering his and his family's lives was worrying. There was every chance Carrie would want to do things her way as far as Belle was concerned and seeing he'd only just learned about Belle, it would be difficult for him to insist otherwise.

"You've raised her alone this last year while holding down what I imagine to be a high-profile job. My head is telling me I have no right to demand anything from you…" He glanced at her and smiled. "My heart is telling me the exact opposite and demanding you bring her to the Cove for Christmas."

Her eyes widened. "What? I can't—"

"I'm joking. I'm just saying that's how much I want to see her."

"Oh." She slumped into her seat. "Well, that's okay then."

He gripped the steering wheel. "When do you go back to work? I'm guessing you're on a break right now for the holidays?"

She nodded. "Yes."

"Then when you start back, when will I see you again? I want to be with you, Carrie. I want us to give this everything we've got and not just shuttle Belle back and forth on holidays and the weekends."

A few heartbeats passed before she spoke. "I work hard and I love my job. I won't jeopardize it for something I don't know for sure will work out. I wouldn't ask you to give up your business. I think I deserve the same consideration."

He glared ahead, his heart thumping. "You're independent, I get it. So am I." He looked at her. "All I'm saying is, I hope you can trust me. I want to be with both of you and, for that to happen, we're going to have to make sacrifices. Take a few leaps of faith…"

"I have a feeling that will be easier said than done."

Scott clenched his jaw. Were the current situations, past hurts and problems too much to overcome for the sake of their little girl and each other? The thought that they could be sent an ugly stain of resentment through Scott's mind and into his heart. Even now, his father's actions affected everything Scott wanted to do. Maybe eventually he would throw caution to the wind and move to be with Carrie and Belle, but there was little chance of that happening anytime soon if his father was waiting for an opportunity to pounce back into their lives.

She eased her hand from his. "Last night was amazing, but it's not enough to base our parenting on. Before Gerard died, Belle's life was stable and secure. I won't lie to you. I want that for her again."

Irritation rose behind his ribcage. "There's more to me than sex, Carrie."

"I know that."

He turned. "Do you?"

"Yes. I know about the women and I don't care because it's in the past. It will only matter to me if they become an issue in Belle's present. You're a good man. Someone who has such obvious passion for his mum and sisters couldn't be anything else. But I still need to know for sure which side of you is the real you."

"What does that mean?"

Her cheeks flushed and she lifted her chin. "I mean, is the real Scott Walker the man who likes to spend his free time with his friends and women? Or is the real Scott Walker the man who cares and provides for his family, no matter what? There's only room for one of them in my life and Belle's."

The insult struck hard and cut deep. He steered the car into Kevin's office parking lot, found a vacant space and killed the engine. Trembling with suppressed irritation, he released his seat belt and glared ahead at the office building.

"Considering everything Amanda's poured into your head, it's no wonder you're thinking the way you are, but the real me is the man who cares about my family. Period." He faced her, anger pulsing through him that she, of all people, could think so little of him. He trusted her, yet she couldn't trust him. He was falling in love with her, but it seemed she wasn't with him. "Where has all this come from, Carrie?" He met her gaze. "I'm taking this, us, seriously. That should be enough for you right now. Everything else, we'll work out as we go along."

He dropped his gaze to her left hand and he swallowed against the dryness of his throat. Her ring finger was still bare.

He raised his eyes to hers, which glinted with unshed tears. "I'm just protecting my baby, Scott."

He took her hand. "I know. Let's get these results and then I'm going to tell you about me and my life. I want you to do the same. I didn't ask you to stay in the Cove so we could have sex for the next two days—"

"Damn it. Now you tell me."

Relief shuddered through him and his heart kicked to see her eyes shining with torment. "You think you're funny?" He laughed.

Her smile wavered and she cupped his jaw, her eyes turning somber. "No. Far from it. I just wanted you to know what I'm thinking. I didn't want to be anywhere else but in your arms last night. I didn't want to do anything else but make love with you, but today…today is a new day and we have to focus on Belle."

He lifted her hand from his jaw and pressed a kiss to her palm. "We will."

She slid her hand from his grasp, yanked on the door handle and got out of the car. Taking a moment to steady his heart and his overbearing need to talk more with her, Scott breathed deep. Everything he had to say would have to wait. He only hoped when he told her about his family obligations it wouldn't send her running. There was every possibility his responsibility to his family... and the impending return of a father he couldn't stand...would be too much too soon.

If a man could split himself in two, there wouldn't be a problem. If he were a different kind of man, there wouldn't be a problem. The cold wind bit at his face as he faced Carrie across the roof of the car. She stared at him, her face somber, her beautiful dark eyes storming with the determination of a successful, independent woman.

He locked the car and came around the hood. He took her hand and together they entered Kevin's office. The reception was surprisingly quiet, considering the last time he'd been there. He approached the desk and Carrie immediately slipped her hand from his and turned to study the various fliers on the wall beside them, her back ramrod straight.

"Scott. Nice to see you again."

He snapped his gaze from Carrie to Julie's smiling face as she looked at him from behind the desk. He forced a smile. "Yep. I roll back and forth like a bad penny."

She laughed. "If all pennies were as bad as you, Scott Walker, I'd take a sackful and be happy." She ran her fingers over the keyboard in front of her. "You can go straight through. He's expecting you."

"Thanks." Scott moved to the side door, not missing the way Julie's suspicious gaze appraised Carrie. He protectively cupped her elbow and they walked to Kevin's office.

Scott paused outside the door. "Everything's going to be all right."

She nodded, her face giving away nothing of what she was thinking or feeling. Swallowing hard, Scott pushed open the door.

Kevin immediately rose from the chair behind his desk and came forward, his hand outstretched toward Carrie. "It's nice to see you again."

Scott lowered himself into one of the two vacant chairs in front of Kevin's desk as he and Carrie shook hands. Her smile unsteady, she sat next to Scott and folded her hands on top of her purse in her lap. The image brought a nervous bubble of laughter to the back of Scott's throat. She hadn't acted quite so prim and proper when they were rolling around in the hotel bed last night.

"So…" Kevin cleared his throat. "The results."

Scott snapped his gaze to Kevin, all thoughts

of his and Carrie's lovemaking disappearing on a puff of stark reality. He stared at his friend.

Kevin looked from Scott to Carrie and back again. "You okay?"

Scott swallowed. "I'm fine. Thanks for getting them so quickly. I've got no idea how you managed it, but I'm grateful."

Kevin nodded. "Are you ready for this?"

Scott sat a little straighter in his chair. "Yes."

Kevin glanced at Carrie before lifting a brown envelope from the top of a stack of trays on his desk. He passed it to Scott. With the envelope clutched in his fingers, Scott turned to Carrie. Her dark brown eyes lingered on the envelope for a moment before she raised her gaze to his. Her eyes were soft but scared and his nerves jolted higher. Did she really know he was Belle's father or just hoped he was?

She nodded and gave a small smile. "It's okay. Open it."

With his gaze locked on hers and his hand ever so slightly trembling, Scott pulled the sheet of paper from inside the envelope. Taking a slow, steady breath, he dragged his gaze from Carrie's and scanned the words. His breath left his lungs with an audible whoosh. He laughed. "Bloody hell."

99.99% positive.

He stared. And he stared…then he stared some more.

99.99% positive.

"Scott?" Carrie's voice filtered through his stunned state.

He faced her, his heart thumping and his mind racing. *I'm a father. I have a little girl. I'm a father.* "I'm her daddy."

Tears blurred her face and Scott quickly blinked before he completely embarrassed himself in front of one of his two oldest friends…but there was nothing he could do about his grin. "I'm her daddy."

Carrie laughed, tears glistening in her eyes. "Didn't I tell you that all along?"

He pushed to his feet and whirled away to pace the breadth of the office. Who would've thought the news he was a father would bring such a feeling of complete pride and love rocketing into his heart? He and Carrie had a child. During that one amazing week they'd created life. Why was he surprised? The intimacy and passion they shared surely couldn't have resulted in anything else.

He strode back to Carrie, tugged her from her seat and into his arms. Her bag fell to the floor as he whirled her around.

"Scott!" She laughed.

He shook his head and put her down. "I'm her daddy."

She laughed. "Yes, you are."

With his entire body shaking, Scott leaned

down and picked up her bag. "Do you have that picture? The picture of Belle?"

Grinning, she opened her bag and fumbled inside. She brought out her wallet and opened it to reveal a photo of his baby. Scott slowly took it, his heart damn near bursting from his chest. "My God, look at her."

Tears burned and no matter how hard he tried, he couldn't blink them back. "She's beautiful, Carrie." He swiped his fingers under his eyes. "I don't think I've seen such a beautiful girl in my life."

She laughed and stole her arm into the crook of his elbow, her head coming down on his bicep. "Except me, of course."

He pressed a kiss to her head. "Sorry, I think you've been upstaged."

She laughed again. "That's okay."

He stepped back and reluctantly handed her back the purse. "Here. You'd better take it before I stand here staring at her all day."

She took the wallet and extracted the photo. "Here." Her eyes shone with unshed tears as she held it out to him. "It's yours. I have another million and one pictures of her at home. I'll share a few more as soon as I can. Promise."

He took the photo and stared at it again. "My girl. My Belle."

Kevin's not-so-subtle cough echoed around the room. Swiping his hand over his face, Scott turned.

His friend raised his eyebrows, a wide grin on his face. "I take it you're pleased?"

Scott laughed and shoved his hand into his hair, holding it there to keep the top of his head from blowing off. "Yes. I'm bloody ecstatic."

"Good." Kevin laughed. "I'm glad to hear it."

Scott's grin faltered as silent communication passed between them that this was far from over. This was just the beginning. Kevin's sensibility permeated Scott's euphoria, bringing him slowly back to earth. This moment was a bigger relief for Scott than Kevin or Carrie could possibly understand. If Carrie had lied to him, made him think about the insecurity of his family and their future, for nothing, God only knows what would have been left of his wafer-thin trust in human nature.

He glanced at Belle's photo once again before sliding it carefully into the inside pocket of his jacket, shoving the negativity firmly away. It was wasted energy even going there. Carrie wasn't lying and she was there, with him, in this life-changing moment. He refused to waste another second of it. He had to make love to her again. He pressed a lingering kiss to her cheek and whispered in her ear. "Let's get out of here."

She looked into his eyes, and comprehension lit her gaze. She snatched her gaze to Kevin, her cheeks flushed. "Umm...thank you. For everything."

Biting back his smile, Scott held out his hand. "I owe you a drink."

Kevin laughed. "A drink? I think you owe me a whole lot more than that. Get out of here. You both have some talking to do."

Scott winked and led Carrie out of Kevin's office, along the corridor and out of the building. Snow fell like confetti, coloring the asphalt white and reminding Scott it was Christmastime. He didn't stop until they reached his car and he pulled her into his arms once more. He kissed her deeply, possessively. He pulled back. "Merry Christmas, Carrie."

She laughed. "What?"

He grinned. "I'm a dad and you're in my arms. It's Christmas Day, surely?"

The blush that darkened her cheeks made her prettier than ever. Desperately wanting to be alone with her, Scott touched her face and slid his hands to her waist. He pulled her closer, relishing the feel of her hands travelling from his shoulders to the nape of his neck.

He needed to make love to her, hold her and feel her skin on his lips and against his body. He wanted to thank her, cherish her. He kissed her again, pouring his need into the kiss so there could be no doubt in her mind of his intention.

"Scott…" She pulled away from him, her breath short and her eyes shining. "I can't breathe."

He laughed. "I need to get you back to the hotel."

She stepped back and held a hand to his chest. "Wait. No more sex. We have to talk."

He groaned. "Seriously? I want you, Carrie. You've just made me the happiest man alive."

She grinned. "And I'm glad to hear it but still, no more sex."

Cursing, he dropped his forehead to hers, his hardened cock aching with frustration. Slowly, his rationale returned and his libido eased to a simmer rather than a raging inferno. With his brain clearer, inspiration struck and he lifted his head to meet her eyes. "Fine. Have it your way, but we need to get you back to your hotel room anyway."

She arched her eyebrow. "No sex, but you want to take me back to the hotel?"

He ran a hand over her crown and down the thick plait of her hair to play with the tip hovering at her breast. She trembled—and his penis twitched. She wanted him as much as he wanted her, no matter her insistence they talk.

He smiled. "I want you to go back to the hotel and get ready for a date. A real date."

She grinned. "We're going on a date?"

"A date. Just you and me."

"In Templeton?" She shook her head, her gaze teasing. "Never going to happen."

He laughed. "How about we at least try?"

She lifted her shoulders. "I can do that... I think."

"Good. I'm going to take you to one of the nicest, fanciest restaurants in Templeton."

"You are, huh? Then I'd better get myself a dress."

He released her hands and pulled his wallet from the inside of his jacket. He pulled out some money and held it out to her, grinning. "Here. It's on me."

Her smile dissolved. "Oh, no, Scott. I didn't mean for you to—"

He leaned close to her ear. "If I pay for it, it doesn't matter if it splits when I rip it off, does it?"

Her groan and kiss was all the answer he needed.

CHAPTER SIXTEEN

CARRIE STARED INTO the full-length mirror hanging from the hotel's wardrobe door and smoothed her hands down the sides of her new dress. Her stomach knotted with nerves and her hands shook. As soon as Scott said the word *date,* panic had set in. Aside of the implication that a date meant he was taking her—and them—seriously, what made her nervous was the fact that she'd brought nothing suitable to wear. She'd rushed from the hotel into town and managed to find a simple black dress with a dusting of sparkle around the neckline. Teamed with four-inch black stilettos and stockings, she'd have to do.

Pressing her hand to her stomach, she whirled away from the mirror and went into the bathroom to give her hair a final check. She wanted so much to trust Scott with her heart, but she'd be foolish to dismiss the depth of his somewhat excessive commitment to his family.

She straightened her spine. Rightly or wrongly, she'd agreed to this date and whatever the outcome, by the end of tonight, she had a decision to make. Either she and Scott gave their relationship everything they had, or they went their separate ways and Carrie left Templeton with her heart only slightly scathed, and Belle's entirely intact.

Everything will be fine. We've had sex and released the sexual tension gathering like a thunderstorm since I arrived. A date will be easy, mature and productive.

Carrie rolled her eyes at her reflection. *Shame your body isn't on board with that insightful reasoning.*

Leaving the bathroom, she paced the room as nerves leaped and dived in her stomach. When she and Scott made love, she'd taken him, owned him, but all the while prayed one night of sex would bring an end to her desire for him. Yet, every time they kissed, every time her hands explored his brick-hard body, she wanted more.

Carrie shivered as memories crashed into her heart. How was she supposed to keep her feelings for him under control? Her body yearned and her heart faltered. The sex had been as incredibly, mind-numbingly satisfying as the first time…and something more intense had grown between them. Emotions soared and trust bloomed; whispered words and heated sighs filled the air and slipped deep into her heart. She was into Scott Walker right up to her neck and then some.

The ringing of the hotel phone beside the bed

shot Carrie's heart into her throat. She hurried forward and snatched it from its cradle. "Hello?"

"Good evening, Ms Jameson. I have a Mr. Walker waiting in Reception for you."

"Thank you. I'll be right down." Carrie hung up and exhaled a shaky breath. "Here we go."

She snatched her purse from the dresser and dropped her cell and room key inside before walking to the wardrobe to grab her coat.

The two-minute trip from the room to the lobby did nothing to steady the beat of her heart. When the elevator doors opened, Carrie spotted Scott immediately. He stood alone, dressed in a black suit with a crisp, white, open-collared shirt. His expression and stance oozed masculinity and easy confidence as his gaze wandered the lobby, seemingly oblivious to the glances of the women around him.

Carrie swallowed as her center pulled with impatient desire. Lifting her chin, she strode confidently forward. As if sensing her approach, he turned and their eyes locked. He pulled back his shoulders, straightening to his full six-feet two-inch height and came toward her.

When he stood in front of her, his blue eyes darkened as his gaze languidly traveled over her body. He let out a low whistle. "I am so going to be ripping that dress."

Carrie arched an eyebrow, even as her stomach

executed a girlish loop-the-loop. "We'll have to see about that." She inhaled, taking in the clean soapy scent of him. "You don't look too bad yourself."

He stepped closer and stole his arm around her waist, pulling her close. Seemingly unconcerned with the people in the lobby, he dipped his head and kissed her deeply, making her heart stumble and her need for him intensify. Fear of getting hurt thundered inside her but still Carrie lifted her hand to grip his biceps and returned his kiss with equal fervor.

His tongue teased hers, his lips firm yet soft. She breathed in the masculine, musky scent of his aftershave, satisfaction warming her breast when he growled softly into her mouth.

Releasing her, he winked. "Let's go."

Enjoying the feel of his hand around hers, Carrie smiled as they walked to the revolving doors at the front of the hotel. Outside, late December made its presence known as a bitter wind whipped thick snowflakes through the air. She shivered and Scott immediately took her coat and moved behind her. He held it open. "Here. I think we'll be having a white Christmas this year."

She smiled with her back to him. "Belle would love that. It will be the first time she's seen snow." She slipped her hands into the arms of the coat and he lifted it over her shoulders. "Thanks."

He gripped her upper arms and pulled her back against the broad expanse of his chest. Carrie closed her eyes. His warm breath whispered across her ear and cheek. "I'm glad you're here."

Her heart turned over and she turned, lifting her chin to stare into his beautiful blue eyes. "So am I." The truth of her words hit her, and Carrie smiled. She wanted to be in Templeton. For her. For Scott. For Belle.

Being there with him felt right and the pressure to do the moral thing and remain faithful to Gerard finally lifted. It was time she moved on a little and got excited about the prospect of a new beginning—albeit one she hadn't anticipated.

Scott stepped to the side and pulled her closer, his arm about her shoulders. "Come on. Let's get to the restaurant before we freeze to the pavement."

He led her a little way along the street to where he'd left his car. They joined the holiday traffic and Carrie sent up a silent prayer that whatever Scott told her about his family tonight wouldn't put an end to what was developing between them. Whether or not that happened, his reaction to the DNA proof he was Belle's father meant he wanted his child. Scott Walker didn't walk away from his responsibilities. He'd told her that from the beginning.

SCOTT'S NERVES ALTERNATELY stretched and relaxed as he drove closer to the restaurant. He needed to tell Carrie about his dad's absence and what it had done to him emotionally. As glad as he was about being Belle's daddy, the issue of him being up to scratch as a father still lingered. In order to embrace the paternal challenges that lay ahead, he had to find a way to leave the Cove happily if that was what Carrie wanted. He refused to make mistakes as far as Belle was concerned, but his heartfelt fears remained rooted in his soul.

And he had no idea what to think or do to banish them.

Carrie was a mother, first and foremost, and he loved her for it.

He couldn't mess this up. His father's abandonment lingered like a long-reaching shadow over his and his sisters' lives, but that didn't mean he couldn't turn on the light. The lack of contact, the missing birthday and Christmas cards and the long nights of listening to his mother cry behind her closed bedroom door had left a bitter stain that needed to go. His resentment had done no good, and by holding on to it, he risked hurting Belle with its passion.

The timing of him becoming a father hadn't been expected, but Carrie was everything he wanted. She'd given him a child and the love he felt for the little girl he'd yet to meet continued to grow. The thought he could ruin the chance to be part of Carrie and Belle's lives was a ball of lead in his gut.

He pulled into The Oceanside parking lot, hoping he'd made the right choice of where to take Carrie tonight. Never before had the dilemma of choosing a restaurant for a date given Scott more grief. Situated on Cowden Beach, The Oceanside was classy and sophisticated and would create the romantic atmosphere he wanted.

There was also little chance of bumping into his sisters, mother, Nick or any other person in Templeton he wanted to avoid. As far as he knew, none of his favorite people were dating right now, and he couldn't imagine any reason they'd turn up there.

He cut the engine and turned to look at Carrie. "Here we are."

She grinned as she peered through the windshield. "It looks lovely."

He smiled. "Come on. Let's get inside."

Scott got out of the car and straightened his jacket as Carrie came to stand beside him. Pride swelled his ego when she pushed her hand into the crook of his elbow. "This place is beautiful. My friends and I walked past it a few times on the infamous hen weekend, but we never ventured inside."

He brushed some snow from her hair and pressed a brief kiss to her lips. "Then I'm glad I get to be the first person to take you here."

She moved her hand into his and Scott led her through the parking lot. With the snowfall growing heavier, he grasped her hand tightly as they descended a set of stone steps onto a planked walkway. The walkway led across the sand to a wooden staircase and the restaurant situated on stilts high above them. The Oceanside held some of the best sea views in the whole of Templeton during the summer months, but in late December, it was the warm ambience inside that mattered.

He glanced down at her shoes and tightened his grip on her hand. "Don't let go of my hand. If you fall—"

She laughed. "I won't. I've told you I live in heels. A bit of snow and wood won't get the better of me. I promise."

True to her word, they reached the restaurant door without incident and Scott pushed it open. He gestured her inside ahead of him and her soft gasp was all the validation he needed to know he'd made the right choice bringing her there. Romance, candlelight and soft music weren't always at the forefront of his mind when he dated...until Carrie. Now, from the shimmering chandeliers to the suited waiters and rich ruby tablecloths, it all mattered because she liked it.

He wanted to romance her, show her he respected and wanted her...show her he could love her as well as make love to her.

"Ah, good evening, sir, madam." The maître d' approached the podium where Scott and Carrie stood waiting to be seated. "Do you have a reservation?"

Scott nodded. "Yes, table for two at seven-thirty. Scott Walker."

The maître d' consulted his clipboard and whipped a line across the page with a flourish. "Excellent. If you'd like to follow me." He took some menus from beneath the podium and led them through the restaurant.

The desire to have time alone with Carrie and her earlier suggestion it would never happen in Templeton pushed into Scott's mind as they walked through the dining room. He darted his gaze back and forth, breathing easier as each face was one that offered no risk to this intimate time with her.

Carrie could easily judge him because of his relationships or reject him for his inability to make things work with Amanda. What else did she really know of him? Scott clenched his jaw. Nothing...and she'd also soon know about the bitter, hardened anger he held toward his father.

He lifted his chin. People changed and he would

do what had to be done to make her see he was a good man. A man who loved his family.

They reached their designated table and the maître d' pulled out Carrie's chair. Scott forced a smile as his fears continued to ricochet through his conscience. He reluctantly released her hand and they took their seats opposite each other.

After ordering wine, their appetizers and mains, they were left alone. Carrie's eyes focused on his and she placed her elbows on the table, lacing her fingers. She smiled. "Thank you."

"For what?" He frowned, trying and failing not to fall a little deeper in love with her as her brown eyes shone with happiness and the gleam of the chandeliers above them edged her blond hair silver.

"This. Tonight." Her gaze focused on his mouth and she smiled almost shyly. "For last night. For everything."

Scott picked up a glass of water from the table and drank, his gaze holding hers over the rim. "You're welcome, but I'm not sure I deserve your gratitude. I wasn't the nicest guy in the Cove when you first got here."

She lifted her shoulders. "Well, the way you were when I first arrived turned out to be good for me. If you had been all sweetness and light, one, I wouldn't have any idea of what you really felt about Belle being yours or anything else that happened between us, and two…I wouldn't have wanted to relive the week she was conceived. You were a bad boy then…and I supposed I wanted that again. At least for one night, anyway." She winked.

The hungry flirtation in her gaze gripped his penis and stroked it wide awake. Scott cleared his throat, glancing around the restaurant. "We keep to family stuff only tonight, remember? Your rules."

She grinned. "Dammit."

A waiter appeared with their wine and Scott waited until their glasses were filled and the waiter walked away before he spoke again. "So, where do I start?"

Her smile dissolved as she took a drink and then played with the stem, her jerky movement belying her nervousness. "Wherever you like."

He closed his eyes and pushed his thumb and forefinger into his forehead, willing the right words to come so he explained everything clearly and Carrie would understand. He took a deep breath and opened his eyes. "My father had numerous affairs throughout the entirety of my mum and dad's marriage. Right up until the day he left he had a mistress. He had debt. He had dealings with Templeton's crime boss. There was no good in him, but…"

He met her eyes, the beat of his heart strong

with adrenaline. "We all loved him as though he was the best dad in the world." He huffed out a laugh. "What do kids know, huh? Mum said to me recently that kids see their parents, especially their dads, as perfect. Someone who can make no mistake. Maybe that's true, but kids grow up. My dad leaving made me grow up a whole lot faster than I wanted to."

"How old were you? Eighteen? Nineteen?"

"Just turned nineteen. I was happy running around with Kevin and Nick. We were there for each other and thought, between the three of us, we had every woman in England covered, let alone Templeton." He smiled, wryly. "What the hell did we know?"

She smiled. "Seems to me you and Nick still think that."

He frowned and reached across the table to take her hand. "Those days ended when a blonde girl named Carrie walked into our local bar and smacked me off the radar as far as every other female on the planet was concerned."

She narrowed her eyes. "Nice try, mister. Amanda and plenty of others came after me."

"Not for a long time afterward, and even then it was Nick's griping that got me agreeing to date again. I didn't leap into bed with all of them."

She smiled. "I'm only teasing."

He stared deep into her eyes, checking for her

sincerity because he had no idea what she thought or felt. "Are you? Because you need to know, Carrie. You need to know what you did to me and still do to me. I haven't felt for anyone what I feel for you. Ever."

She nodded and closed her eyes.

His gaze drifted over her face and lingered at her lips. He exhaled a long breath. "So, with Dad gone, I took on his role and stepped up to the plate."

She opened her eyes. "You took care of your mum and sisters?"

"Yes, and as sad as it sounds, my mum and younger sister still live with me, in the house I bought. When Dad left, Mum was devastated and my sisters confused and distraught. We were in danger of falling apart. I had to do something to keep us together, so I gave them me. I gave them everything they needed, whenever they needed it. I guarantee you and Belle will get the same commitment as my family does, but as much as I might want to, I won't be able to easily leave Templeton. I need to be sure my mum and Lucy are okay and right now, that means being here where they need me."

The skin at her neck shifted as she swallowed. "I understand."

Scott tightened his fingers around hers. "And you have Belle and your work where you live.

It's another huge thing working against us, and I hate it."

Her eyes darkened with determination and her cheeks flushed. "We'll find a way. If we want to be a family bad enough, we will." She squeezed his fingers back. "As long as we talk to each other and promise to always tell the truth." She briefly looked at their joined hands before meeting his gaze once more. "There's just one thing I need to ask…"

Scott tensed. "Go ahead."

"It's not about your family, it's about Amanda and the way she was when I spoke to her."

Scott closed his eyes. "God, Carrie, don't let her come into this. Forget her."

"Look at me."

He opened his eyes.

She smiled. "I'm just looking out for Belle, remember? Please, Scott. I need to ask these questions and have you answer them so I know you better."

He nodded. "Okay."

"I've met Amanda twice, and the woman isn't happy. From her point of view, it's all about her child. I saw your face at the doctor's office…I know you're happy about Belle being yours, but still I'm scared—"

"That I'll walk away? That I won't be able to hack it for the long term?" Scott shook his head and frowned. "I understand why you'd think that considering what you've learned about me. I love women, Carrie. I'm not denying that…but I haven't had such an overwhelming need to be with one as I have when I'm with you. And as for Belle?" He smiled, his heart beating faster. "She's mine. Rhys was Amanda's son and she made sure I knew that. Belle is mine and I intend giving her everything she needs."

"Including you?" Her eyes were somber. "*All* of you?"

Scott swallowed, possession filling his soul. "All of me."

She nodded and released his fingers to pick up her wineglass. She took a sip before replacing it on the table. "We haven't time to find out things about each other like people normally do. We haven't the luxury of twenty dates and weekend breaks away to make sure we're a good fit. You said my staying here for a few days was about getting to know each other. Well, this is what getting to know each other looks like."

Fear shone in her eyes that she seemed to be trying so hard to disguise with attitude.

He leaned forward and cupped her jaw. "We have time. I'm not going anywhere. Admittedly, I haven't exactly been a saint in the past, but Amanda's the only woman I've any friction with,

I promise. She doesn't want me, Carrie. She wants someone to manipulate and mold into her idea of a partner."

Her pretty brow creased. Eventually, she nodded. "You and her little boy spent quite a bit of time—just the two of you?"

"Yes, and I didn't sign up for that, but that doesn't mean I didn't want children eventually. I told you from the start it was the timing of Belle that shocked me more than anything else." He took his hand from her face and stared into her eyes, willing her to believe him. "Amanda was so busy doing what she had to do, I never got the impression she even wanted to be Rhys's mum. What mum is happy for her date to babysit her child?"

She raised her eyebrows, her jaw hardening. "Not me."

"See? This, between us, is entirely different. You are perfectly capable of raising Belle alone, I know that…but, from now on, I'd rather we were side by side raising her."

She lowered her gaze to the table.

Scott took a deep breath and reached across to take her hand. He squeezed her fingers. "I'm happier than I've been for years, and I'll do everything in my power to keep feeling this way for the rest of my life. How about you? Can I ever be to you what Gerard was?"

She snapped her eyes to his, a tiny pulse flickering in the shallow hollow at the base of her neck. "What?"

"I want to look after you like he did. I want you to love me as you loved him."

Her gaze drifted over his face as Scott's heart beat painfully. Slowly, her mouth curved with a soft smile. "I've never met two more different people."

Scott closed his eyes. She loved Gerard. Loved him enough to marry him and now inferred Scott would never be anything like a man she trusted enough to look after her and Belle.

"But you're you, Scott, and I think you're all I ever wanted."

He opened his eyes. She grinned at him, her eyes shimmering with tears. Smiling, Scott lifted out of his chair and leaned across the table. She met him halfway and they kissed. He poured himself into her, hoping to God she understood he was sealing his commitment to her and Belle. That he would see this through to the end, no matter what.

"Ahem."

They jumped, separated and turned. The waiter grinned beside them. "Your appetizers, sir, madam."

Scott looked at Carrie as they dropped sharply into their seats. "Thank you."

He looked about the restaurant, his smile wide

as hope for the future burned inside him. The waiter straightened their cutlery and glasses and laid down their plates. He walked away and Scott was just about to pick up his knife and fork when his gaze fell on a couple across the restaurant. He froze. Everything around him faded into the background as his stomach lurched with acid vengeance. He slowly curled his hand into a fist, instantaneous rage tearing through him and obliterating his previous hope and happiness.

"Scott?" Carrie's voice filtered from a faraway distance. "What is it?"

He couldn't look at her, couldn't drag his gaze from the sight ahead of him. He swallowed. "My father." His voice was a low rumble deep from his chest. "My father is having dinner with my mother right over there."

CHAPTER SEVENTEEN

A RED MIST of anger momentarily blinded Scott as he rose from his chair, his pulse thumping. He stood stock-still and stared at the man who had dared to come back to Templeton and sit in a restaurant where any of his kids could walk in at any moment. No pre-arranged meeting, no consideration. How could his mother think this was okay?

He shot his gaze to her just as she tipped her head back and laughed like he hadn't heard in years. When was the last time he'd heard her laugh like that?

"Scott?"

He turned. Carrie's face was etched with concern, her cheeks flushed and her gaze darting manically from his to the table where his mother and father sat. The right thing to do was to get Carrie out of there and deal with this situation when he was alone, but the right thing was a stretch too far.

"Don't do this here. Let them have their meal."

Carrie's gaze shot from him to his parents and back

again. "This isn't the place. Trust me. How about we leave? Get out of here and back to the hotel?"

His heart thumped and his hands shook. Hadn't she heard him when he told her what his family meant to him? How his father's disappearance splintered them and he'd spent a third of his life fighting to keep the wafer-thin glue that held them together in place?

He shook his head. "I can't just leave. How can I not talk to him? Tell him to get the hell back to wherever it is he came from? He's sitting there as though he belongs here, for crying out loud." He tossed his napkin onto the table and strode across the restaurant.

The heat of Carrie's gaze burned into his back, but he couldn't stop, couldn't control the need to confront the man who had walked away from his wife and children so easily…and now seemed to be able to walk back into their lives with the exact same level of ease and complete disregard.

Scott didn't know whether his mother sensed his approach or saw him in her peripheral vision, but she turned when he was about five feet away. She immediately stood and held her hand in front of her like a shield, her eyes wide. "Scottie, wait."

Her defensive, almost scared posture sent a stream of guilt vibrating through him. Scott ground to a halt, his chest rising and falling as his harried breaths scratched at his throat. He glared straight at the man he hadn't laid eyes on in ten years. "What the hell do you think you're doing?"

His father slowly put down his wineglass and leaned back in his seat. His blue eyes darkened to what Scott assumed was the same shade others told him could be equally as threatening in his own gaze. "I'm having a meal with your mother. My wife." His father shot his glare around the restaurant, before turning it on Scott and gesturing to a vacant chair beside him. "Why don't you join us?"

Anger ebbed and flowed through him as Scott drank in every detail of the face he remembered so well. The lines around his father's eyes and mouth were deeper, his dark brown hair peppered with more white than gray, but still the familiarity tore a pain deep in Scott's chest. He squeezed his eyes closed, blocking any weakness and the need to know where the hell the man who should have taught him so much had been. The only thing that mattered was why he was here now. "You lost the right to call her your wife when you walked out on her." Scott opened his eyes and glared. "What do you want from her that you couldn't ask for in front of your daughters or me?

His father's gaze was steady, his pallor neither flushed nor pale. The corners of his mouth lifted in an amused smile. "I don't want anything from her that she isn't willing to give. We're taking this one step at a time, and if your mother wanted to include you and your sisters, I would have been fine with that. As it is, she didn't—"

"Ask us to be involved because she doesn't want you near us until she knows what you're up to."

His mother stepped forward and gripped his arm. "Scottie, stop this now. I told you I can handle this."

Scott tried and failed to drag his eyes from his father to look at her. He shook his head and pointed a finger at him. "You thought you'd get back under her skin and in her damn heart before any of us stood a chance of showing her how insane it is to trust you again." His body trembled with suppressed anger. "You're a cheating waste of space. Go back to where you came from. We don't want you here."

His mother pinched her nails into his arm. "Look at me right now."

Scott turned, his heart beating fast, his face hot. "This is wrong. He's going to hurt you."

"And if that happens, it will be my fault. Not yours." She glanced behind him. "You're supposed to be entertaining a beautiful girl you have real feelings for. That should be your concern right now, nothing else. Now go and sit down before she leaves."

"Excuse me, sir. Is there a problem?" The maître d' subtly slid in between Scott and the table where his father remained sitting. "Anything I can help with?"

Scott flicked his gaze to the maître d', his blood running hot through his veins. "This won't take long." He looked at his father. "He's just leaving."

His father shook his head, his eyes storming with angry determination. "I'll leave when your mother tells me to leave. I understand why you and your sisters might hate me, Scottie, but right now this is between your mum and me. Now, why don't you go and sit with your girl? Your mum has my number and you can call me anytime you want to fight this out." He glared. "I'm not doing this here. Not now."

Scott locked his eyes on his father's and curled his hands into fists at his sides. Pressure bore down on his chest as his gut burned with vengeance and protection for the people he loved most in the world. If his mother took his father back, then what?

The maitre d' coughed. "I suggest you deal with your personal problems somewhere else, sir, rather than in full view of others who have come here to enjoy their evening." He waved toward their table. "If you would like to return to your friend..."

Scott snapped his head around. "I will when I'm done."

"Scott, I'm leaving."

Carrie's icy-cold tone slipped through his blaz-

ing hot anger and Scott turned. Her eyes flashed
fire and her cheeks were red. He stood thigh-deep
in a situation he had no idea how to control. Was
this what love did to a man? Made him crazy?
Made him lose his mind and prevent him dealing
with his problems one step at a time as he always
had before? He faced his mother again and his gut
knotted when she brushed past him to stand beside his father. She slid her hand across the back
of his chair. United.

Words scorched and burned his tongue. Angry,
bitter words that would only wound the woman
who loved her children so damn much. How could
he walk away and give his father free rein to rip
her heart out a second time? He'd known Carrie
for a few days—no matter how much he felt he'd
known her a lifetime. The choice was simple.

He faced her. "I'm not leaving, Carrie. You go.
I'll see you tomorrow."

She stared. "This is a bad decision. If you don't
come with me now, there will be nothing else for
us to talk about. If you don't come with me now,
you're showing me exactly who you are."

"I can't leave him with her. I thought you'd understand that after everything...." He shook his
head. "I'll catch up with you later."

"No, you won't. I am asking you to come with
me now." She glanced at his parents. "What happens between your mum and dad isn't your choice

to make. If you feel the need to do this now, in front of everyone, what does that tell you?"

He looked at her, frustration running through him. "You don't understand."

"I understand more than you think. You love your mum and sisters. I get it. You want to be here for them, to protect and provide for them. I get it. But where does that leave me, Scott?"

"What do you—"

"I need you to be with us now. Not in weeks or months when you've come to terms with the changes in your family." She glanced toward his mother and father once more. "This isn't fair for any of us." She snatched her purse from the table. "I'm sorry, Scott. I need more from you than this."

His heart thundered as loss gripped him. Every moment he was with Carrie was better than the last. Every moment he looked into her eyes, the pressure lifted. He whirled away from her beautiful, powerful gaze and pinned his father with a glare Scott hoped optimized every ounce of rage burning inside him.

"Go, Carrie. This is too important."

"Scottie, what are you doing?" His mother gripped his forearm. "Go with her. Go now. I won't let you ruin this chance to be happy. What's the matter with you? Your father and I are just having dinner. Do you really think I will make any serious decisions without talking to you and your sisters? Do you?" She fisted her hands on her hips. "The one person who's made you happy for the first time in God knows how long has just walked away. If you don't go after her, you'll be making a bigger mistake than I ever thought possible. Do you hear me?" Tears ran over his mother's cheeks. "Don't risk losing her over this."

Scott blinked and dragged his gaze from hers to the maître d' and then around to the entire gawping restaurant.

The things that had happened, the mistakes he'd made for the last three years came hurtling back to him and hit him full force in the chest.

He'd given his family all he had, everything he was, while purposely holding further commitment to anyone else at bay. Where had that gotten him? His father here now, seemingly worming his way back into their lives. He looked at the determination in his mother's eyes. Could he really stop their reunion from happening if this was what she wanted? And what of Bianca, Ella and Lucy? What if they wanted their dad back, too? He briefly closed his eyes as tiredness settled over him before looking at his mum.

"You're right. I'm not letting Carrie go, Mum. She's too important to me. I'm done here. I love you, Bianca, Ella and Lucy, but I want my own life, too. I want Carrie. You do what you have to do. I'll always be here when you need me, but I'm letting go."

His mother nodded and smiled. "About time. Go find her, sweetheart, before it's too late."

He faced his father. "As for you and me? We're not done. Not by a long shot."

"I didn't expect any different from you once you found out I was talking to your mum again. I deserve everything you, your mum and your sisters throw at me." He took a hefty gulp of his wine and the glass trembled, indicating his father's true state. "But if you let my being back in the Cove ruin whatever you have going on with that girl, you've given me more power than I deserve."

Scott stared at him, as anger and resentment fought against the incoming stream of knowledge that his godforsaken father was right. He snatched his gaze to his mum. "I'll see you at home. Alone. Do not bring him to my house. Christmas or no Christmas, it's too soon."

She nodded, tears glinting in her eyes. "Okay. Just go."

Scott stormed through the restaurant, banging the door back on its hinges. Outside, he breathed deep and concentrated on cooling his anger. He ran through the thick snow for his car, his heart and mind a jumble of questions, rights and wrongs. No more living entirely for his family. No more worrying about his mother and not going after the life he wanted with every ounce of his being and every beat of his heart.

He gunned the engine and fought his frustration as the wipers lifted the snow from the windshield and the heater blasted the condensation inside. When his vision was the best he could make it, Scott slowly crawled from the parking lot. Once on the main road, he headed for The Christie Hotel, praying that's where Carrie had gone and she would still be by the time he negotiated the panicked British public as they drove home through heavy snowfall.

CARRIE FELL THROUGH the doorway of her hotel room, her tears blinding her and her heart breaking. What she'd witnessed in Scott at the restaurant couldn't be ignored. His anger and unresolved issues with his father still ate him from the inside out. How could he possibly embrace everything Belle had to offer if his heart and mind were still wholly committed to protecting his mother and sisters to the extent that he tried to control them and their decisions?

He'd chosen to stay where he was and not move forward.

She refused to spend her life feeling as though she had pulled Scott away from his family. His reaction at the restaurant proved he was far from ready to leave them to live their own lives and move forward with her and Belle. Tears burned. Belle deserved a father who gave all of himself to her, not one who could only spare what remained after his family's needs had been taken care of… especially when that family consisted of adults.

Grabbing her suitcase from the wardrobe, Carrie whipped clothes from hangers and drawers, tossing them haphazardly into the case. Frustration and disappointment swept through her as she made for the bathroom and snatched hair bands, makeup and jewelry.

She had to get out of Templeton. Go home and be with Belle. She had no intention of stopping Scott from seeing Belle in the future, but he had a long way to go before she allowed that to happen. Her child's happiness was the important thing, and he had to prove he'd be a light in Belle's life before any kind of meeting took place.

Heartbreak threatened and Carrie swiped angrily at her face. Scott was protective, strong and committed. He fought for his family, no matter what. His loss of control at the restaurant was something she thought she'd never witness in him. It could only be a sign of how much he hurt from his father's betrayal, and how roughly the role of protector was thrust on him from such a young age, preventing him from being able to see past it into making a life of his own, but she could not weaken as far as protecting Belle was concerned.

He could have offered his amazing virtues to his child but had chosen to turn the other way. Carrie couldn't ignore, or forgive, that. The risk to Belle was too great.

Scott's love—his passion—clearly held two sides. The ugly side was his protection sometimes went too far. He might think he was helping when really he could be hindering his relationship with his mum beyond what he could see or understand. Carrie gripped the bottles in her hands and took a long, steadying breath. God damn it, Scott needed to step back and let his mother make the decision about his father. The only decision Scott could make was what relationship he would have with his dad from here on in.

Carrie stormed back into the room. *He has to realize that himself. I can't stay here. I need to be with Belle.*

She tossed everything into her suitcase and zipped it shut. With a final glance around the four walls that had been her home for too long, she heaved her case to the floor and rolled it straight out the door. On the way to the elevator, she halted, pulled her cell from her back pocket and dialed her mum's number.

"It's me." Carrie pressed the button for the elevator, the phone balanced between her chin and shoulder.

"Carrie? What's wrong?"

"I'm coming home. Things have taken a U-turn. Scott's not ready to be in Belle's life yet."

"Oh, darling. I'm so sorry."

"I'm okay. It's for the best he showed me who he is now rather than later."

"Are you crying?"

Carrie huffed out a laugh and shut her eyes. "Of course not. I'm fine. Things haven't turned out any differently than I expected. He has my number if he wants to call in the New Year..." The elevator pinged and the doors swept open. "I've got to go. I'll call you when I get to the station and find out how soon I can get out of here, okay?"

"Okay. Just be careful and keep calm. You sound upset, and people don't think straight when they're upset."

"I will."

With her heart aching and her head pounding, Carrie dragged her suitcase into the elevator and smiled at the attendant. "Lobby, please."

Upon reaching the lobby, she hurried to the reception desk and the young girl there smiled. "Can I help you?"

"I need a cab to the train station. As soon as possible."

The girl raised her eyebrows. "Aren't you booked in until Christmas Eve, Ms. Jameson? I hope everything has been satisfactory during your stay with us? The Christie prides itself—"

"Everything's been great. I've just changed my mind about staying and want to get home in time for Christmas." Carrie's smile was so strained, her cheeks ached. *Just call the damn cab. Please.*

The receptionist grimaced. "And you're hoping to travel home by train?"

Carrie's smile dissolved as unease rippled through her. "Yes. Is there a problem?"

"I'm so sorry, Ms. Jameson, but I don't think you'll be leaving today. We had a call from the train station earlier saying that due to the increase in snowfall, they've chosen to close the line in view of public safety. The forecast is for the snow to stop in the early hours, so hopefully the line will be open tomorrow. Can I book you a cab for midday? If the station tells us there is still a problem by mid-morning, I will make sure a message is sent to your room."

"But I don't want to be here." Carrie cursed the crack in her voice and pulled back her shoulders.

"I'm so sorry. If there was—"

"Is there any other way out of the Cove?"

The girl shook her head, sympathy showing in her gaze. "The only other way is by car through two neighboring towns to the next train station. I wish I could suggest some alternative—"

"Carrie."

Carrie's heart leaped into her throat and she spun around. Scott stood a few feet away from her, his dark hair wet with snow, his jacket drenched and his expression dangerous, broody and determined.

Her stomach knotted and her body trembled as joy, attraction, irritation and protectiveness for her and Belle's hearts simultaneously tore through her. He couldn't be here. She didn't have the strength to walk away from him when he stood in front of her, looking so full of resolve and purpose. She loved him. It was pointless denying it…but she loved Belle more, and the depth of Scott's resentment toward his father, and the stringent ties to his family were too much for her to want or have to fight against.

He glanced at her suitcase on the floor beside her. "Don't go."

Her weak heart urged her to run forward into his arms, but she stood firm. "I have to."

"No, you don't."

Glancing over her shoulder toward the receptionist, Carrie walked forward and gripped his elbow, steering him to the side. She tipped her head back to look into his eyes. "I'm not giving up on you, but you have to deal with your issues with your dad before I can let you be with Belle."

"I'm ready to do this. Don't shut me out because of what just happened. I haven't seen him for ten years." His dark blue gaze searched hers. "Ten years."

"And I can't imagine how you're feeling, but that doesn't change what I'm saying." She pushed the longing to comfort him far away. "I'm leaving. You have too much to sort out."

"And I can't do that and be with you and Belle? You really think my family, *any* family, ever stops having problems?" He came closer. "I want to be with you, Carrie. I want to be with our child."

She shook her head. "You can call me in the New Year and we'll try again."

"Carrie, please don't do this."

The open and pleading tenderness in his eyes was the furthest thing from the anger he'd shown in the restaurant. Time and again, his strength and virtue struck at her heart and his Steve McQueen eyes brought her totally undone.

She straightened her spine. She had to be stronger than this. "I have to go. I'm sorry."

He stood close enough for her to smell the scent of snow on his skin, close enough for her to hear the soft pant of his breath as though he'd run from the restaurant to the hotel to be with her.

He gripped her hands, his beautiful blue eyes boring into hers. "Yes, I have things to sort out with my family, but I have a daughter and a woman I've yet to convince she can trust me, but you can. Don't leave like this. At least stay for tonight." He glanced toward the revolving doors at the front of the hotel. "The snow is coming down too hard for

you to travel. I'll speak to my mum and I promise I'll listen to what she has to say about my dad
without judgment." He smiled wryly. "And I hope
she offers the same to me when I tell her about
you and Belle."

Carrie stiffened. "Now isn't the time to tell her
about us. Not with all this going on with her husband."

"It's the perfect time. I'm sick to death of feeling angry and bitter, so unsure what the hell to do
next." He ran his gaze over her face. "When I'm
with you, everything's better, easier. The problems are still there, but together, I know we'll get
through all of it. I love you."

She slumped her shoulders, tears burning her
eyes. "I love you, too." He moved to pull her closer
and she pressed her hand to his chest. "But you
have friends and family who care about you. You
have a business, money and your home. I don't
want you to change your life for me. How can we
move forward in a relationship when I'll worry
every day you're not being who you really are, and
that you're resentful of me taking you away from
your commitments?" She shook her head. "I won't
risk that. That's what was never right between Gerard and me. No matter what he did, he wouldn't
have ever made me truly happy, because it was
you I thought about every time I looked at Belle.
I refuse to let you live a single day like I did."

His gaze burned with intensity as he cupped her jaw. "This is me, Carrie. Right now. With you. I would happily be this man, feel this way, for the rest of my life."

CHAPTER EIGHTEEN

SCOTT WAITED FOR her to reject him and rip his heart from his chest in front of the audience in the lobby.

Her brown eyes were wide, her cheeks flushed and her mouth…was stretching into the most gut-wrenching smile he'd seen yet on her beautiful face. "You're making this too damn hard."

His heart stuttered and he released her. "You'll stay?"

She covered her face with her hands as though she couldn't bear to look at him. "How can I be with you, make this decision to fight or flee when our daughter is so far away? If Belle was here… our life was in the Cove, then maybe we could work at this, but—"

"We'll deal with that. What happens with me leaving the Cove can come later. We don't have to think that far ahead. Not yet."

She snatched her hands from her face, her smile gone and her gaze hot with passion. "*I* have to think ahead, Scott. *You* have to think ahead. You're a parent now. Everything's changed. What you want or what you don't comes second to Belle. At least until she's an adult." She lifted her eyebrow and stared at him. "Then she'll come second to what you and I want. She'll have her life and we'll have ours, and she'll have to learn to accept our decisions, and we will hers."

He frowned for a split second before he understood the tone of her voice and the way she looked at him. "In other words, exactly what I told my mum before I left the restaurant. I get it, Carrie. I really do."

"You're going to leave your mum to her own decisions? Her own life?"

He inhaled. "Yes. Finally. My sisters, too."

She smiled. "Then I'll stay until Christmas Eve. I'll even meet your family, but I have to see a change in you before I'm convinced what we have is worth fighting for. I have to know for sure Belle isn't going to be hurt. I'm sorry."

He smiled and pulled her tightly into his arms. "Don't be. You make me better, Carrie. We'll work it out, I promise."

Her arms came around his waist and she settled her head on his chest. "It was always you, Scott. I think it always will be."

He eased her back and kissed her. *She's mine. I'll never, ever let this woman go as long as I live.*

He took. He savored. He loved. He needed to touch her, show her what she did and meant to him. Slowly, he eased her back. "Can I help you back to your room with your suitcase?"

She blinked and looked around her, her pink cheeks instantly darkening to a shade closer to red. He followed her gaze around the lobby. There were curious glances, some more blatant than others, directed at them from every corner.

She laughed. "Yes. Now. Before I die of embarrassment."

He picked up her suitcase as she drew from his embrace and returned to the reception desk. The girl behind the counter smiled. "Shall we forget the worry about the train, after all?"

Carrie glanced over her shoulder. "I'll…um… stay for tonight and call down in the morning about that cab."

The receptionist winked and flashed Scott a smile. "I don't blame you."

Scott grinned after Carrie when she marched past him toward the elevator like a woman on a mission. Despite the sneaking feeling it was out of mortification of losing her cool in front of strangers, rather than her need to rip his clothes off, he followed. She was the one. The woman to dispel the resentment and anger toward a man he'd once idolized.

Scott drew his gaze over the back of Carrie's head, lower over her exquisite body, still tantalizingly concealed in black silk. He inhaled a long breath, imagining the scent of her perfume and the feel of her skin. He loved her and from then on he only had himself to blame for his future choices and decisions.

Tomorrow he would see his father and lay down the rules once and for all. *It's time I moved on. My time is now. With Carrie and our baby.*

Carrie stepped into the elevator and turned to face him. He tipped her a wink and leaned against the back wall. The sexual tension between them increased with every floor they passed. Scott clenched his jaw and hungrily drew his gaze up and down her body. She leaned against the opposite wall; out of his reach and clearly tormenting him, judging by the look in her eye.

His mother had given him a strong, loving upbringing and taught him about real love, no matter how much she was hurting over her husband. Later, he'd make sure she understood everything she'd done for him and how much he loved her.

He'd also make sure his mother understood he wasn't staying put anymore—the life he wanted might just be away from Templeton and everything he'd ever known and loved. That didn't mean he was abandoning her or his sisters. They'd stay in Templeton and be happy here—his happiness would only be wherever Carrie and Belle were.

He cast his gaze over Carrie from the top of her head to the sexy heels on her feet once again and his cock twitched with impatience. As soon as they were inside her hotel room, he'd show her just how much he desired every single inch of her. He wouldn't stop making love to her until she shouted his name. They could have a great future if only they held on…

The elevator came to a stop and the doors opened. The attendant stepped back to let them exit. Once the doors drew closed again, Scott clasped her hand and tugged her to him.

She frowned. "Are you okay?"

"I'm great." He stared at her mouth then lower to the ample cleavage revealed above the neckline of her dress. "I want you. Now."

Her skin turned pink, but she held his gaze. "Then let's go."

Every step to her room stretched his need for her to breaking. The sexual tension had been scorching hot since the first moment he laid eyes on her, but now something more profound, more needful, existed between them. He wanted her for the rest of his life and short of banging on his chest and tossing her over his damn shoulder, there was little else he could do but make sweet love to her.

Her body called to him on a primal level, her heart on an emotional level he equally feared and coveted. He wanted every part of her forever and the knowledge she'd carried and given birth to his child escalated every emotion and primitive instinct within him. The look of fear in her eyes when she spoke in the lobby was clear. She was putting not only her faith, but also Belle's, in him and he would not let them down.

She stopped outside her door, flicked him a glance from beneath lowered lashes and unlocked it. The door barely closed behind them before Scott dropped her suitcase to the floor and gripped her hand.

He tugged her sharply against his chest and her breath left her lungs on a gasp. He kissed her and she moaned into his mouth, her nails digging into his biceps. She met his intensity, sending his arousal soaring. He fumbled with her coat belt as she fumbled with the button on his trousers. Finesse and care had been left in the lobby. He was sealing the deal, pledging himself to her, and prayed she did the same.

She drew her mouth from his, her brow creasing in concentration as she shimmied his trousers down his thighs, his boxers following. Her mouth reclaimed his and her fingers smoothed over his cock to massage the length of him until he thought he'd come right there and then.

He eased her back, bringing his lips to her neck. "Slow down. You're killing me."

The tendons in her neck shifted as she laughed. "You need to get back to your family. We don't have much time."

He laughed. "You're concerned about my family now?"

"Yes, but I'll still take what I need before you go."

"Will you, now?"

She grinned. "Oh, yes."

He pushed her coat to the floor and eased down the thin straps of her dress. Kicking off his shoes, he kissed her shoulders as she unzipped the dress and it pooled at her feet. Lifting her into his arms, Scott carried her to the bed and laid her down. His cock ached at the sight of her dressed in a bra, panties and lace-topped stockings.

"God, you are…" He shook his head as he yanked off his socks and crawled onto the bed. "Everything."

"My bag. There's a condom in my purse. Quickly."

He strode back to the door where their clothes and Carrie's purse lay jumbled on the floor. He found the condom, ripped it open and sheathed his erection. He came back to her and climbed onto the bed.

Taking his time, he unclasped her bra and eased it from her body, kissing her full breasts, sucking one pebbled nipple into his mouth. He teased it with his tongue, while inching her panties from her hips. She writhed, her impatience clear as she moved his hands away, and eased her panties lower. Her beautiful, chestnut gaze locked on his as she lifted her body and discarded them with a sharp kick of one shapely leg.

He lifted his eyebrows and forced a glare. "The stockings stay on."

She grinned. "Perv."

He laughed and locked his lips to hers. His body humming and his heart thumping, moving between her thighs, Scott smoothed one hand down the side of her body, over her hip until he touched her where he wanted to the most. She was hot and wet. He gritted his teeth. How could one woman be so damn sexy?

"Scott, please."

He met her heavy-lidded stare. Her desire had turned her eyes the darkest brown. Her bottom lip was caught between her teeth. Keeping his body close to hers, he positioned himself and firmly massaged her, sliding his fingers in and out of her warmth until her breathing quickened and her cheeks flushed. Moving his body over hers, he locked his eyes with hers and slid inside.

"Mmm."

Her soft, satisfied moan smoothed his ego and caressed his heart. He would make it his life's work to hear that sound come from her pretty lips every time he made love to her. He drew in and out, slowly, carefully, bringing her with him to the place they both wanted to be.

Her hands slid over his shoulders and down his

back, her nails scratching lightly over his skin until she reached his buttocks. Her light, feminine touch disintegrated when she clutched his ass and pushed him deep.

She stared into his eyes, her gaze blazing with erotic intention. "Take me."

He clenched his jaw and surrendered. He thrust deep and drew back. Gave again...and again until she met each of his motions. Together they moved. On and on, the sensations burned and rose, their bodies moving in rhythm. Slowly, fantastically, the pace increased and then her moist core tightened around him. She closed her eyes, her mouth dropping open as she trembled with the rush of her climax.

Scott watched her, his body perspiring and his heart soaring. Then, and only then, did he take his own pleasure. He exploded inside the woman he loved more than any other, the strength of his passion and love ripping through him. The force of his orgasm caught like fire in his blood. He squeezed his eyes shut and gritted his teeth as its potency stripped him bare. Slowly, he spiraled back to solid ground and dropped his forehead to hers. Their harried breaths joined and Scott lifted his eyes to hers. Her smile was as bright as a summer sun. She was everything.

Growling, he gathered her close and held the woman he always knew should be his.

DESPITE THE HOUR Scott finally climbed into his own bed. Sleep eluded him for most of the night as thoughts and the ramifications of his father returning to the Cove haunted his dreams. When he woke at nine-thirty, his semi-naked body was bathed in sweat and his bedcovers tangled about his body. Scott lay still and waited for his heart rate to slow and his mind to regain its equilibrium.

Normally, he would've bolted from bed, panicked and knocked off-kilter for being late for work. Carrie's arrival had kicked the garage to the curb and, for the time being, all that mattered was getting his life in order before she left again to spend Christmas with Belle. His gut clenched. He wanted to spend Christmas with them, too.

He belatedly realized his mother had never stopped loving her husband. All the anger, frustration and fear that showed time and again in her eyes was because she was separated from the man she loved. Scott stared at the ceiling. It wasn't his place to mess with that, but it was his place to protect her if the bastard skipped town again.

The dilemma was what he said and did next. How was he going to deal with his father's return in a rational and mature way? The more he considered, the more Scott realized the huge shift inside himself. He was calmer and more in control of his feelings than he'd been for as long as he could remember. Being around Carrie and seeing his mum with his dad had clarified things in his heart. It was time to step back and let fate take over.

His longing for Carrie over the last three years was most likely nothing compared to what his mother must have suffered being separated and rejected by his father. He now had a second chance with Carrie and wouldn't allow anyone to stand in the way of making that possible. So, why did he think he had the right to tell his mum whom she should be with or love? Lord knows, she wouldn't listen to him any more than he would to her if she tried to forbid him from seeing Carrie.

He closed his eyes. That didn't mean there was any chance his father would have his feet under the Christmas dinner table—or arrive at his house unannounced without his sisters being prepared for the prodigal's return. Scott clenched his jaw. He had to take action and vanquish the power his father had by solely communicating with their mum. If he was serious about wanting his family back, he had to face Scott and his daughters, too. They would each have questions they wanted answered.

Scott threw off the bed covers. It was time to get the ball rolling. He walked to his bedroom door and yanked it open. Just as he reached the bathroom, Lucy emerged from her bedroom.

"What time did you come in last night?" She lifted an eyebrow, her bright blue eyes shining with their ever-present happiness.

Anxiety gripped him as the uncertainty of how the next few days and weeks would pan out battled inside him. He pulled her in for a hug. At eighteen, she was the age Scott had been when his father went for a drink at The Coast Inn and never came back. Ten years Scott's junior, Lucy was the baby of the family and would always be his special girl, as she'd once supposedly been their father's. Clearly not special enough, considering the bastard left her at barely eight years old.

"What's going on, Scottie?" Lucy spoke into his chest. "You okay?"

Scott squeezed his eyes shut. "Not really."

She pulled back and tipped her head back to look into his eyes, the brightness fading. "What's wrong?"

He ran his gaze over her young face, and loathing for his father rose again, despite his intention to move on. The one thing his sisters had in common was their integrity. They might be too honest and forthright for their own good sometimes, but there weren't any two sides to them. What you saw was what you got. He owed them his honesty and needed to tell them what little he knew about their father—and about Carrie and Belle, too.

Forcing a smile, he touched his finger to Lucy's chin. "I want you to go downstairs and put on a pot of coffee." He glanced at the grandfather clock across the landing. "Wait half an hour or so and then call Bianca and Ella. We need a family meeting. Ask them to come here for lunch."

She frowned. "Why?"

He sighed. "It's about Dad, Luce."

His mother's bedroom door opened and Scott stiffened. He lifted his gaze and met his mother's glare. She shook her head and the pile of laundry she carried trembled. "You don't think it was my place to let her know about her father?"

Lucy turned around. "Dad's back?"

She sucked in a breath and Scott held her close, his arm across her shoulders. He frowned. "This involves all of us. You said I can't stop you from talking to him, and I can't. What I can stop is you bringing him back into our lives without any of us having a say in whether we want to see him or not."

Their gazes locked and Scott's heart picked up speed. Couldn't his mother see he was trying to protect her? Protect all of them?

She put the laundry on the floor. Ignoring Scott, his mother took Lucy's hands. "I've been speaking to Dad over the last few weeks and he'd like to visit on Christmas. There's nothing to worry about. I haven't agreed to anything yet." She glanced at Scott, her gaze cold. "Your brother is making a mountain out of a mole hill."

Scott glowered. "You haven't just been talking

to him. He's here. I want us to talk about this. What happened after I left last night?"

Lucy touched his arm. "What happened last night? You've seen him? Did you speak to him?"

Her eyes were wide with confusion.

Scott inwardly cursed. This was not the way he wanted her to find out. Her hand slipped from his arm and she stepped back, anger burning in her eyes. "Have you spoken to him, Scottie? Yes or no."

He opened his mouth to respond, but their mum got there first. "Yes, he has." She shot Scott a glare. "In a roundabout way. Scott ran into your father and me at The Oceanside last night."

Lucy's mouth dropped open. "You were having a meal together? Why didn't I know about this? Am I the last to know, as usual?"

Scott stepped forward, this time managing to grasp his sister's elbow. "No, you're not. Bianca and Ella don't have any idea yet, either. That's why we need them to come here ASAP." He looked at his mum. "We have to talk about this now. Where's he staying?"

His mother looked from him to Lucy and back again as two spots of color darkened her cheeks. "I don't know."

Scott stiffened. "Why wouldn't he tell you where he's staying?"

She looked past him. "I don't know."

"Did you ask him?"

She glared. "I know what you're thinking, and it's not like that. He wants to take this one step at a time, just like I do."

Scott shook his head. "Fine, then let him take his time. All I care about is you, Bianca, Ella and Lucy. If you want to try again with him, we can't stop you, but we can decide if we actually want him to be our dad again." He turned to Lucy. "What happens between you and Dad is up to you, Luce. If you want to see Dad, you can. Okay? If you don't…that's okay, too."

Her gaze flitted over his face. "What about you? Will you see him again?"

Scott inhaled a breath. "I don't know."

His mum cleared her throat and he turned. Her eyes were dark with determination. "You made your feelings pretty clear last night. I've told him no to Christmas and we'll see how things go in the New Year." She faced Lucy. "Come on, sweetheart. Let's call Bianca and Ella and start thinking about what we can make for lunch." She picked up the laundry and tossed a scowl at Scott. "While we leave your brother to have his shower. Maybe he'll cool off a little."

Scott stared after them as they descended the stairs, a voice screaming in his head that the longer his family had no clue about Carrie and Belle, the more he was a hypocrite for confronting his mum. When lunchtime rolled around, all the cards would be laid out on the table. In the meantime, he'd spend what was left of the morning running his business before he lost that on top of everything else.

He stalked into the bathroom and closed the door.

CHAPTER NINETEEN

AFTER THE MORNING from hell due to ruffled customers calling the garage wondering where Scott had been hiding for the last few days, he was cranky and in the worst mood possible to face his family as he pulled into his driveway at one o'clock. He got off his bike and stowed his helmet in the rear box. As he walked up the drive to the house, Scott glanced at Bianca's and Ella's parked cars...and then halted as he stared back toward the street. The hairs at the back of his neck rose. A black sedan was parked at the curb.

He clenched his jaw and turned to glower at the house.

His father was here. Inside his house.

Sending up a silent prayer for the strength for whatever came next and the ability to hold his already simmering temper, Scott strode forward and pushed his key into the lock of his front door. As soon as he stepped into the hallway, the unusually muted and strained blend of female voices filtered from the kitchen. Scott toed off his work boots and approached the kitchen. He paused with his hand on the door, took a deep breath and pushed it open.

He entered the battlefield, determined to start the discussion with a sense of calm civility. This unachievable notion was kicked into oblivion as soon as he saw his father sitting at the kitchen table.

His self-control vanished on a puff of air. "What the hell are you doing here?"

His father's blue eyes darkened and he rose to his feet, his hands lifted in a gesture of surrender. "This was your mum's idea, Scottie. Not mine. She thought it best we get everything out in the open and I see all of you again at the same time, in the same place."

"And you agreed?" He glanced around the kitchen at the pale faces of his mother and sisters. "Are you okay with this?"

His sisters stared at him.

He clenched his jaw. "Well?"

Bianca pushed away from the counter. "It's for the best. We've all got things we want to say to Dad, but ultimately, this is about Mum, not us."

Scott's blood burned with frustration, but he couldn't deny Bianca's words. He snatched his gaze to his mother. She stared back at him, her gaze steely but laced with pleading. "Sit down, Scottie. Please."

Asking him to sit with his father was a step

too far, so Scott strode between Bianca and his mother, straight to the sink. He cursed the tremor in his hand as he lifted a clean glass from the drainer and filled it with water. He needed to get a handle on the overwhelming need to shout and curse before ejecting his father from his home. He took a fortifying gulp and turned. "So, where do we go from here?" He trained his glare on his father. "I hope to God you're not here expecting a white Christmas reunion?"

His father lowered back onto his chair. "I'm expecting nothing more than you kids are willing to give me." He drew his gaze from Scott's to look at each of his daughters in turn. "I'll take whatever it is. Good or bad. You're…" He shook his head and briefly closed his eyes before opening them again. "You're all so grown up. I can't… I won't insist we work this out right now, but I'd love for us to start working on something to make up for what I've done."

Scott gripped his glass so tightly, how it didn't shatter he had no idea. "I'd love to hear your summary of what you've done. Why don't you sum up the last ten years for us?"

His father met his glare. "I ran, Scottie. I ran and didn't look back. I own that. That's my fault and looking at you kids now, I know I messed up big time."

Scott glared, not trusting himself to speak or

refrain from spewing his resentment all over his sisters and mother. It wasn't his place to tell them what they should or shouldn't do as far as their father was concerned. He glanced at them.

Ella and Lucy stared at their dad with awed fascination, whereas Scott imagined the hot glare coming from Bianca pretty much mirrored his own expression.

Silence followed.

He could count on one hand how many times his sisters and mother were quiet for more than two seconds when he saw them individually, let alone when they were together. The tension was palpable and his eldest sister's temper was notorious. The insane urge to laugh rose inside him. Maybe their father was braver than he ever gave him credit for.

Scott lowered his shoulders and faced his mum. "What do you want, Mum? Do you want to try again with him?"

Her mother glanced from Scott to her daughters, to their father, before moving closer and resting her hand on her husband's shoulder. "Yes, I think I do."

The joined tut of his younger sisters and the curse of Bianca permeated the room. Scott inhaled through flared nostrils. "Then I don't see there is a lot any of us can do to stop you." He met his father's eyes. "But that doesn't mean you're forgiven. I can't speak for everyone else, but it's going to take a hell of a long time for me to even come close to trusting you. A hell of a long time."

His father nodded. "I understand that."

"Good." Despite the adrenaline pumping through his veins, Scott casually leaned his butt against the kitchen counter and took another sip of water. He met Bianca's gaze as she watched him. He swallowed. "Anything to add?"

Bianca turned to her father and walked closer, fisting her hands on her hips and staring him down. "I'm with Scott. Ella and Lucy don't remember or know you like Scottie and me. Their forgiveness might be easier to come by. You've got a lot of work to do and if for one single, tiny moment you hurt Mum again…"

"I won't." He looked up at their mother, standing rigid by his side, her face a mask of determination. "I might be an idiot but I've learned from my mistakes." He met Bianca's gaze and then Ella's and Lucy's before concentrating on Scott. "You have my word. This time I'm here for keeps, whether you want to see me or not."

Wariness edged up a notch as Scott's wafer-thin hold on his need to smack the man in the face took a hairline fracture. "Do not say that out loud. Do not say we have your word on anything." He glared. "Your word means nothing to any of us.

Not yet." He faced Ella and Lucy. "What do you two think about this? You're very quiet."

Ella continued to stare at their father rather than look at Scott. "I don't know what I think yet, but I do know I want Mum to be happy."

His gut clenched. Ella was right. That was what he wanted, too. What they all wanted. He swallowed and turned to Lucy. "Luce?"

Lucy blinked and faced him, her big blue eyes shining with unshed tears. "I want the same as Ella." She faced their father. "I don't know you. You're a stranger to me so this is going to take time. A lot of time."

Scott looked to their father. He nodded and his cheeks turned red, but there was no denying the relief in the slump of his father's shoulders. "Thank you. Thank you all…" He looked around the kitchen before he reached up and clenched his wife's hand where it lay on his shoulder. "I won't ask for any more than that."

Nausea coated Scott's throat in bitterness and he took another drink of water in an attempt to dilute it. He pushed away from the sink. "Fine. Then we take this slowly. You and Mum are entitled to do what you want, when you want, but I think I speak for the rest of us when I say we take this one step at a time."

"Scottie?"

His mother's voice was like a vise around his heart. He met her eyes. "What?"

"What about Christmas? I'd like your father to come for lunch."

The seconds beat with each dangerous thump of Scott's heart. He looked to Bianca and she shrugged; he looked to Ella and Lucy and they nodded in unison. Shit. He faced his mother. "Do what you want. I've got more important people to worry about at Christmastime than him." He dumped his glass in the sink and made for the door. He needed to get out of there so he could breathe.

"Where are you going?" Bianca's question halted him.

Scott turned. "I'm going to see Carrie. My time with her is too precious to waste."

Bianca smiled. "You really like her, huh?"

He nodded, cursing the gleam of satisfaction in his sister's eyes. "Yes."

"I heard on the grapevine she has a kid too. A little girl."

Scott tensed and cast a glance around the kitchen before meeting Bianca's gaze once more. "Who told you that?"

"Oh, the wonderfully delightful Miss Arnold, of course. She was practically peeing her pants with excitement when she caught me at Marian's yesterday."

The weight of his mother's, Ella's and Lucy's stares pressed down on Scott's chest. Unasked questions hovered like an unexploded grenades around him. "Yes, she has a daughter. Her name's Belle."

He opened his mouth to speak, but Bianca got there first. Her steady gaze pinned him to the spot like the accused in the box. "Is she yours?"

His heart picked up speed as he stared at his eldest sister, her tone as calm as it always was, but her gaze told him in no uncertain terms she wanted the truth.

He pulled back his shoulders. "Yes."

The collective gasp of his mother, Ella, and Lucy bounced from the kitchen tiles and smacked him right in the gut. He focused entirely on his mother. It was her feelings he cared about the most in that moment. This was not the way he wanted her to find out about her very first grandchild.

"How can you be so sure?" Bianca demanded. "The woman hasn't been in town more than a few days."

Swallowing the need to apologize to his mum, to go to her and put his arms around her, he turned to his eldest sister. "Kevin rushed through a DNA test. Belle's mine. I have a daughter."

He looked back to his mum.

Her eyes glistened with tears and she pressed a

hand to her heart, her mouth stretched to a grin. "You're a daddy?"

In spite of everything and everyone in the room, including his father, Scott smiled. "Yes, Mum. I'm a daddy."

A sob caught in her throat and she immediately left his father's side, her arms coming around Scott in an embrace. "I'm a grandma. Oh, Scottie, this is the happiest day of my life."

Closing his eyes to his father's smile, Scott grinned. "You're going love Carrie, Mum. All I want is her and Belle."

"I am so happy for you, sweetheart." She pulled back and held him at arm's length. "When do we get to meet Carrie? Could you invite her over now?"

Scott tensed and shot his gaze to his father. "Not now, but soon." He smiled to ease the worry that immediately clouded his mother's happy gaze. "I love her, Mum. I've loved her since the moment I first laid eyes on her. I waited for her to come find me instead of going to find her. I was an idiot to let that happen and waste every damn minute we could've had together." He stole an arm around her shoulder and met his father's eyes. "You and I share the same gene pool, have made similar mistakes but from here on in, we have a lot of work to do. No more playing around. No more women.

You and I are going to do it the right way from now on and not lose the women we love. Deal?"

His father smiled. "Deal."

Scott nodded, his heart beating hard. He pressed a kiss to his mother's temple before stepping back, only to be embraced in a family hug by Bianca, Ella and Lucy. When they released him, he exhaled. "Right, I'm out of here. Christmas doesn't wait for anyone, including Carrie, and she's desperate to get home in time to be with Belle. I'll see you later." He glanced at his father for a final time. "And I'll give some thought about Christmas lunch."

CARRIE REACHED FOR her third latte of the day, her mind busy with the words and ideas flowing through her brain like the snowflakes running down the bakery window. She grinned as her pen flew over her notepad. She hadn't been this creative, this energized or excited about her work in months. It was as though the darkness since Gerard died had lifted and a sliver of light for a possible, happier future had kick-started her heart and mind.

She sucked on the end of her pen and stared across the bustling bakery toward Marian and Stacy as they worked behind the counter. Carrie smiled and her heart swelled with fondness for the good people she'd met in Templeton. When she arrived, her defenses were high and her mind set on nothing more than clearing the air with Scott. She hadn't expected to feel like anything more than a stranger visiting an even stranger town.

Yet slowly, the pull of this small town with its beach and promenade, quaint shops and restaurants and colorful characters were seeping under her skin and making her understand Scott's reluctance to leave.

Templeton Cove was his home. Her smile dissolved as Marian blurred in her vision. Carrie hastily swiped at her eyes and turned back to her work. She was leaving. The receptionist had rung Carrie's cell an hour before, telling her the Cove was now open to incoming trains but as yet hadn't given the all-clear for departures. She would call again as soon as she knew more.

Carrie closed her eyes and prayed God stopped throwing snow down on them and let her go home to her baby for Christmas. The alternative, to be stranded here without Belle, was something she couldn't contemplate. Tears threatened and she blinked. It wouldn't happen. No God would be so cruel as to bring her to Templeton to find Belle's father and not let her return in time to sit with her by the tree and open their presents together.

As soon as she got the call from the hotel, she'd book a cab for first thing the next day. Christmas Eve. Carrie blew out a breath. In the meantime, she needed to call her mother and explain the reason for the delay. She snatched up her cell and dialed home.

Her mother picked up on the second ring. "Carrie, I'm so glad to hear from you. Any news from the station?"

Belle's delighted laughter resounded in the background, along with her father's bad impersonation of a train. She smiled. "They're allowing incoming trains but no departures. The hotel will call as soon as anything changes." Her breath caught. "Mum, I need to be there for Christmas. I can't be without Belle—"

"Come hell or high water, you'll be with her. You mustn't think that way."

"What if nothing changes? What if the line is still closed tomorrow?"

"Then your father and I will bring Belle to Templeton."

Carrie snapped her eyes open. "What? You can't. It's too soon for Scott to meet Belle. We've got so much to talk about." *But, oh, God, it would be wonderful*. She dropped her shoulders. "It's too soon."

"Sweetheart, if he wants to see his child, how can Christmas not be the perfect time? Your father and I can bring Belle to Templeton and we'll be there with you the entire step of the way. I'm not suggesting for one minute Scott sees her alone, but by having us bring her to him, with you, it will prove how serious you are about making up for lost time."

"Maybe." Her stomach quivered with anticipation. "But we won't go there yet, not until it's definite I can't get home. Okay?"

"You call me as soon as you hear anything."

"I will. Love you."

"Love you, too."

Carrie ended the call and slid her phone back onto the table. *Please, God, get me home to my baby.* Shaking off her melancholy, Carrie drew in a long breath. Everything would work out how it was supposed to, but for tonight, she'd be with Scott.

She owed him some time to tell her what happened with his family when he'd told them about Belle. If he wanted her to speak to them too, she would. Nerves rolled through her. Belle was her daughter and as much as she feared her new extended family encroaching on what Carrie thought she'd always view as her territory, she understood Scott came as a package, and his family had every right to know their granddaughter and niece.

She glanced at her watch and frowned. She'd expected him to call by now but her cell had remained ominously silent all day. She picked up her phone.

"Hey."

Carrie's stomach flip-flopped as she looked up and met Scott's smiling face. She grinned. "Hey. How did you know I was here?"

"A little bird told me they saw you come in here."

She laughed. "Once again, Templeton's residents show their talent in knowing everything and everyone."

His gaze slid from hers to the notepad in front of her, and his smile faltered. "What's that?"

"This?" She put her hand on the notebook. "Just some ideas I'm working on. It seems Templeton's a lot more inspiring than I ever thought it would be."

He slid onto the chair opposite her and nodded toward the notepad. "May I?"

"Of course." Apprehension rippled through her. His face was devoid of humor and his shoulders stiff. "Is everything okay?"

He didn't answer and instead scanned the pages she'd filled with ideas and lines of dialogue, his eyes manically flitting back and forth. Carrie frowned as his cheeks reddened and his jaw grew tight.

"Scott?" She covered his clenched hand with hers. "What is it?"

He looked up. "Your work's important to you, isn't it?"

She glanced at the notepad, trepidation rippling through her. "Yes, but yours is important to you too." She took his hand. "Please don't worry about our work. It's Christmas."

He raised her fingers to his lips and kissed her knuckles before meeting her eyes. "I just saw my dad. In my kitchen."

Carrie grimaced. "Oh."

He drew in a long breath and exhaled. "They know. They know about you, about us…and Belle."

Nerves knotted her stomach and her heart picked up speed. "Were they…happy?"

He smiled. "More than you could ever imagine."

Relief pushed the air from her lungs and Carrie grinned. "Good. That's really good. And your dad? How did things go with him?"

He released her hand and ran it over his face. "Better than I expected, I suppose. We've got a long way to go and I don't trust him, but we'll see."

"You're willing to give it everything you've got, though? For your mum."

His gaze focused on her mouth. "And you."

Carrie frowned. "For me? This has nothing to do—"

"You were right. I can't let my resentment toward him control my life anymore. I've done everything over the last ten years because I love my family so much. This, us, is new to me." His fiery gaze bored into hers. "You loved Gerard and you know how much real love can hurt. I'm still learning. So just promise you won't turn away from me while I stumble."

She trembled, his words rolling over her and into her heart. Tears pricked hot behind her eyes. "We can work through any problems as they come. Do you trust me, Scott? Trust yourself?"

He smiled. "Yes."

She leaned forward and he met her halfway across the table. Taking his jaw in her hands, Carrie pressed a long lingering kiss to his lips before pulling back and dropping back into her seat, her body hot. "Good."

"So are you ready to meet Mum, Ella and Lucy, talk to Bianca again? They love Belle without even meeting her."

Carrie briefly closed her eyes. "How could I have forgotten you have *three* sisters?"

He dropped his chin, his eyes glinting with mischief. "I have every faith they'll be putty in your hands."

Carrie's heart beat with fear of the unknown, fear for how much she loved this passionate, strong and caring man. "I love you, Scott."

He smiled and slid from the booth, his eyes still on hers. He took her hands and pulled her to her feet, his gaze drifting over her face and hair as he pushed some strands from her face. "I love you too."

He pulled her into his embrace, his lips touching hers and Carrie melted against the man she longed to love for the rest of her life. The man she suspected Gerard knew all along was her destiny.

CHAPTER TWENTY

SCOTT RELUCTANTLY EASED her back. He needed to see her eyes, her face. "When I told my family about Belle, all hell broke loose, but they were so damn happy. The questions and reproofs will come, but for now, neither my mother nor sisters can think past the potential of having a two-year-old little girl to spoil."

She smiled, but her anxiety was clearly reflected in her dark brown eyes. She took a deep breath. "Then I guess we'd better go and say hi."

They stood and Scott pulled some notes from his wallet and pushed them under her plate. "I've got this. Let's get out of here."

Hand in hand, they left the bakery and Scott carefully watched Carrie as she glanced along the street. She exhaled. "I really didn't expect this to happen quite so fast."

"Hey, you're going to be fine." He brushed his lips over hers. "They'll love you. You make me happy. They know that already."

She nodded. "Did you bring your car?"

"It's parked just along the road. Let's get the

introductions to my mum and sisters out of the way, and then we can decide how best to spend tonight." He wiggled his eyebrows.

She laughed. "Hmm…like you haven't already thought that through."

He grinned and tucked her hand into his elbow. There would be no more times that he doubted her or himself. They would stumble and fall, hurt and love, but Carrie and he were meant to be together. He'd never felt surer of anything in his life. In less than half an hour, Carrie would meet his mum and sisters before she left Templeton to spend Christmas with their baby.

He had every intention of being on that train with her.

They reached his car and got in. The atmosphere grew more fraught with tension as they neared his house. The fifteen-minute drive passed in silence, but Scott constantly glanced at Carrie and squeezed her hand in way of encouragement. When he met her parents, he'd be full of nerves, needing them to like him. Carrie's self-assurance usually came from her in waves, but the clenching and unclenching of her hands right then told him this meeting was something equally as terrifying for her as being without Belle on Christmas day.

He pulled into his drive, relieved to see his father's sedan had now gone. He parked his car behind Bianca's, cut the engine and turned in his seat. "You okay?" Carrie stared at his house and he followed her gaze. "Sorry about the decorations. Mum's like a kid at Christmastime."

She smiled. "It looks amazing. Belle would love it."

He cast his gaze over her profile. She looked amazing. Her skin glowed from the flickering white and red bulbs covering his porch and windows, not to mention the lights strung all over the trees and bushes in the front yard. "Maybe next year she'll get to see it."

She met his eyes and smiled. "Maybe she will."

He leaned closer and kissed her, inhaling the soft scent of her skin and gliding his fingers through her hair to hold the back of her head and pull her closer. He poured his entire heart and soul into the kiss, hoping it gave her the strength and tenacity to believe in him and whatever the future might hold for them.

Eventually, they parted and she blew out a shaky breath. "Okay. I'm ready. Let's do this."

With a final kiss to her cheek, Scott yanked on the door handle and got out of the car. Carrie met him in front of the hood and slid her hand into his. Together, they approached the front door. Before he had a chance to push his key into the lock, the door swung open.

Scott didn't know whether to laugh or curse.

His mum and sisters stood in a line, their faces

identically drawn into comical expressions of complete ecstasy, each frozen to the carpet and not speaking.

Scott cleared his throat, "Mum, this—"

"I know who she is." Her paralysis broke and his mum came forward and took Carrie's hands in hers, urging her inside. "Welcome, Carrie. Welcome to Scottie's home. You are…" She pressed a hand to her breast. "Just beautiful."

Carrie laughed, albeit shakily as she allowed his mother to drag her over the threshold and into the throng of his now chattering sisters. If he hadn't put his foot in the door, Scott could've sworn it would've been slammed in his face.

He shut the door and fought his smile into a frown. "Mum, won't you at least let Carrie take her coat off?"

His mother laughed. "Of course. Sorry, Carrie, it's just so exciting to have you here. I'd like to say I've heard a lot about you…" She flicked a meaningful glare in Scott's direction. "But all I've heard has been secondhand. I can't wait to get to know you better."

Carrie smiled. "You're very kind to have me here, Mrs. Walker."

"Mary, please. Here, let me take your coat and bag."

Scott exchanged a series of facial expressions and wide-eyed glares with each of his sisters before his mother practically threw Carrie's coat and bag into his arms. "Here, Scottie. You take care of these, will you?"

Glaring at his mother's turned face, Scott did as he was bid and was just about to tell them all to let Carrie have a bit of breathing space when Carrie spoke. "I love how you've decorated the house, Mary. It's amazing."

His mother beamed with pride. "Fit for a little one, don't you think?"

"Mum!"

Scott joined his sisters' chorused reprimand and then they all laughed when Carrie laughed louder than all of them. "It certainly is, Mrs. Walker... Mary."

His mother clasped Carrie's elbow, her smile as wide as her face. "Would you like some hot chocolate?"

Carrie nodded. "Sounds perfect."

Scott stared after them, shaking his head as the five women who made up his entire life disappeared into the kitchen. He clenched his jaw. Add just another small female and he had a funny feeling his life would be complete.

When a unified cackle of laughter rose and burst from the open kitchen door, he quickly hung Carrie's coat and bag before shrugging out of his coat and scarf. He took a couple of steps toward the kitchen and then halted when Carrie's phone rang from inside her bag.

Turning around, he grabbed the bag and carried it through to the kitchen. He had to shout above the volume of female joviality. "Carrie, your phone's ringing."

She turned and he held the bag aloft.

When she came to him, his heart kicked to see her eyes shining with happiness and her smile wide. It felt so right to have her in his home. She took the bag. "Thanks."

She rummaged inside, but the phone had stopped ringing.

Scott frowned. "Do you want to go into the hallway to call whoever it was back?" He glanced at his sisters and mother dotted about the room in varying stages of making hot chocolate or setting the table with bowls of sweets, crisps and nuts. "They may be a while. When guests come at Christmastime, Mum tends to go a bit overboard. Actually, scrap that, she tends to go overboard whatever the time of year."

When Carrie didn't answer, he faced her. She was already calling back whomever it was she'd missed. She pushed her bag into his chest with the phone to her ear. "Mum? It's me. Where are you? Mum? Can you hear me? What's that noise?"

She wandered into the hallway, her free hand pressed to her other ear in a futile attempt to block out the noise of his boisterous family. Scott strode after her and she reached back to grasp his hand. "Mum, you're going to have to speak up, I can't hear you." She screwed her eyes shut in concentration…and then snapped them wide open. "You're on your way here? To Templeton. Oh, my God. Is Belle with you?"

Scott's heart thundered and his mouth drained dry. He stared at Carrie, his entire body wired with adrenaline and hope. Each second felt like an hour. *Please let them be bringing my daughter to me.*

Carrie met his eyes. They stormed with love, disbelief, laughter and fear. "Oh, Mum. I don't believe it." She nodded, her eyes locked with his. "You're bringing her to us."

To us. For a moment Scott couldn't move. Belle was on her way. He was going to spend Christmas with a daughter he never knew existed until four days ago. Smiling, he pulled Carrie closer and pressed his lips to her forehead. The rest of Carrie's conversation with her mother faded into the background…

CARRIE ENDED THE call and pulled back from Scott's arms to look him in the eyes. "She's coming to Templeton. I don't believe it."

Scott grinned. "That's good, right? It means you don't have to leave. We can spend Christmas together…as a family."

Fear skittered through her and Carrie pulled out of his grasp. She turned her back to him, her mind racing and her heart aching. "This feels too soon. You still have so many unresolved issues to sort out with your father. How can I be sure that Belle won't be hurt in the end? How can I be sure that things won't go wrong between us and we end up hating each other?" Tears burned and Carrie wrapped her arms tightly around her body.

"Carrie."

She shook her head, refusing to turn around and face him. She had to think of Belle. Her baby was her constant. Her baby wouldn't leave her. Her baby would never die…Her sob caught in her throat and Carrie covered her mouth with her hand. Where was all this panic coming from? She closed her eyes. It was now or never. Scott would soon see his little girl for the very first time. There would be no going back for any of them after that most precious moment.

Scott came behind her and the scent of the man she loved encompassed her. He wrapped his arms around her, pulling her in close. "Hey, don't cry. We're going to be okay. We're going to make it, and Belle will be at the center of everything. Look at me."

Trembling, Carrie turned in his arms and met his eyes. He lifted his thumbs to her cheeks and wiped at her tears, his lips gently brushing hers.

"You're afraid." He smiled wryly. "I'm terrified. Let me just ask you one thing."

She sniffed. "What?"

"When you found out you were pregnant, did you jump for joy? Shout it from the rooftops? Or did you have the exact same feeling you're having now?"

Shame infused her. "I had the same feeling as now..." She shook her head. "But that lasted for a matter of days. This isn't the same. Once I accepted I was pregnant, that I could raise a baby alone, I wasn't afraid anymore. I wanted my baby, your baby."

"And what you've just described is the exact journey I've been on since you walked into my garage four days ago. I'm ready, Carrie. I'm ready to be Belle's daddy for the rest of my life." He grinned. "Let me meet her. Let me see her." He glanced toward the closed kitchen door. "Let us all spend Christmas together. Your family, my family, our family. We'll spend a few days together and then you'll see what I already know. We'll be okay. We'll have the elusive happy-ever-after. I know we will."

"You can't know that. Neither of us can." Cursing the doubts and fear rushing through her, Carrie stepped away from him. "Gerard always said Belle and I were his happy-ever-after." Her breath caught. "And look what happened to him. He's dead, Scott. He's dead and a year later I'm here with you, and my daughter is on her way to Templeton with my parents. How did that happen? How did my trip here become so big?"

"Because it was meant to be this way all along. Gerard was the right man for you at the time, Carrie. He was what you needed when you found out you were pregnant and had a baby. He was what Belle needed for the first eighteen months of her life. If I had been there, who knows? Maybe I would've royally messed up. But now?" He pushed his fist against his chest. "Now I know I want you and her more than anything in the whole damn world. I'm the right man for you now. I'm the right man for Belle. If it takes me my entire life to prove it to you, I will."

Carrie's heart swelled for the man standing in front of her, opening his soul and baring his vulnerability, yet standing strong and refusing to let her fear override a second chance at long-lasting love. She took a deep breath. "I told my parents to take Belle to The Christie when they arrive."

He pulled back his shoulders. "Ring your Mum back. Ring her back and ask them to come here."

"What?" Her eyes widened. "But—"

He grinned. "We can eat together. Mum will have more food on the table than any of us could possibly manage once I tell her your family are coming." He rolled his eyes. "She started making food for Christmas in April, I swear."

Swiping at her face, Carrie smiled. "Okay."

"Okay?"

She laughed. "Okay."

Smiling, Scott took her in his arms and when he kissed her, his silent promise seeped into Carrie's soul and nestled in her heart. They would be okay. She felt absolutely certain of it after coming full circle in a matter of days. God only knew how much better they could be together in the years to come.

"I love you, Carrie."

She smiled and her desire for him heated her body as he lifted back her hair to leave a trail of kisses down the curve of her neck…just how he knew she liked it. She inhaled a shuddering breath. "I love you, too."

SCOTT GLANCED AT Carrie for the thirtieth time in as many minutes as she stood staring through his living-room window. When she'd called her mother back, they had already left Templeton train station in a cab and were on their way to The Christie. After a hurried delivering of Scott's address, he, his family and Carrie now nervously waited for Carrie's parents…and Belle's arrival.

Inhaling, Scott rose from the sofa and went to join Carrie at the window. She held back the curtain and together, they watched the falling snow in silence. The muted onslaught of shuffling and not-so-subtle coughing behind him told Scott his mother and sisters had tactfully decided to leave him and Carrie alone. He put his arm around her and pulled her close. "You okay?"

She looked up at him, her brown eyes wide and anxious. "I don't know." She smiled. "I think so."

He smiled and pressed a kiss to her hair, inhaling her scent. "I know the feeling."

She turned and put her arms around his waist. "You meeting Belle was my sole intention when I came here and now it's happening...."

He lifted an eyebrow. "Your sole intention? Wasn't there even a part of you that wanted to know if I was still as irresistibly handsome as I was three years ago?"

She scowled and playfully swatted his arm. "Good God, that is one gigantic ego you have there, Mr. Walker."

Scott grinned. "Is that a yes or no?"

She laughed. "Fine. Maybe a small..." She put her finger and thumb barely a centimeter apart. "Was curious about you and me."

He dipped his head and brushed his lips over hers, relishing the feel of her breasts on his chest when she leaned close to him. His Carrie. In his arms. Just where she should have been for the last three years. Just as the urge to beat himself up about their lost time together filtered his heart, a stream of headlights lit up the room.

Carrie leaped from his arms and yanked back the curtain. "Oh, God. They're here. It's a taxi."

Scott stared out the window, his heart pumping fast and his entire body tense. "Well, let's go meet your family."

She snapped her head around and pressed her hand to her chest. "Let me go. On my own. Just give me a minute with her. Okay?"

Nerves and excitement leaped in his stomach; impatience hummed in his blood but he nodded. "Sure. Whatever you need to do."

She smiled and cupped her hand to his jaw. "I love you."

Carrie rushed from the room, leaving him standing alone and immobile. Seconds later, the living room reopened and his mother and sisters crashed into the room. Bianca stormed toward him as the others shot manic glances toward the window. "Carrie just went outside. Are they here? Is your daughter here?"

My daughter. Scott's mouth drained dry. "She's here."

Silence descended and Scott snapped his gaze to the door. Even the excruciating wait for it to open again and Carrie to enter with Belle was preferable to the intense, feminine scrutiny of his family.

The muted sound of female conversation, mixed

with the deeper voice of a man and the soft, melodic squeak of a little girl sounded outside the door. His mother's breath caught beside him. "She's here, Scottie. Oh, your little girl is here."

The door opened and Carrie came in carrying the most precious Christmas gift Scott had seen in his entire life. He clenched his jaw and silently cursed the burn of tears in his eyes. He tried to look at Carrie but couldn't drag his gaze from Belle. Her beautiful shiny curls were ebony-black and her eyes were the brightest blue as they darted from him to his mother and sisters and back again. She grinned, revealing teeth as white and perfect as her mother's. "Hi."

In that single word, Scott fell in love harder and faster than he even fell for Carrie. He pressed his hand to where his heart had been a moment before. "Hi, Belle."

Carrie came closer and stopped in front of him. "Belle, this is Mummy's friend, Scott. Can you say Scott?"

She smiled and shook her head, her cheeks flushing pink. "No." She glanced from Scott to the huge Christmas tree in the corner, its flickering lights dancing over her face. "Tree."

Scott grinned. "Do you like it?"

"Uh-huh." She faced him once more and leaned forward from Carrie's embrace, her arms outstretched. "I go see."

Scott looked from her arms to Carrie, his heart pounding. "Does she—"

Carrie nodded, tears rolling softly down her cheeks. "She wants you to show her."

Scott swallowed and stepped forward, gently sliding his hands under his daughter's arms and lifting her against him. She was as light as a feather and pretty as a picture. Their eyes locked and she placed her tiny hand on his shoulder, staring deep into his eyes "You show me."

"I'll show you the tree, Belle." He whispered. "I'll show you the whole, wide world, if you let me."

She grinned. "Okay."

Leaving his family to the introductions, muffled with more than a few smothered sobs, Scott carried his daughter to the Christmas tree. As she pointed to all the ornaments, Scott stared at the star on top as his whole world fell into place at the most perfect time of the year.

* * * * *

LARGER-PRINT BOOKS!

HARLEQUIN *Presents*

PASSION GUARANTEED SEDUCTION

GET 2 FREE LARGER-PRINT NOVELS PLUS 2 FREE GIFTS!